# The First Mistake

Sarah Ward is a critically acclaimed crime and gothic thriller writer. Her book, *A Patient Fury*, was an *Observer* book of the month and *The Quickening*, written as Rhiannon Ward, was a *Radio Times* book of the year. Sarah is a former Vice-Chair of the Crime Writers Association, Trustee of Gwyl Crime Cymru Festival and an RLF Fellow at Sheffield University.

## Also by Sarah Ward

### A Mallory Dawson Crime Thriller

*The Birthday Girl*
*The Sixth Lie*
*The Vanishing Act*
*The Death Lesson*
*The First Mistake*

### Carla James Crime Thrillers

*Death Rites*
*Quiet Bones*
*Grave Intent*

# THE FIRST MISTAKE

SARAH WARD

canelo
CRIME

DK | Penguin Random House

First published in the United Kingdom in 2026 by

Canelo Crime, an imprint of
Canelo Digital Publishing Limited,
20 Vauxhall Bridge Road,
London SW1V 2SA
United Kingdom

A Penguin Random House Company
The authorised representative in the EEA is Dorling Kindersley Verlag GmbH.
Arnulfstr. 124, 80636 Munich, Germany



A CIP catalogue record for this book is available from the British Library.

ISBN 978 1 80436 939 5



Cover design by Andrew Smith

Cover images © Shutterstock.com: Leighton Collins

Printed and bound in Great Britain by Clays Ltd, Elcograf S.p.A.

Look for more great books at
www.canelo.co | www.dk.com

1

FSC www.fsc.org MIX Paper FSC™ C018179

*For Karen Meek*

# 1

A bitter wind swept through the town. January was the worst month – ice competed with the wind to bring plummeting temperatures and a slick of sleet settling on roads and pavements. In these conditions, it was hard to remember that in the summer, Ceigwyn was a tourist destination packed with visitors attracted to its locally made honey ice cream and picturesque harbour. No seaside town thrives in the dark months, and Eleri was yearning for the red midsummer sunsets and warm July breezes. Still, they made the best of it, and tonight was a festival of tradition and laughter that everybody could enjoy. Across the streets and up the steep hill, a sense of anticipation hung over the town. Elsewhere across Wales, other places had enjoyed their *Mari Lwyd*. Tonight was their turn.

Eleri had spent the afternoon making loaves of *bara brith* to sell at the stall by the quay. She'd brought them to the table still wrapped in greaseproof paper and cut the slices under the twinkling lights that, according to the priest from the local church, should have been removed by Twelfth Night. He was a new man: Welsh, but brought in from Cardiff with a high-minded view of what should and shouldn't be done as part of the winter festivals. He'd asked the church warden to take down the green man in the church porch, remonstrating that such things had no place in a house of God, which showed how little he knew about these things. Wales had always embraced both the sacred and pagan, adopting new practices brought to them by *Dewi Sant* while clinging on to the old ways. Poor man – he'd learn soon enough. When he'd heard about what was taking place that night, he'd asked the woman who came to make his tea to get it ready for six p.m., after which he'd retire to bed early. The thought made Eleri laugh. She could imagine him in his striped pyjamas, reading some improving work with his ears plugged to muffle the cries of the revellers in the night.

Eleri pulled up her scarf to cover her mouth as she spread the butter on the thick slices of cake. She'd warmed the spread on the car dashboard on the way to the quay, but it was already hardening in the cold. Eleri swore as it snagged on her slice, tearing a hole the size of a penny. More haste, less speed was needed. Her daughter, Gwennie, had promised to come down and help her with the work, but the little minx was probably out on the town with her friends – and her latest fling. Another out-of-towner, she'd heard, this one from England, but the thought didn't raise a smile.

Gwennie was a problem, and the fact she'd been going around with a self-satisfied smile on her face over the holiday season made Eleri anxious. She even had money to buy a new orange puffa jacket, although when challenged, she claimed she'd picked it up in a charity shop for pennies. Gwennie and secrets were a toxic combination. Add a man into the mix and the trouble was multiplied. She'd been behaving oddly that morning, hanging about the house and even rooting around in Eleri's bag. If she thought she could nab a tenner for the evening's festivities, she could think again. Eleri had left her purse at a friend's house the previous evening and had gone to retrieve it that afternoon en route to the quayside. If Gwennie wanted money, she'd have to come and work for it. Nothing came easily to Jones women. Nothing.

By seven p.m. the town was in full swing. Music from the band wafted over as Eleri sold her coffee, mulled wine and *bara brith* to families following the *Mari Lwyd* effigy of the horse, its skeletal head bobbing up and down as it passed from pub to houses, accepting coins and jousting with made-up, silly verse. Gwennie was still nowhere to be seen. At first, Eleri had been too busy to notice her absence, but now she felt the prickle of anxiety as she scanned the groups of people passing along the quay. She rang Gwennie's mobile, but it was switched off, and Eleri's WhatsApp message was unanswered.

In the crowd, Eleri spotted her daughter's ex-boyfriend Huw out with another girl, his arm around her shoulders. Eleri swallowed her instinctive dislike of him and left the nearly empty stall to ask after Gwennie.

'Have you seen her? She's supposed to be helping me out this evening, but I've not seen sight nor sound of her.'

Eleri saw that Huw's new girl had disentangled herself from his embrace and was drifting towards a van selling popcorn and doughnuts, imported crap rather than her own home-cooked fare. Eleri turned her attention back to Huw. The scent of cannabis hung over him like an aftershave splashed on too liberally. It was one of the reasons she'd tried to stop Gwennie seeing him, as well as his reputation for spreading himself around the town's teenagers. He took a step back, his eyes on the popcorn stand.

'She was outside the old cinema next to the pharmacy a while back. She ignored me when I said "hi". She waiting for her new boyfriend?'

'I'm only her mother,' said Gwennie, spotting a queue forming at her stall. 'I'd be the last to know who she was meeting.'

'I heard she was seeing someone else,' said Huw, removing his vape from his pocket and sucking on it furiously. He breathed out a plume of bubble-gum-scented vapour. 'She moved on quickly.'

'So did you, I see,' said Eleri, turning back to her customers.

It was probably that new boyfriend, thought Eleri sourly, as she sold her last slice of cake and began to pack away her plates. He was probably another wrong-un, though, if Gwennie didn't think him good enough to introduce to her mother. Eleri wondered, after Huw's frequent glassy-eyed appearances in her living room, what she'd have to look forward to with this new fella. The thought made her unexpectedly weary, and she pinched her cold cheeks to get the blood flowing to her head. She wondered why she couldn't shrug the sense that something was off kilter. Apart from Gwennie's absence, it had been a good evening. She'd seen some old friends in passing and had chatted with them. The takings would bring in some welcome extra income for Eleri over the next week.

In the dark night, she frowned as she saw blue flashing lights in the distance. Police presence was sparse in this part of Wales. The wild west, she sometimes called it, residents flouting the law because of the unlikelihood of actually being caught. The blue lights snaked along the road by the harbour. It was probably some random act of violence by one of the local lads, although it was a little early in the evening for the after-hours fights. Perhaps there had been a car accident, which wouldn't surprise her, given how people drove on the roads. Eleri's heart thumped as she thought about her absent daughter. Jeesh, this wasn't like her. She wasn't one of those over-anxious mothers who demanded to know their child's every movement, although, God knew she had enough history to be that helicopter parent. This was Ceigwyn, though, not London. Women walked the streets in safety.

Eleri watched as the two cars turned right and climbed the hill, her anxiety turning to nausea. What had Huw said? Gwennie was waiting for someone outside the old cinema next to the pharmacy. Eleri knew the place well. She'd had a Saturday job in the shop, selling face creams to the older women who swore by the Evans's special formula. It was opposite the garage whose owner had decorated his building with a huge Santa Claus to annoy the town council and hadn't bothered to take it down as the new year arrived. She could see the edifice from here, its huge arm waving over the celebrations with false cheer.

When the blue lights passed the figure, a panicked Eleri bargained with herself: she would relax a little and try Gwennie's phone one more time. There was no reason to fear the flashing lights that would continue out of Ceigwyn towards Lampeter to deal with any trouble there. She watched as the blue lights reached the giant Santa and stopped. For a moment, the night stilled and Eleri was deaf to everything except the pounding in her ears.

'Mind my stall,' she shouted to no one in particular, and began to run towards the light.

## 2

Mallory didn't like the sea. She hadn't since she'd wound up in it following a series of tragedies on the island of Eldey. A suggestion by an old colleague that she take a post as a night manager in the hotel there had brought her to Wales and to Harri, so it wasn't all bad. The sea, however, never failed to overwhelm her. She stood on the deck of the Irish Ferry hand in hand with Harri after their post-Christmas holiday in County Cork. They had eaten and drunk their weight in wine and cheese and Mallory was seized with an irrational fear of docking in Fishguard and facing the new year ahead.

All should be fine. After eight months living in a caravan near the coast – the only short-term let she'd been able to find over the summer – she'd finally found a cheap-ish rental in Ceigwyn. It had been on the market for five months because the owner was selling up as a result of the steep rise in council taxes being levied on second homes, but the glut of properties had meant it hadn't sold, so it had been offered to Mallory on a six-month lease. The house was only a temporary solution though, and not just because of its short lease. The problem was – and she'd told no one this – the town had a flicker of significance from a past, never-forgotten case.

'Do you want to go inside?' asked Harri, shivering.

'You go,' said Mallory, removing her hand from his and pulling up the zip of her coat over her chin. 'I'd like to see us dock.' She was aware that his diabetes made it difficult for him to tolerate the cold. He liked warm offices and coffee shops, not ferry decks and sea spray. 'Seriously, go inside.'

'I'll go get a drink to warm up. Sure you don't want one?'

Mallory shook her head, and he left her to her contemplation of the nearing dock. It wasn't only in respect of her living arrangements that there were decisions to be made. DI Harri Evans was unofficially her boss. If she'd worked as a regular police detective, he'd need to declare his relationship with a subordinate. One of them, probably her, would be moved to a different team and that would probably be that. But Mallory was a civilian investigator, under contract to Dyfed Powys police during murder inquiries. It was an odd dynamic, and as her relationship with Harri progressed, she became more aware of points of tension. The worry was hypothetical at the moment, given there were no current murder investigations, which also meant she was officially unemployed and reliant on her police pension to tide her over until she was needed again. Realistically, she needed to look for some part-time work for expensive January and February when her heating bills came in.

Within ten minutes, Harri was by her side with a hot chocolate for them both.

'I thought you were cold,' she said. The drink was sweet and artificial tasting, but she was glad of the warmth. She glanced across at him and saw his expression was grim.

'I'm going to need to go straight to work,' said Harri. 'If I drop you off in town, can you get home from

Carmarthen on your own steam? You can leave your luggage with me if you want and I'll bring it up when I get a chance.'

'Of course I can,' said Mallory. 'What's up?'

'There's been a serious assault in Ceigwyn. A young female is badly injured, possibly the result of a domestic with her new boyfriend, although he's not yet been tracked down, so that's just guesswork on the part of the victim's mother. I'm needed there straight away.'

Bloody hell. She'd only just moved into the town and had left her son Toby housesitting while she went away. She looked for her phone and checked for messages from him but there was nothing at all, just a spam text from a car finance company. 'I spoke to Toby yesterday and he said he was going to wander into town to look around the festival. I couldn't quite make out the details. Something about a horse skeleton.' It had sounded a bit too gothic for Mallory's tastes but that was teenagers for you. Toby had also sounded a little more wired than usual. A coil of tension in his voice that Mallory had wanted to question him about but hadn't liked to mention over the phone.

'The *Mari Lwyd* was on. The thirteenth of January is the old Welsh New Year's Eve, although *Mari Lwyd* is separate to that and Ceigwyn celebrates it on the Sunday before. It's an old wassailing tradition, where a horse's head is carried to houses and pubs where residents are challenged to a *pwnco*, a kind of rhyming challenge, for the right to enter the house.'

Mallory shivered. The thought of the skeletal remains of a horse's head being paraded through town wasn't doing anything for her. Funny Toby hadn't texted her with some photos.

'Need a hand in the case?' she asked, making her voice as casual as she could. Winter bills, Toby's travel expenses, petrol. It all depleted Mallory's meagre income.

'I don't think so,' said Harri. 'It sounds like it's just a case of tracking down her boyfriend.'

'That's a shame.'

Harri looked like he wanted to say something but thought better of it. Mallory guessed he too had reservations about the logistics of their working and private relationship, and also wasn't ready to have that conversation yet.

'When's Toby going back home?' he asked, putting his arm around her shoulder.

'I'm dropping him off at the station tomorrow.'

'Sure he didn't mind being left alone while we had our trip away?'

Mallory shook her head. 'He brightened up when I suggested that he might like the house to himself. I remember feeling the same when I was a teenager. Not quite ready for the outside world but straining for my freedom.'

'He's not been in touch, has he? The news of the attack will be all around town.'

Mallory looked at her watch. 'He'll still be in bed, I guess. He'll be safely back in London tomorrow.'

'Isn't he supposed to be at college?'

'He's got his mock exams soon. He's been given two weeks off to revise for them, but your guess is as good as mine as to how much work he's actually done.'

'He enjoying it?' asked Harri, throwing the dregs of his drink into the sea.

Mallory shrugged. 'More than school, I'd say, and they've got a good counselling service, which he's using alongside the private one we pay to address his bulimia. But you never really know, do you? He seemed a little distracted and hyped up when I called him from Ireland.'

'He probably didn't like speaking on the phone. It's the same with my kids. They'd let the bloody thing ring rather than speak to me, but send them a message and they're happy to chat all night.'

The explanation gave Mallory some relief. Harri was probably right. She took a breath. 'You know, if there is any work going...'

Harri nodded. 'I'll see what I can do but it's not always my call.'

They stood together watching as Fishguard approached, the white houses of Goodwick in the distance and the grey port building ahead. No, Mallory wasn't looking forward to going home.

# 3

Harri's holiday bonhomie disappeared as soon as he entered the foyer of the police headquarters. The place was busy, energised by New Year's resolutions and a serious crime to solve. West Wales was generally a safe place to live. Drugs were an issue – both dealing and using – but by and large, policing involved intervening in local disputes, traffic offences, petty crime and the odd disorderly conduct. His entrance into the hubbub was delayed as he'd left his building pass at home and had to wait while he was given temporary access to the site. One of his detective constables, Siân Lewis, was hovering by her desk as he walked into the CID room, her expression apologetic.

'I'm sorry, boss. I did tell the super you were on holiday and would be back in tomorrow, but she wanted you here straight away. We're a bit pushed here at the moment. Flu's going round.'

Flu? Harri shuddered and made a mental note to avoid anyone coughing or blowing their nose. 'What's the rush? From the message you sent me, it sounds like a domestic incident. It would have waited until I'd had a shave.'

Siân grimaced. 'It's now a murder inquiry. Gwennie Jones died of her injuries this morning and we need to move fast on this. It was the *Mari Lwyd* yesterday in the town and we have hundreds of potential witnesses. Some will have left Ceigwyn already.'

'Shit.' Harri's mood shifted. 'Come with me into the office.'

The room had a stagnant air, even though it had only been a week since he'd last been there. Despite the cold outside, he pulled up the blinds and opened a window, letting the heat of the radiator escape across the car park. He flapped the window three times and then shut it again, turning up the dial on the radiators. Siân shivered and took the seat opposite him.

'OK, I'll give you a quick rundown of what we know so far. Gwennie Jones, aged seventeen and a student at *Coleg Ceredigion*, was found with head wounds outside Evans's Pharmacy on Mwnt Street at ten past seven yesterday evening. She was discovered lying on her side by a dogwalker by the name of Andrew Price, who lives on an adjoining street. He tied his dog to a lamppost and administered first aid while calling for an ambulance. He was joined within minutes by another passerby, a woman named Sue Davis, who helped comfort the victim.'

'Was she conscious?' asked Harri, the image of the stricken teenager bringing to mind his own daughter Ellie.

'According to both Mr Price and Ms Davis, she was moving slightly and her eyes were flickering but she wasn't able to speak. They initially thought she'd simply fainted, although neither could bring her round. Gwennie's condition was stabilised by paramedics and she was taken to Bronglais A&E. I went there early this morning and she was in an induced coma. According to the consultant, she hadn't spoken since the paramedics arrived on the scene.'

'Did you talk to the paramedics?' asked Harri.

'One of the uniforms took a statement from the pair and they confirmed that Gwennie was in a critical condition when they arrived. She wasn't able to speak to them in the ambulance so there's no clear explanation for her injuries. She was admitted with indications of a traumatic brain injury and fractured skull. The working assumption is that she was attacked and sustained head wounds. A fall from standing is unlikely to have caused the injuries and there's no evidence that she accessed the roof of the pharmacy, so we're ruling out the possibility that she fell from there.'

'And when did she die?'

'At nine twenty this morning. She'd been booked in for various imaging tests today, but she had a seizure and was unable to be revived.'

'Damn,' said Harri. 'Who's her next of kin?'

'She has a mother, Eleri Jones, who's a single parent. She was in the hospital with her overnight and was with her when she had the seizure.'

'How is she?' Harri saw Siân hesitate.

'I don't think the investigation is going to be as straightforward as we originally thought. Gwennie had been seeing someone, according to her mother, although she didn't have many details. He's English; that's about it.'

Harri snorted. 'That narrows it down. What else?'

'I dunno. She's a bit, well, reticent in relation to Gwennie's personal life, although she did mention an ex called Huw Roberts. There's no love lost there, apparently. She knew Gwennie was waiting for someone in that spot because Huw told her so during the celebrations. Gwennie was supposed to be helping her with her coffee stall down by the quay and she failed to turn up.'

'Does he have an alibi?'

'I need to speak to him. It's a priority, alongside tracking down her new boyfriend. As I said, Eleri was pretty cagey about Gwennie's love life.'

Harri frowned. 'Cagey? Her daughter's dead, for Chrissakes. Does *she* have an alibi for the evening? You say she was down at the quay?'

Siân, for the first time, consulted her tablet. 'She says she last saw Gwennie at around two o'clock when she came downstairs after finishing off a college assignment. Gwennie was studying catering, although wasn't very interested in the subject; it was just something to do. Eleri runs her own food company and Gwennie occasionally helped out, which is why she was expecting to see her at some point that evening.'

'How was she at two? Did Eleri notice anything different?'

'Apparently not. She says Gwennie went into town at some point in the afternoon – Eleri thinks around three – but she's not sure of the reason for the trip. She liked experimenting with make-up, so it might have been to buy a new lipstick or something. Eleri had to leave around four thirty to set up her coffee stall, and she fully expected to see Gwennie at some point.'

'Wasn't Eleri worried when she didn't turn up?' Harri, the father of two teenagers, already knew the answer to this. He had no idea what either of his children were up to at this moment in time.

'She says not, but I'm not so sure. She seems to be holding something back, but at this stage it's difficult to say what.

'OK.' He massaged his forehead, all his holiday goodwill now gone. 'Concentrate on interviewing Huw Roberts and tracking down her current flame. Talk to friends, family, anyone. I'll come with you to visit the crime scene and I'll take it from there. I guess the super will want to talk to me. Who was put in charge last night?'

'DI Williams was the temporary SIO, but he's needed in Aberystwyth after a stabbing last night.'

'Two deaths in the same evening?' Harri froze. 'Are they connected?'

'It doesn't look like it. The Aber one was a stabbing in a pub and it looks like it might have been racially motivated. The victim was an asylum seeker recently given settled status.'

'Do they have the perpetrator?' asked Harri.

'Not yet. There was a gang of four youths caught on a camera outside a shop. It's probably only a matter of time but tensions are running high.'

Harri folded his arms. 'I'm surprised Steph didn't ask me to take that case on, given that Jon Williams had already been assigned to this one.' Did he actually want that particular investigation? Probably not, and he wasn't local to Aber in the way Jon Williams was. He was inclined to trust his superintendent's decisions when it came to the allocation of cases.

Siân shrugged. 'That decision's well above my pay grade. I've been told to brief you on this one.'

'All right.' Harri stood. 'Let's go, shall we?'

–

On the drive to Ceigwyn, Harri caught up with his emails. DI Williams had scheduled a call for two p.m. to update Harri on his progress. In his heart, now he'd had time to think about it, Harri was relieved he hadn't been given the Aberystwyth case. Tensions had begun to rise in the town, whipped up by agitators determined to blame anything wrong on the immigrants being housed in temporary accommodation. It was a powder-keg situation and Jon Williams would need all the resources at his disposal to identify the killer and defuse tensions.

As they reached the town, Harri saw it had a bleak air to it, different from its usual affluent self-satisfaction. It was probably due to the grim weather and the vans lining the road that remained closed to traffic. There was a gaggle of onlookers kept away from the police tape by two cold-looking officers. Thankfully, no press yet. Siân parked up and pointed to the old cinema across the way that had become a Chinese takeaway and was now, once again, derelict. In contrast, there was an old-fashioned pharmacy next to it with bottles of potions in the window.

'Gwennie was seen standing outside Evans's Pharmacy at around six p.m. This was the sighting by her former boyfriend Huw, which he conveyed to Eleri Jones when she began to ask where her daughter was. As I've mentioned, his impression was that she was waiting for someone.'

Harri frowned and looked at the homely window with its large glass bottles and old-fashioned scents. He hadn't seen the place before, but it reminded him of a chemist from his childhood in Carmarthen that had a similar vibe. 'Any reason why Gwennie would have chosen this place for a meet up? It's an odd place to choose.'

'We don't know. It was sleeting briefly so perhaps she felt happier waiting outside a shop which has a small canopy over the front door. It's near a streetlight too.'

Harri was unconvinced. 'It would give her a good view of the approach of whoever she was waiting for, which is just about the only thing going for the spot. The cinema, however, is in darkness, and it's derelict. I just can't see Gwennie suggesting it as a meeting spot. When you speak to Huw, ask him if it was a regular rendezvous point for them when they were together.'

Siân nodded. 'I asked Eleri and she said she had no idea why Gwennie might have been waiting there. There's only that thing over there, which might account for it.'

Harri looked at the giant Father Christmas, left up long after the festive season had passed. It was waving across the town, and the cheeriness made him nauseous. 'Can't we get that thing turned off?'

Eleri nodded. 'I'll ask the owner. One possibility is that whoever she was meeting was from out of town. It's probably the one landmark in town, even if temporary.'

'Possibly,' Harri grunted. 'We've only got Eleri's view that Gwennie might have been meeting someone based on the assumption of Huw Roberts. I'd like to speak to her first before we get a statement from Huw and his new girlfriend. I need to see how reliable they are.'

Siân gave a shrug, not offended by Harri's need to interview the witnesses himself. As a DI, it was below *his* pay grade, but they did things a bit differently out here.

'Eleri is at home and has sent away the family liaison officer. Wanted to be alone, and I said we'd keep her updated. You'll have to watch your step, though, as I've already told you.'

'Does she have a record?' asked Harri as he got back into the car, turning up the heater.

'Nothing came up, but I suspect there's some history there. She's a single mum; Gwennie's father isn't on the scene and never has been. Shall we go?'

Harri wondered if the hundred-metre drive to Eleri Jones's house further up the hill was for his benefit. All right, it was raining, but that was nothing special for a January in Ceredigion. He'd never mentioned his diabetes to Siân, and he liked to think he kept it under control with the occasional lapse after eating one of the birthday cakes that did the rounds in the office. But there were no flies on Siân, and she probably saw his haggard expression in the mornings when he'd overindulged the night before. He'd also seen her smuggle in a box of doughnuts for the team and conspicuously fail to offer him one. These things had a way of leaking out.

Eleri Jones lived in a small terrace painted an indigo blue. The multicoloured houses were a feature of the town and Eleri had gone further by placing pots of cyclamen with trailing ivy outside her front entrance. She opened the door before they had a chance to knock. She was about Harri's age, with thin blonde hair tied back in a ponytail.

'Got any news for me?' she asked, pulling the door to behind her to keep them outside. Harri let Siân do the talking, given she'd already met the victim's mother. Siân had been right. Eleri didn't like the police, and Harri wondered what was behind that closed door.

'Could we come in, Ms Jones?' asked Siân, moving forward an inch.

Eleri hesitated and nodded. 'All right.'

She opened the door and took them into the front sitting room, which bore the hallmarks of a teenager in the house. A hoodie was thrown over an armchair, printed with Taylor Swift's Eras Tour dates, and two pairs of expensive-looking trainers were lined up at the bottom of a bookcase. Eleri was waiting for her daughter to come home.

'Are you sure you don't want anyone with you?' asked Siân, her eyes also on the trainers.

'I can manage.' Eleri's tone was taut. 'I've given you my statement. If you've no updates for me, why are you here?'

'We're here because of me,' said Harri, conscious of the woman's cold blue eyes on him. 'I'm the senior officer in charge of the investigation and I wanted to introduce myself.'

'Well, you've done that now. Feel free to leave.'

Harri felt a rush of anger towards the mother whose daughter's clothes lay around them. 'I can understand you're upset but I do want to talk to you.'

'I've said everything I'm able to. Gwennie's dead and it's all your fault.'

'I'm sorry?' Harri frowned. 'Why is it my fault?'

'I don't mean you personally. I'm talking about you lot. You're so fucking useless, people can do what they want out here. There's no police presence, you don't attend incidents unless we force the issue and no one is ever caught.'

A little harsh, thought Harri, a wave of weariness washing over him. Sometimes he wondered why he came to work. 'We're going to solve your daughter's murder,' said Harri, surprising himself. It wasn't the sort of thing he usually said to victims' relatives, but Eleri's cynicism had got to him.

It didn't pacify Eleri, who sat on the arm of the sofa shaking her head. 'You'll be of no use, like you were useless when it came to Jaci's death.'

'Jaci?' Harri was trying to remember a recent case involving someone called Jaci. Not on his watch, he was sure. 'Who's Jaci?'

He saw Siân was also frowning, the source of the woman's hostility also news to her.

'Jaci Jones. Remember? Not much use you lot were then too. And don't tell me you're any different from the Met Police because you're all the fucking same.'

'Jaci Jones?' Harri swallowed. 'You knew her?'

'Knew her? That's an understatement. She was my sister, and a fat lot of use you were investigating her death.' Eleri stood, brushing down her trousers. 'Come back when you've got something useful to tell me. And if you're going to pick my daughter's personal life apart like you did Jaci's, you'll have me to deal with.'

# 4

Mallory was bad tempered when she saw the police tape at the bottom of Mwnt Street. She appreciated Harri needed to get to the station as a matter of urgency, and she'd happily boarded the T1 bus at Carmarthen bound for Ceigwyn. She'd promised herself she wasn't going to sit and wait for the call to join the investigation, but the sight of police officers going about their business reminded her of how much she'd come down in the world. There was just an afternoon of washing and tidying up after Toby to look forward to.

Her son, to his credit, was up and showered, not always a given at midday. Mallory had thought long and hard about taking four days' holiday while her son was staying with her. But it was he who was keen to have the house to himself, and at seventeen, with no friends in the area, she was pretty sure he could be trusted. He was on his phone when she walked into the kitchen; nothing unusual there, she supposed, but he hastily put it in his back pocket.

'There's been a murder, Mum,' he said, giving her a brief hug. She could feel the tension in him, his body taut. 'It's all over the internet. I can't believe it.'

She pulled back despite the unexpected physical closeness. 'Murder? I thought it was an assault.'

'It's been on the news.' Toby's voice trailed off. 'She died. Will you be working on the murder?'

'Oh God, I don't know. It's up to Harri or his boss, I suppose. Have they named the victim?' she asked, although, given she'd only been here a few weeks, she was unlikely to know the name.

'I think she's called Gwennie Jones. That's what it says on the news sites. She apparently died during the *Mari Lwyd* festival. It's so stupid a murder happened when everyone was having so much fun. I went down to the quay to watch what was going on and the town was packed.' Mallory heard the high-pitched note of anxiety. Toby wasn't the most robust of teenagers and she needed to offer him some comfort.

'You're not concerned, are you? I don't think it was a random attack, if that's what you're worried about.'

Toby winced. He suffered from mental health issues mainly connected to his intake of food and body image, and there was a vulnerability about him that was distinctly lacking in her or his father. Mallory felt her gung-ho parenting style just wasn't what he needed sometimes.

He took a deep breath. 'It just feels, I dunno, weird that it's happened here. I mean, in London, I'm always careful, especially on the Tube at night. It just feels safe in Wales.'

'It *is* safe here, but if it's a relationship dispute, for example, these things can blow up at any time. Look, let's go and grab a burger from the cafe in the quay. You can tell me what you've been up to.'

Toby wavered, and Mallory could have kicked herself. Using food as a reward or means of bonding was generally a bad idea with her son, but there was precious little else to do in the town for a boy his age in the depths of winter. She could hardly offer to take him to the beach.

'If you're not hungry, we could just have hot chocolate.'

'Sure,' said Toby, picking up his coat. 'A drink sounds good.'

–

In the cafe, Toby ordered a plain hot chocolate with skimmed milk while Mallory got herself a burger, suddenly ravenous now she was on terra firma. The place was quiet, probably reeling from the events of the previous night. At the corner table, she could hear two women discussing the murder.

'They say her head was caved in.'

Mallory caught Toby's eye and grimaced. 'Do you want to move to another table?'

Toby shook his head. 'Have they caught who did it? Maybe it was a boyfriend.'

Mallory shrugged. 'I don't know. I'm not involved in the investigation unless something comes up that I can help them with.'

Toby fiddled with the zip of his coat. 'I saw the blue lights last night and went to see what was going on. There was blood everywhere. The girl was lying on the floor and there was this dark red liquid by her skull. They put a tent up afterwards, but not before I'd seen her injuries.'

'God, Toby. You didn't need to see that. Why did you go to look?'

Toby shrugged. 'I dunno. I was a bit bored, to be honest. I've been thinking, do you think I'd make a good police officer?'

Mallory froze but kept her expression neutral. Even though Toby was the son of two officers, she had never given any thought that he might be attracted to the force. There were plenty who came into the job as a result of family connections, but Toby was, well, different. He was sensitive and emotional, unlike either herself or Joe. While she was all for the constabulary recruiting more emotionally intelligent officers, she wasn't sure Toby was up for the rough and cut of everyday policing. He was too physically frail, if nothing else.

'I think if you join the police, it needs to be because it's something you want to do, not just because your parents are in the job.'

Toby screwed up his face. 'I don't know what else to do.'

It was as Mallory had thought. Toby had no great desire to become an officer; he was just seeing what was around. She noticed she'd lost his attention, his gaze directed towards the doorway. Mallory turned and saw Harri and DC Siân Lewis coming in out of the cold. Harri looked freezing, rubbing his hands together to get warm. Mallory turned back to Toby.

'Don't wave, he's working.'

But Siân had already spotted them, and Harri, after a moment's hesitation, made his way towards them.

'Enjoy the house to yourself?' he asked Toby as he reached their table.

'It was all right,' Toby mumbled. Although he and Harri got on perfectly fine, he looked embarrassed at the question.

'I hear the victim of the assault last night died,' said Mallory. 'I'm sorry to hear that.'

Siân glanced at her boss and Mallory wondered what was going on. There was some kind of tension between the two of them, both absorbed in their own thoughts.

'I need to ask you something, Mallory,' said Harri. He was looking at Toby, who took his cue.

'I just need to use the bathroom.'

This wasn't particularly what Mallory wanted to hear, given Toby's bulimia, but at the same time it looked like both Harri and Siân wanted to speak to her, which was something.

Harri took a seat opposite her. 'I'll be quick, as this is a question that can be answered "yes" or "no".'

'OK. I'm intrigued.'

'Other than what you might have read or heard in the media, does the name Jaci Jones mean anything to you from your time in the Met?'

'Jaci… Jaci Jones? Christ, of course it means something. I worked on that investigation when I was a DC, and it's been on my mind recently with the move to Ceigwyn. I heard the name of this town a very long time ago, and I sometimes can't believe I'm living here.' Mallory swallowed, dreading what might be coming next. 'Why are you bringing up Jaci?'

'She grew up in Ceigwyn. I hadn't realised the connection myself until I spoke to her sister this afternoon.'

'Her sister?'

'Eleri Jones is the mother of the victim who was killed last night. She's got a poor view of the police, which isn't going to help the investigation.'

Mallory sat back in her seat, suddenly chilled. Keep calm, she willed herself. 'I remember Eleri. I'm afraid there was a catastrophic break between the police and the family in the aftermath of Jaci's disappearance.' She stopped, spotting Toby coming out of the bathroom. 'I don't really want to talk about it all in front of Toby. Do you have a suspect for this one?'

'Not really, but we're going to speak to her ex-boyfriend and discover who her new boyfriend was. Her mother thinks she was seeing someone.'

'You don't think the two cases are connected, do you?' Mallory was beginning to feel nauseous. Jaci Jones was a name she thought she'd left far in the past. She hoped to God Jaci's mother was nowhere in the vicinity. She was a person she'd happily never meet again.

Harri glanced at Siân, clearly desperate to get back to the investigation. 'I don't know, but I might have a job for you, given your knowledge of the Jaci Jones case. Can we speak tomorrow? I want you to dredge up everything you can remember about Jaci, and I'll see what I can do about getting you onto the team.'

Toby sat back down at the table, wiping his mouth. 'Are you going to give Mum a job?'

Harri smiled across the table at him. 'I like to have the best people in my team.'

# 5

While he was in Ceigwyn, Harri wanted to sit in on Siân's interview with Huw Roberts and his girlfriend Daisy, whose last name they didn't yet know. Superintendent Stephanie Morris wanted to see him that night, and he needed a feel of the possible suspects while door-to-door enquiries continued. He was surprised that more people hadn't come forward with sightings of the victim. In a town bustling with an evening celebration, there must have been plenty of witnesses to Gwennie's wait for her meetup. Given Huw's attendance at the festival with his new girlfriend, Harri doubted he was the person Gwennie was meeting, but that didn't rule him out as a killer. Jealousy was a powerful motive in homicide. As they sat in the car contemplating the harbour, he wondered if he had any other suspects to bring to the super.

'The two that found Gwennie as she was dying, Andrew Price and Sue Davis. What do you know about them?'

'DI Williams asked me to check them out first. His thinking was that there wasn't much time between Gwennie being attacked and her being found. Either her attacker was extraordinarily fast, lucky or perhaps one of the people administering first aid. Andrew Price, who discovered Gwennie, is a retired dentist. He lives alone and was widowed last summer. He gives the impression of someone still coming to terms with grief. He says he didn't know the victim, and he seemed shocked and upset.'

'And Sue Davis?'

'She did recognise Gwennie and said she knew Eleri, but only from school. They said hello when they saw each other in the street and that was it.'

'We've no idea at this stage what weapon we're looking for?'

Siân shook her head. 'If there is even a weapon. Plenty of people have died from single-blow punches.'

Harri looked at his watch. 'I'd like them both reinterviewed. This is a small town where people often know more than they think about the dynamics of a place. We need to establish a motive as quickly as possible.'

Siân nodded and started the engine. 'You don't think the Jaci Jones case has got anything to do with it? I'm going to have to read up on that one.'

Harri thought back to Mallory's stricken expression. 'I'd like to leave Jaci Jones to one side for the moment. We don't have any reason to connect the cases yet.'

–

Eleri had given Huw's address as 24, The Terrace. The street was towards the edge of the town, a good twenty-minute walk to the harbour, and if that's where the couple had started from, their journey into town would have taken them right past the spot where Gwennie had been standing. It was a shabby area, mainly rental properties with key safes next to front doors. Tourism hadn't reached this part of town, and as they approached the house, a strong smell of cannabis wafted towards them. Siân glanced at Harri and winked.

'I think this might be the source of Eleri's disapproval.'

They rapped on the door, there was a brief face at the window and a good two minutes later, Huw appeared on the step. He was a gangly lad with a spotty complexion, but underneath, Harri could see how he might be attractive to women. A girl stood in shadow behind him, only her long fair hair visible.

'Can we come in?' asked Siân.

Huw took them into the street-facing living room, where a large cheese plant blotted out most of the light. Unasked, Harri and Siân took a chair each, with Huw and Daisy perching on the sofa.

'Is it about Gwennie's death?' asked Daisy.

'You knew her?' asked Siân.

Daisy nodded. 'She was the year below me in school. We occasionally hung out together.'

'Hung out?' asked Siân. 'What did that involve?'

Daisy fiddled with the toggle on her hoodie. 'We'd get the bus into Aber and look around the shops or sit on the seafront. Huw too.'

Harri watched Huw nod. He knew the scenario well; it had been the same in his day. A group of friends hanging out. Some interchanging of partners, all very casual.

'Did Gwennie smoke weed?' he asked the pair. Daisy glanced at Huw, who shrugged. Harri suspected he might be able to arrest Huw for supplying as well as using but wanted to examine the group dynamics before going down that route. Huw wasn't bothered by the question.

'She didn't like it. She read something online that it gave you acne and wouldn't touch it.' Huw scratched his pimply chin. 'Do you know who killed her?'

'Not yet,' said Harri. 'Do you?'

Huw shook his head. 'It wasn't me or Daisy. We spent most of the evening inside The Feathers pub, apart from when we walked around the stalls at the quay.'

Siân pulled out her notebook, although she likely knew the facts off by heart. 'You said to Gwennie's mother, Eleri Jones, that you saw Gwennie outside the pharmacy around six. Did you walk from this house?'

Huw nodded. 'We spent the afternoon here and left after five thirty. We saw Gwennie as we were walking down to town.'

'And she looked like she was waiting for someone. What made you say that?'

Huw shrugged. 'Makes sense. Why stand there otherwise?'

'Can you describe how she looked?' asked Siân.

'She was wearing this orange jacket that I hadn't seen before, and she had a bag across her body. It had a silver strap.'

Siân glanced at Harri. She hadn't mentioned a handbag to him, only that Gwennie's phone had been found in the pocket of her coat.

'Was that where you'd meet when you were together?' asked Harri.

Huw laughed. 'There? Why would we meet in that cold place? She used to come here or I'd pick her up from her house, although that old bitch Eleri didn't like me there.'

Harri looked around at the bohemian living room. 'Do you live with your parents?'

'Just Dad. Mum left years ago. He works at the meat factory.' Harri nodded. It was the local employer – a slaughterhouse-cum-meat-processing plant that stunk on a hot summer's day. Come to think of it, it reeked every day.

'Do you know anything about a new boyfriend? Eleri thought she was seeing someone from England.'

The pair of them shook their heads. 'We haven't seen much of Gwennie over Christmas,' said Daisy. 'I think she had someone as she didn't seem that bothered about me and Huw. So there must have been someone else.'

'But you don't know who.'

'Nope,' said Huw, unconcerned. 'No idea.'

Harri looked at the pair. They were dry eyed and calm, but he detected an undercurrent of shock. Ceigwyn wasn't a place where you'd come to harm. 'What was Gwennie like? Describe her to me.'

Huw opened his mouth and closed it again, unable to form a sentence. Harri wondered if it was a lack of intelligence or an over-indulgence in class B drugs. He suspected a mix of both. Daisy, however, sucked in her breath and exhaled noisily.

'She was a bit different like she didn't mind being on her own. Most of us spend most of our time outside our homes, but Gwennie would say she wanted a night in, and we wouldn't see her for ever. She also wanted to get away from here. Talked about moving to London one day to work in a posh hotel.'

'Did she ever mention her aunt, who was killed in London?' he asked. 'Jaci Jones?'

Daisy's eyes widened. 'We knew all about Jaci's murder, but no one ever spoke about it because it was so terrible. I mean, it was a long time ago, before Gwennie was born. Except…'

'Except what?' asked Harri.

'Except about a month ago, we were talking about murders because there was something on the news and Gwennie said that there was money to be made from Jaci, if you knew how.'

'Money to be made?' asked Harri. 'Who would be giving her money?'

Huw made a scoffing sound. 'Not someone from round here. Maybe find that guy from England.'

–

They were back in the car when Siân received a call to say the 'guy from England' had shown up at the crime scene distraught at the news of Gwennie's attack and was having trouble articulating himself. Harri, used to dealing with teenagers, drove back to the pharmacy and took him into the car. Fat blobs of tears coursed down his face as he heaved out his full name.

'It's Liam Ball. I'm nineteen.'

'And do you live in Ceigwyn, Liam?' asked Siân.

He shook his head. 'Not now. I came down here over the summer to work at The Feathers as a pot washer. I'm taking a year out before uni and I like it here. They said they'd need to lay me off after the holiday season, but then they said they could keep me on until Christmas.'

'So you left at Christmas, did you?' asked Siân.

Liam shook his head. 'I thought they'd lay me off, but no one said anything. Last week, though, my dad had a heart attack and Mum called me to say he was in Salford Royal. Jo, my boss at The Feathers, let me go straight away and I left that day.'

'How's your dad doing?' asked Harri.

'He's had stents put in yesterday and we think he'll be OK.'

'And you left… when?' asked Siân.

'Monday this week.'

'OK, and where were you last night, say, between six and seven fifteen?'

Liam wiped his cheeks with his sleeve. 'With Dad in hospital. My mum was with me too.'

Harri watched the lad. He was definitely a step up for Gwennie, clean shaven with short curly hair. Presentable and with a place at university.

'Tell me about your relationship with Gwennie,' asked Harri. 'When did you start seeing each other?'

'About mid-December. She'd broken up with her boyfriend, Huw, and she came for a kitchen job at The Feathers. She didn't get it as Jo, my boss, wanted someone who could serve at the bar too when needed, but I asked Gwennie if she wanted to get an ice cream sometime and that's what we did. We met for coffee and ice cream.'

'Was it a sexual relationship?' asked Siân.

Liam nodded. 'Towards the end. We only did it twice, though, over Christmas. She didn't seem bothered about it.'

'Would you still have called yourself boyfriend and girlfriend when you left on Monday?' asked Harri, studying his reaction closely.

Liam shrugged. 'I don't know. I messaged her to say I had to go back to see my dad and she replied that she was sorry. The thing is, when I left, Jo said she could employ me again from mid-March if I wanted, but January and Feb would be too quiet to need me. I wasn't sure if I'd ever see Gwennie again.'

'You didn't want to come back to resume your relationship with Gwennie.'

Liam shook his head. 'She seemed distracted, maybe excited even, but wouldn't tell me what it was about. She kind of got bored with me after that.'

'And you didn't make any arrangements to meet Gwennie outside Evans's Pharmacy yesterday evening,' said Harri.

'Definitely not. I was at the hospital all day.'

'OK,' said Harri. 'So, how did you find out that Gwennie had died?'

'Jo at The Feathers called me. She was crying as everyone knows the family around here. She's given me my old room back in the pub for a few days while I came down to see what had happened, but I need to go back to help with Dad soon. Do you think I should call to see Gwennie's mum? I never got to meet her as Gwennie said she was a bit odd.'

Harri thought back to the reception he'd got. 'Maybe leave it a day or so. Eleri's got a lot to deal with at the moment.'

# 6

Jaci Jones. It was a name Mallory had repressed for years. Even when she'd visited the house in Ceigwyn, the only property on the rental market she could afford, she'd resolutely refused to think of Jaci. She'd seen Eleri once in Carmarthen a year or so ago and the woman had passed her without recognition. She doubted that would be the case with Eleri and Jaci's mother, Marion, who had reserved a special ire for Mallory, but she'd last heard Marion lived somewhere in Somerset and rarely came home.

Mallory sat on the sofa in her living room and tried to think. She needed a clear head if she was going to agree to become part of the current murder investigation, and that was by no means a given. But she was one of the few people who knew the ins and outs of Jaci Jones's disappearance, and they must surely want her. Despite the hunt for Jaci being one of her failures, she had been a junior member of the team, and it had propelled her career forward, giving her the hunger for solving crimes to atone for failing to bring a conclusion to the Jones family agony. In some respects, Toby had his own connection to the case. While Mallory was working on the investigation, she had met his father, Joe, and they had got together, with Mallory falling pregnant shortly afterwards. Toby owed his existence to the case.

Although desperate to get on her laptop and remind herself of the essential facts of the investigation, Toby needed her attention until he returned to London the following morning. She took him for a drive into Aberystwyth, picking up some ready meals from M&S for their supper. He was quiet for the trip, not glued to his phone or listening to music, but in a world of his own.

'Are you OK?' she asked him when they were back at the house. 'You know, I wish you hadn't gone out to see the victim on the street. I could arrange for some counselling if you'd like.'

Toby folded his arms. 'I'm already having counselling, aren't I? I don't want to see another one.'

'I meant someone who's experienced in trauma. Police get to see them sometimes after a violent crime. I could ask around.'

Toby shook his head. 'Don't bother. I'll be all right.'

After picking at his food, he went to his room while Mallory thought out a plan of action. After a ten-minute internal debate, she got out her mobile and called her ex-husband, Joe.

Relations between them had significantly improved since he'd begun a relationship with a new woman called Jennifer, who Toby seemed to like but rarely mentioned, perhaps to spare Mallory's feelings. Joe answered his mobile on the first ring, a common occurrence that spoke volumes about his addiction to his smartphone.

'Is everything all right?' He failed to hide the alarm in his voice, probably as damaged by stress over Toby's bulimia and anorexia as she was.

'Toby's fine and looking forward to getting back to London, I think. He quite enjoyed being in the house on his own. I'd never have gone if I thought it was going to be an issue.'

'That's all right then.' Joe relaxed. 'How are you?'

'Post holiday blues, I think. However, something's come up. First of all, a girl was attacked and died in the town yesterday evening. I was getting the overnight ferry so Toby was on his own. He saw the blue lights and went out to take a look.'

'Is he all right?'

'He seems to be. He's not exactly, well, open, but he seems to be OK. I thought I'd better mention it, but there's a second issue which he doesn't know about. It means I might be contracted on another investigation.'

Joe groaned. 'You know, you spend as much time in a police station as I do. When it comes to my retirement, I'm not going near another criminal inquiry. Why can't you do the same?'

Because I'm bored stiff, Mallory thought. 'Jaci Jones,' she said. 'Remember her?'

Joe whistled down the phone. 'That's a name I haven't heard for a long time. What about her? Has someone come forward with new evidence?'

'No, unfortunately. It was her niece, Gwennie, who was killed last night during a local celebration in this town. Investigating officers hadn't made the connection until the SIO visited the victim's next of kin this afternoon.'

'Bloody hell, I bet that wasn't an easy conversation. It wasn't Marion Jones, was it?'

Mallory winced at the name. 'The person Harri spoke to was Eleri, Gwennie's mother. Marion is the victim's grandmother, but I don't think she's currently in Wales.'

'If you're hoping to be co-opted onto the investigation, I'd pray Marion isn't close by. Neither of us were her favourite people, and she isn't the type to forget a name or a face.'

The sting of outrage pinched Mallory, and she remembered the shame every time she'd spoken to Marion. Joe was wrong, though, about Marion disliking them both. Jaci's mother had placed the blame squarely on Mallory for the team's failure to discover Jaci's whereabouts, even though she'd been the most junior member. There had been an unfortunate TV appeal that had gone down badly with the family; they felt that Jaci's reputation had been besmirched. Perhaps it was because Mallory was a woman that she'd drawn most of Marion's ire, which was bloody unfair. She'd been a mere detective constable, and it had been her first major case, so she'd been desperate to do things the right way.

'I'm going to look over the case from back in 2008. Just news articles and whatever else I can find on the internet. I might even look at Reddit to see what the conspiracy theorists are saying.'

Joe sighed down the line. 'You'll be unpleasantly surprised to find both our names there. I took a look a few years back and there was a whole thread discussing the perceived failures of the investigative team, you and me included.'

Mallory felt her face flame and a prickle of tears appear. She dabbed at the corner of one eye with her finger. 'But we did our best, didn't we? We looked and looked and Jaci couldn't be found. I can understand why it's still a matter of interest for armchair detectives, given Jaci is still missing, but why blame us? Not all crimes are easy to solve, are they?'

'You don't need to tell me that, Mallory. Look, CID never suited me, which is why I'm better off in uniform.

We don't have the glamour of detectives, but I'm not working into the nights any longer. You know that investigation was the catalyst for my change in direction. We looked at every possible avenue, drew a blank and upset the family in the process. I have none of that in my current job and sleep easy at night.'

'So why were you looking at Reddit conspiracy threads?'

Joe sighed again. 'It was always hard to hoodwink you. Just look after yourself, won't you? Toby loves you and I still care. Our first and only investigation together was a poisoned chalice and neither of us want to be living through all that again.'

'You'll keep an eye on Toby?'

'Of course.'

After finishing the call, Mallory couldn't help herself and looked at various Reddit threads to do with Jaci Jones. Some of it was old hat, but there was stuff there that bordered on the defamatory – rumours of father figures, sex tapes and drug use. The team had found no evidence of any of that whatsoever. All they knew was that Jaci was an ordinary, single girl who seemed to be keeping a big secret. They just never found out what or who it was.

# 7

*3 November 2008*

Jaci put her key in the lock and pushed open the glass door of her first-floor flat. She'd specifically asked her landlord to replace the door with a wooden one so her silhouette wouldn't be visible to whoever was outside when she opened it at night, but after three months' tenancy, she'd done nothing to sort it out. The outside walkway was brightly lit, though, and her neighbour Eddie Novak usually looked out for her coming home from work. As if on cue, he banged on the partition wall, two hard raps. She gave the agreed answer, a corresponding three knocks, and all was silent. Eddie wasn't one to intrude; he just liked to make sure she was home safely from work. Three knocks and all was well.

Jaci went through to the small, square kitchen and dumped the shopping bag on the counter. She placed the apples and clementines in a bowl and turned on the oven for the fish pie she'd treated herself to. Her mother, Marion, would have been shocked at the meal, coming from a generation that made everything from scratch. Fish pie had been one of her specialities, too, with freshly caught mackerel, a creamy sauce and mashed potato. This ready meal wouldn't be a patch on Marion's, but it would be filling on this chilly November night.

At seven o'clock, she took a shower and opened the new perfume she'd bought – another treat. It hadn't been her usual fragrance until six months ago, when she'd been gripped by a nostalgia for the first bottle of scent she'd ever had, even if it had been one of Marion's cast-offs. It had been offered first to Eleri but, two years older than Jaci, she preferred to wear Dewberry, bought in a little bottle from the Body Shop with her savings from the Saturday job she had in Ceigwyn. At twelve, Jaci had no savings and had taken the bottle off Marion with a kind of reverence. It had been the start of a love affair with perfume, and the sight of the familiar blue and white packaging in a supermarket glass cabinet had stopped her in her tracks. She'd worn it and worn it and had even kept the perfume bottle after it was empty. Now she had a new package to open. *Je Reviens*. I'll be back.

She sprayed herself with the scent and wrinkled her nose. It smelt more acidic than she remembered but perhaps it was simply because it was a new bottle. It would hopefully settle down to the powdery smoothness that she remembered once it was on her skin. She put on her new pyjamas and took the fish pie out of the oven, putting it on a tray so she could eat it while watching the Scandi drama she'd been recording. She had no other plans for the night but to eat her meal and watch the detective in the knitted jumper solve the crime.

She took her phone and texted her mother to say she'd call at the weekend. Marion usually liked a chat and Jaci was too tired to cope with her mother's uncertain moods. Instead, she found the recording she'd made of Saturday's *Strictly Come Dancing* and watched Tom Chambers waltz his partner around the dancefloor. She loved the romantic dances, evoking a long-lost age of glamour.

She'd just scooped up the last morsel of mashed potato when the doorbell rang. She frowned and turned down the TV, listening. The doorbell rang again, this time a fraction longer. Jaci, feeling vulnerable in her pyjamas, pulled on a jumper and walked towards the door.

'Who is it?' she asked, ready to bang on the partition wall for help. Eddie might be getting on a bit, but he'd be able to call the police easily enough.

'It's me.' It was a voice she recognised. A surprise, but still welcome. She banged three times on the wall – all is well – and opened the front door.

# 8

Toby, with the resignation of many a police officer's child, accepted with good grace Mallory's proposal that he get an earlier train from Carmarthen back to London so that she could attend the police briefing at 9.30. She bought him breakfast at McDonald's and watched him eat a few mouthfuls before he stuffed the rest back into the paper bag, promising he'd finish it on the train. At the station, while she was buying his ticket, she saw Toby put the bag into the refuse bin. She said nothing, giving him a hug while he tensed in her arms. She felt that they were leaving on bad terms, a reaction she put down to having poured cold water on his suggestion of joining the police. Mallory, however, had seen many a police career ruined in relation to someone not right for the role. Toby was too young and too... Mallory couldn't think of the word, but just not right. Once more, she wondered if Toby would have flourished under a more emotionally sensitive mother.

At the police station in Carmarthen, she felt on safer ground. Even as a civilian investigator, this was familiar territory, and she could bring something to the inquiry into the death of Gwennie Jones, even if it was the details of her own place in what she saw as the failed investigation into the disappearance of the dead girl's aunt. Unusually, it was Siân who met her in reception, dangling Mallory's lanyard in her hand.

'Harri's been called upstairs, as it were. There was supposed to be a meeting last night that was cancelled, so I've been asked to update you on the investigation before we get started so you're up to speed.'

'All right.' Upstairs meant Superintendent Steph Morris, which suggested the investigation was going to be high profile, and Mallory had a pretty good idea why.

'Fancy a decent brew?' Instead of leading her to the open-plan CID office, Siân steered her to the coffee shop and bought them both lattes. 'We'll sit in the corner so we're not overheard, but we might as well be comfortable while I fill you in with what little I have. How much do you know?'

'Only what Harri told me in the cafe yesterday. That the victim was Gwennie Jones, who lived in Ceigwyn, and was the niece of the still-missing Jaci Jones.' It wasn't much really, but it had set off a train of memories for Mallory.

'We'll leave Jaci to one side at the moment, because that's where you come in.' Siân took a swig of her coffee and dabbed foam from the side of her mouth. 'The problem is that not much has happened since we saw you yesterday afternoon. You know what it's usually like at the beginning of an investigation with events moving fast. That's not happening here. Harri and I think we're in for a long slog.'

'Are there any suspects?'

Siân shrugged. 'Not obvious ones. Gwennie had an ex-boyfriend called Huw Roberts, who is one of the witnesses in establishing her last movements. She was last seen by her mother around three yesterday afternoon going into town, and friends have come forward to say they saw her around four thirty walking towards her house. She was wearing a distinctive orange jacket, but these are positive IDs from girls who knew her.'

'And the ex saw her too?'

'Yes, at around six he passed Gwennie with his new girlfriend. He was under the impression that she was waiting for someone. The couple went on to The Feathers pub and, according to the statement, they stayed put until they walked around the stalls at the quay following the *Mari Lwyd*.'

'Christ.' Mallory sat back in her chair. 'I'd never heard of the festival before I came here. It sounds bizarre, parading around the streets with a horse's head, but even Toby went down to see it.'

Siân laughed. 'Never been to one myself. Part of a revival of an older tradition, if you ask me. They weren't doing it when I was growing up. Anyway, we're now looking to establish the alibi of Huw and Daisy, his girlfriend. The pub apparently has CCTV inside, after a vicious fight last year, so we should be able to confirm that side of their story.'

'They couldn't have killed Gwennie and then gone to the pub?'

'Overnight, we've had another witness who's come forward. She saw Gwennie by Evans's Pharmacy around ten to seven and she was still waiting for someone, looking at her watch. The witness knows both Gwennie and Eleri's mother, so is reliable. In addition, house-to-house enquiries have unearthed two further witnesses who've said they saw a girl in an orange coat standing in the spot. One estimates around six-ish, the other can't really remember but thinks it's before quarter to seven.'

'So that suggests Gwennie was waiting for at least three quarters of an hour for whoever she was meeting. It must have been important to her – most people would have long given up. Is there a current boyfriend?'

'We interviewed Liam Ball last night after he came forward looking pretty distraught. He'd been seeing Gwennie since mid-December and said she'd kind of lost interest in him. He sounds like he might have a good alibi, with his father undergoing surgery the day Gwennie died, but we're checking it out.'

'What about her phone? Are there messages to suggest who she might have been meeting?'

'We have her mobile and her password was her date of birth, so it's been straightforward to access. There are no messages as far as we can see, so there's the possibility that the arrangement was made verbally. We're going through recent calls now.' Siân bit her lip. 'Last night Huw said she was carrying a cross-body bag with a silver strap. We're checking with Eleri, but we think it's missing.'

'God, could theft be a motive?' How utterly tragic, thought Mallory, if Gwennie was killed for the contents of her bag. 'Could she have been dealing, for example?'

'Her ex says not and I can't see why he'd be protecting her. He's definitely a user himself. His place stank of the stuff.'

'What kind of girl was Gwennie? I remember Jaci being ambitious, desperate to get out of Wales. Was Gwennie happy with her lot?'

'She'd talked about moving to London. I'm wondering if her relationship to Jaci might have prompted this. She told Huw that there was money to be made from Jaci's disappearance.'

'What?' Mallory swallowed her hot coffee in surprise, burning her throat. 'What did she mean by that?'

'We don't know. I wouldn't even know where to start with a comment like that.'

'You weren't serving when Jaci disappeared, were you?'

'Nope.' Siân looked across at her. 'I was a teenager at the time, but I remember being intrigued by the case. It just seemed so… unlikely.'

Mallory winced. 'Do you know how many people are reported missing each year in the UK? Around 170,000, and they think that figure isn't a true snapshot of those who have disappeared as many are just never reported. Our problem back then was that, because Jaci had a relaxed approach to dating, we thought she'd just gone off with someone and would turn up in due course.'

'We?'

'Well, most of us, I suppose.' Mallory pushed her coffee to one side. 'The senior investigating officer was Terrence Foster. Old school, liked his holidays in Marbella and kept his tan permanently topped up with a sunbed at home. But on it, if you get my drift. Nobody's fool. Whatever the failings of the case were, Terry was sharp as a tack but kept his intelligence hidden like a dirty secret. Preferred to be one of the lads.'

'I know the type.' Siân looked across the coffee shop to check no one was listening. 'He was competent, though?' she asked in a lower voice. 'Not corrupt or anything?'

'Very competent, I would have said, but his background held him back. He couldn't understand someone with as complex a love life as Jaci and that proved fatal to the case.'

'I…' Siân stopped as Harri came into view.

'Mind if I join you?' He pulled out a chair and extracted a bank card. 'Get us another round of drinks, would you, Siân?'

Siân frowned at his tone but took the card.

'Toby get off all right?' Harri loosened his tie a fraction, his face creased with lack of sleep.

'He did and seemed fine about being dropped off a little early. Am I on the team?'

Harri grimaced. 'Unofficially, no. Things have got a bit hairy with the press. But we do have a job for you.'

Mallory puffed out her cheeks. 'Anything.'

Siân returned with the coffees.

'There's something I need to tell you first. Siân is hearing this for the first time too. Eleri Jones was pretty pissed off yesterday when we spoke to her, but she's clearly been doing some thinking in the meantime. She called my mobile this morning and told me about a documentary being made into the disappearance of Jaci Jones. Gwennie was clearly excited about it and had begun to ask questions about her aunt.'

'Oh no,' said Mallory, the bitterness of the coffee suddenly unbearable. 'I've not heard anything about this.'

'No reason for you to have, if plans are at an early stage. We're checking everything out now. It could have been some blogger or podcaster trying it on, but Gwennie thought it was going to be the chance of a starring role. The niece's perspective, that kind of thing. She had aspirations to be an actress and was applying to do a drama course at Llanelli.'

'Next stop, Hollywood,' said Mallory, unable to help herself.

Siân coloured. 'Catherine Zeta Jones made it to LA via Swansea. No need to sneer.'

'Sorry.' Mallory pulled a face, a wash of shame making her grow hot. 'A documentary is bad news. Is it just coincidence that Gwennie is now dead?'

Harri crossed his arms. 'The crime has a local feel to me. I'm not convinced by either boyfriend's story until it's proven otherwise, but I'm not ruling anything out. That's where you come in.'

# 9

Harri watched Mallory's reaction to the news. This was going to be a tricky case – weren't they all? – but Mallory in ordinary circumstances was someone he'd have asked to assist the team. However, there was clearly some unfinished business with the Jaci Jones investigation, and there was also the issue that they were now a couple. After doing some hard thinking overnight, he'd fought hard with his boss to have Mallory on the case, and it had been nothing to do with his personal life. He needed someone on the team who knew the Jaci Jones case inside out, and that, he realised after checking her work record, was Mallory. He wasn't yet convinced that Gwennie's death was related to her aunt's disappearance, as experience had taught him that there were weird coincidences in everyday life. However, he needed someone to check that angle and Mallory was the person best placed to do this. The fact that she'd not mentioned the case to him before this week was neither here nor there. Mallory had a past and so did he and neither of them was inclined to dwell there. First, however, he had to deliver the bad news.

'OK,' he said, leaving his coffee untouched. 'The first thing is you're not officially co-opted onto the team. The super was adamant about that, and I happen to agree with her. The case was well contained from a media point of view, with only the *Western Mail* pushing us to release information to pad out their story. That changed this morning.'

Harri glanced at Siân, who would also be wondering where he was going with this. He continued. 'Gwennie Jones's grandmother, Marion Jones, went to the *Daily Mail* to tell them that Gwennie was the niece of Jaci Jones, a woman missing due to, and I quote, "the rank incompetence of the police officers in 2008".'

Mallory folded her arms. 'That's bullshit. Are you going to take the word of one disgruntled family member?'

'No, I'm not, and neither is the boss. We do, however, have to contain the news story.'

Harri watched Mallory inspect the contents of her coffee cup. She asked, 'Are the newspapers on their way down here? I haven't seen any around Ceigwyn.'

'I'm not so sure. It's not like the old days where we'd get journalists haring down from London. A lot like to do the work online, plus there's some uneasy history with this case. I have a local press contact who Marion tried to contact and he mentioned she has a difficult relationship with the press.'

'She has a difficult relationship with everyone,' said Mallory.

'Anyway, we're scheduling a press conference at three p.m., by which time, Mallory, you need to be out of the building.'

'You think Marion Jones will be there? She won't have a press pass.'

'No, but by then any journalists who are coming down here will be genned up on the case, including who was on the original investigating team. We can't have anyone making the connection with you.'

Harri realised with a shock that Mallory looked ill. It was only a day since they'd been on the ferry, hinting at plans for the future. Now she looked stricken, something far worse than the dogged tiredness he felt as a result of a restless night.

She half-rose. 'If I'm so toxic—'

'Sit down, for God's sake.' He saw that Siân was watching them. 'I'm warning you because even if Marion can't get into the press conference, you can damn well be sure she'll be on her way down here. I've heard she still lives in the Bristol region so it's not far for her to come, and she has Eleri here. As far as she's concerned, though, no one from the original investigating team is in the vicinity, and that's how I'd like to keep things.'

'And yet the super agreed for me to be involved in the investigation.'

'Steph knows that whatever happens, journalists will be digging around and will know you've been contracted to help us in the past. They'll find you eventually and make the link. We say you're not on the current investigating team, which will be the truth. However, she's looking for a scenario where you help us see if there's a connection with Jaci Jones's disappearance without us officially having you on the payroll.'

'Aren't you being a bit public having coffee with me here?' Mallory's expression was sour.

'It would invite more comment if you were up in my office. Now listen, Siân's a youngster and too many late nights have fried my brain. I want you to give us a quick recap of what went on in 2008 and then I'll tell you what I want you to do next.'

'All right.' To Harri's relief, Mallory settled back down. He hoped he was doing the right thing, even though she clearly wanted the work. He was sure she'd once told him that she'd met her ex-husband on the investigation. That, along with a professional failure, must be churning up some unpleasant memories. 'Where do you want me to start?'

'With an overview of the case. Forget, for a moment, your own part in the investigation; tell us how everything started, as if you were briefing a journalist.'

'Fine. On the third of November, Jaci Jones returned home from her work and let herself into her flat. She lived in a former local authority block in Wimbledon but most of the units were now under private ownership, including Jaci's, which she rented from her landlord. She gave a series of knocks to her neighbour, a prearranged signal between friends who looked out for each other in a strange city. Her neighbour, Eddie Novak, was from the former Czechoslovakia. He had arrived here in the Sixties and was a retired road sweeper. He kept an informal eye on all the residents of the estate.'

'Jaci was around thirty, wasn't she?' asked Siân, scribbling notes into her book.

'Thirty-one, so an adult with her own life and a good job as a PA in a large insurance company. She kept in touch with her family in West Wales.' Mallory stopped. 'Her mother, Marion, had temporarily been living with her over that summer for reasons we never got to the bottom of, but had returned to the Somerset area. Marion said she wanted to spend some time in London, which seemed entirely natural, but…' Mallory looked at Harri.

'There are times you need your mother, but, given Jaci's subsequent disappearance, it's natural to probe a bit deeper into the mother–daughter relationship.'

'Exactly,' said Mallory, 'but we never found anything suggesting Marion's presence was anything more than a long-ish holiday.'

'Was she able to give you any information in relation to Jaci's love life or friendships?'

'Marion said she'd met a work colleague of Jaci's called Lizzie Cates. The two of them went out for a drink regularly and it seemed a pretty normal friendship. What was interesting, though, was that neither Marion nor Lizzie could furnish names of any of Jaci's boyfriends, past or present.'

'Which is unusual,' said Harri, 'for a young, single woman.'

'Yep.' Mallory grimaced into her coffee. 'We'll come back to Marion shortly, but the main thing is that Jaci was alive at around seven p.m. because she texted Marion to say she was at home and going to have an early night after she'd caught up with *Strictly Come Dancing*. And that was the last communication with her.'

Siân stared impassively at Mallory. 'When did people realise she was missing?'

'Almost immediately. At nine a.m. Jaci didn't turn up for work, which was very unusual, and her boss, a woman named Julie Edge, phoned Jaci's mobile and home phone and left messages on both. When they hadn't heard from her by the end of the day, Lizzie, Jaci's friend, said she'd drop by on her way home to see if Jaci was poorly, given the flu was circulating the office. When she reached the flat, Eddie Novak opened his door and spoke to her. He was concerned because Jaci's curtains had remained drawn all day, and she was very particular about opening them before leaving for work.'

'He didn't have a key to check?' asked Harri.

'She'd promised to give him one but had proved reluctant to hand it over. It was our first sign that Jaci was a private person who didn't like the idea of someone in her flat. She'd even insisted in her lease that her landlord give her fourteen days' notice before a visit. Anyway, there was no answer at the flat, and when Mr Novak and Lizzie realised that Jaci might be ill, they called the police who, after knocking, forced open the door.'

'And...'

'And nothing. Jaci wasn't there. The attending officers were inclined to think Jaci had gone off with a boyfriend and just failed to tell her place of work. Neither Eddie nor Lizzie were happy with that explanation, and Lizzie went back to the office and obtained Jaci's personnel files, which she gave to Marion as next of kin. And here's the first weird part. Marion, too, was inclined to dismiss the bother. It was a Tuesday night and Jaci had probably thought she'd already booked the day off work. Apparently, she was in the habit of taking mid-week breaks because they were cheaper than weekends.'

'That's interesting,' said Siân, scribbling furiously. 'So presumably no one knew who Jaci liked to take these mid-week breaks with.'

'Exactly that. It was the nub of the whole case and one we never got to the bottom of. In terms of an investigation, it was a complete and utter failure.'

Harri noticed that Siân had put down her pen and was looking at Mallory in astonishment. She was probably around the age Mallory had been while on the team. 'So what was the issue?' asked Siân.

'The problem,' said Mallory, 'was Jaci's "complicated and hidden" love life.' She made speech marks with her fingers. 'That's where all the trouble started.'

# 10

Daily Mail, *15 January*

## JACI JONES'S NIECE SLAIN. HAS THE KILLER STRUCK AGAIN?

The niece of missing Jaci Jones was brutally killed on Sunday evening during a Welsh festival known as Mari Lwyd. Seventeen-year-old Gwennie Jones, a catering student, was found outside a pharmacy with head wounds. She later died in hospital. Police say they are hunting a 'vicious and cowardly killer' who callously left the girl dying from her injuries.

Gwennie's grandmother, Marion Jones, who has remained at the forefront of efforts to find her daughter, Jaci, who went missing in 2008, has rushed to the seaside town of Ceigwyn to comfort her daughter, Eleri. She told the Mail last night, 'Police incompetence at the start of the investigation into Jaci's disappearance meant vital time was lost and clues overlooked. Investigators were obsessed with what they described as Jaci's 'complicated and hidden' love life, despite there being little evidence to suggest this. I'm determined to ensure that the same thing doesn't happen in Gwennie's case. I've asked for an urgent meeting with the person in charge.'

A spokesperson for Dyfed Powys police said that they were keeping an open mind as to the motive behind the fatal attack and would be updating the family regularly. They also stated that there was no evidence of a threat to the wider community, but asked that everyone stayed vigilant until the killer was caught.

## 11

Mallory made a phone call as she walked back to the car. She'd expected to be in a warm conference room listening to Harri allocate tasks for the case, but was instead cast out into the cold, even though they'd agreed a plan of action. She was to meet the current lead on the investigation into Jaci Jones and act as intermediary between Harri's investigation and the cold case team. It was a job, a good one at that, but she still felt deflated. She missed the buzz of the office and chat amongst colleagues. The moment she finally had a nice place to stay, in the very town where a murder had taken place, she'd be on the road trying to find a connection between the two cases.

Harri WhatsApped her the newly published *Mail* article, which she skimmed over before sliding behind the wheel. Despite Harri's optimism, she was pretty sure that sooner or later (and probably sooner) Marion would sniff out Mallory's involvement in the case. Marion wouldn't be able to disguise her spite towards Mallory, and she'd likely be taken off the investigation. In the meantime, she'd crack on as fast as she could, which would begin with meeting the Jaci Jones cold case lead.

Unusually, DCI Çal Bentley was coming to Wales to speak to Mallory and had already left early that morning following a phone call from Harri. She must have had other business in Carmarthen to justify the trip, possibly a meeting with Harri's boss and a briefing on Gwennie's death. In the meantime, she agreed to meet Mallory at a restaurant in Carmarthen, an upmarket Welsh chain that served locally sourced food. Mallory had been too wired during the catch-up with Harri and Siân to eat anything, but now her stomach told her she needed refuelling for the days ahead.

She thought back to the details of the murder. On the face of it, there wasn't much to link Gwennie's assault to the disappearance of her aunt. Jaci's body had never been found, plus she'd been living a long way from home and was a woman of independent means. Gwennie, on the other hand, was a student, living at home with her mother, and had been attacked in a public place. With the exception of the blood connection and the possibility of a new documentary looming, there was little to link the two deaths.

Cal Bentley was waiting for Mallory when she pushed open the door of the restaurant. Mallory was adept at spotting one of her tribe – a fellow law enforcement officer. They were usually alert, eyes on the door and disinclined to linger. Cal was a tall, taut woman with Nordic blonde hair pulled tight against her head. She reminded Mallory of one of the English Lionesses who had recently won the UEFA Women's Euro championship. Mallory had once been athletic like this woman but the injury that had invalided her out of the force had made exercise a painful reminder of her former fitness.

Cal spotted Mallory at first glance; clearly recognising one of your own went both ways. She motioned her over and they shook hands, leaving Mallory in no doubt that it was Cal who was leading this meeting.

'It's good to finally meet you. Since I took over as lead on the Jaci Jones disappearance, I've been looking deep into the files. I believe you were one of the first detectives on the scene. Must have been an interesting case to start your career.'

'Interesting is an understatement. It nearly put me off a career in CID, given the pushback we had.' Mallory's stomach rumbled. 'Are you hungry?'

Cal grinned at her, showing a set of teeth bound by a clear brace. 'I'm always hungry. The server has told me the burgers are good here.'

'Fine by me.'

After ordering, Mallory sat back in her chair. 'You know, I'm surprised that you've come all this way to meet me. I thought I'd be travelling at the very least to Cardiff, given the press are likely to be sniffing out some of the personnel from Jaci's investigation.'

Cal shrugged. 'I've only been brought into the cold case team, so I'm low profile. Even Marion Jones doesn't know me by sight, but I have spoken to her on the phone. Six months down the line, we would have had you coming to London, but for the moment, we're both incognito.'

'And long may it last.' Mallory picked up her glass of Pepsi and drank half of it in one go, enjoying the sweet fizziness. 'Where do you want to start?'

'The purpose of this meeting, as you know, is to find a potential connection between Jaci Jones's disappearance and the murder of her niece Gwennie. Investigations into that attack are in the early stages, but we both know speed is of the essence, which is where you come in. I believe you are on the books at Dyfed Powys. Do you like being a civilian investigator?'

Mallory shrugged. 'It's really the only thing that I know how to do well. I suppose sometimes I worry what the future will be like, but everyone does that, don't they?'

'I guess so. I believe you were injured in the line of duty. That must have been tough. I'm glad you're still putting your skills to good use. Your career didn't suffer because of your involvement in the Jaci Jones investigation, but I'm keen to hear how the early stages of the investigation played out. It's all in the files, of course, but I'd like your take on it.'

'I'll do my best. Some of what I say might not sound that great in 2026, especially post #MeToo attitudes.'

Cal sat back in her seat. 'Don't worry about that. I think it's worth me saying upfront that I've found no trace of incompetence in what I've read, just, I dunno, old-fashioned responses, which is odd because we're only talking about just over seventeen years ago.'

'You probably don't realise how much has changed in those years,' said Mallory, trying not to focus on the woman's youth. Cal Bentley was about ten years younger than her, possibly still at school in 2008. 'We've had Black Lives Matter, the killing of Sarah Everard, the undercover policing scandal and so on. Institutional shifts have taken place in policing and all for the better. Back in 2008 there were still old timers like Terry Foster.'

'We'll come back to him,' said Cal crisply. 'Let's start with you. The case was referred to CID twenty hours after Jaci was deemed to have disappeared. I believe you were a newbie in the department.'

'That's putting it mildly. I'd been on the team for three weeks. Terry Foster had taken me under his wing because I looked more fragile than I actually was. On the Wednesday morning after Jaci Jones had been reported missing, officers returned to her flat, saw she still wasn't at home and at that point escalated the missing persons report to detectives with the suspicion that a crime had potentially taken place.'

'Jaci had last been seen at work on the Monday and was on CCTV buying a ready meal for her tea. So she'd been missing all of Tuesday. Was there a sense in the team that they'd have liked to have been notified earlier?'

'Not at all. According to Terry, these things were routine and he still expected Jaci to return home at some point in the week. She liked mid-week breaks, according to work colleagues. Because she was single, she had plenty of annual leave to take, so she'd just take herself away for a night or two. Everyone thought that she'd forgotten to book that leave.'

'But you were one of the first detectives on the scene, weren't you?'

'Terry thought it would be a good routine case for me to cut my teeth on. We went to Jaci's flat and it looked as if she'd popped out for something. She'd had a shop-bought fish pie for her dinner and the foil container was soaking in the sink, probably in preparation for recycling. There were no signs she'd had a drink or had company. Her handbag was slung over a post on the side of her bed and it still contained her wallet.'

'But her phone was missing. Back in 2008, however, to pay for anything, she'd have needed her debit cards or cash.'

'Yes, exactly. There had been no significant withdrawals on the days leading up to her disappearance and, given that she might have gone away for the night, there was the assumption that a partner or friend might have paid for the room.' Mallory stopped, aware she was on fragile ground. 'Which is where we started to look into the nature of Jaci's relationships.'

'Which is entirely natural,' said Cal neutrally. 'Tell me what you found initially.'

'We spoke to the family, namely Marion, her mother, and her sister, Eleri. Marion had spent the summer with her daughter, don't forget, and she confirmed that Jaci, rather than take full week-long holidays, as she'd done in previous years, that summer had decided to go away mid-week on a number of occasions. Marion assumed there was a man or men in the background. She'd asked Jaci, who'd refused to say who it was.'

'Was this normal?'

Mallory shrugged. 'Apparently yes. Jaci didn't share details of her love life with Marion or Eleri. She was a private person when it came to relationships. While Marion was still speaking to us, she did mention that she wondered if Jaci was seeing a married man. It would explain the mid-week trips, which might coincide with their business activities, plus the reasons for her reticence.'

Cal sat back in her chair and regarded Mallory. 'But no one came forward.'

Mallory shook her head. 'No one. We briefly looked into whether Jaci might have been a sex worker or even an escort, but found no evidence of that either. We couldn't even find which hotels Jaci might have gone to. We circulated her details, including an up-to-date photo, everywhere from upmarket hotels to hostels and found nothing.'

'And at what point did it change from a missing person to a murder investigation?'

Mallory frowned. 'Within a week or so. We realised early on that Jaci had come to some form of harm and we guessed it might be due to this secretive relationship or relationships.'

'It's funny,' said Cal, 'but you've mentioned men in the plural for the second time. At what point did you consider she might have been seeing multiple men rather than being in a single, if secret, relationship?'

Mallory rubbed her head. 'I don't remember. Marion was prepared to admit to her suspicions that Jaci might have had a single secretive lover, but work colleagues gave a more nuanced picture of her. She liked to have fun – there were a couple of men she'd had brief flings with at the office, for example, and both said Jaci had been free spirited and uninterested in relationships. She'd spoken to these men about not wanting exclusivity.'

'You considered these men suspects?'

Mallory shook her head. 'No. We looked in depth at their alibis. Both were single and counted Jaci as a friend, and their alibis stacked up. It did lead us to think maybe Jaci saw other men outside the office.'

'And DI Foster went on TV and appealed for these men to come forward, calling Jaci's past "complicated and hidden".'

'Exactly. And at that moment we lost the trust of Marion, who turned on us, accusing us of failing to investigate her daughter's disappearance properly because of our prejudice against women who weren't in settled relationships. She didn't think we'd have used the phrase in relation to a man, and she thought we were trashing Jaci's reputation. She also refused to admit to the possibility of multiple men in Jaci's life.'

'Hmm.' Cal leant back in her seat as two burgers were set down in front of them. The multi-stacked kind that you'd probably have to eat with a knife and fork. 'And who actually came up with the phrase "complicated and hidden"? Was it Terry Foster?'

Mallory stilled. A confession coming that she'd wanted to make for years. 'That would be me.'

## 12

'Eleri Jones is in reception,' said Siân, standing at the entrance of Harri's office. 'She wants to talk to you properly. My guess is some of the shock has worn off and she's had time to think.'

Harri puffed out his cheeks. 'An hour earlier and she'd have bumped into Mallory. Is it me specifically she wants to see?'

Siân nodded. 'Apparently so. I think you must have gone down better with her than DI Williams. She contacted you this morning about the film company, didn't she?'

Harri nodded. 'She did, but there was no mention of a visit to Carmarthen. Can you go down and get her yourself and bring her to me?'

Siân and Eleri appeared five minutes later. Eleri's face bore the creased look of a sleepless night, but she'd put on a burgundy felt coat and smart knee-length boots for the visit.

Harri gestured to a chair. 'Take a seat. Is it all right if Siân sits in on this chat?'

Eleri grimaced, squeezing her eyes tight. 'I'd rather she didn't, if you don't mind. This won't take long.'

Harri considered for a moment and nodded to Siân. 'I'll call if you're needed.'

When Siân had gone, he put down his pen and regarded Eleri. 'I'm happy to see you this once, but I can't spare the time as my attention needs to be focused on the investigation. You've been offered and refused a family liaison officer, which is how we usually speak to family members of victims.'

Eleri shrugged. 'I won't want to see you again, but I need to tell you something. I've been awake all night. I should have told you about the TV documentary yesterday when we first met, but I was so angry. It felt like history was repeating itself and it felt almost unbearable.'

'Because of Jaci? I can see that, but we currently have no evidence whatsoever that Gwennie's attack is linked to Jaci's disappearance.'

Eleri exhaled sharply. 'You haven't?'

Harri shook his head. 'Not at this moment. Do you think there might be a connection?'

'I don't know.' Eleri bit her lip. 'There's a sense of things coming around again. First the TV company try to contact me, then Gwennie is… is killed, Mum has gone to the newspapers shouting about police incompetence. I'm not sure I can bear it again.'

'I'm interested that you started by mentioning the TV company. Tell me what happened.'

Eleri scowled, looking at her fingernails. 'I was approached in November by a man named Beck Cowan. He claimed to be an award-winning documentary maker. Very legit, not those ones who post pictures online of Jaci's old flat.'

'You search to see what people are posting?' asked Harri. 'Is that a good idea?'

Eleri snorted. 'Very little is a good idea at three in the morning, but believe me, that's what you do. No one's ever actually contacted me because there's nothing to see in Ceigwyn, is there? Jaci went missing in London. This guy was different, though. He said he was no armchair detective but wanted to do a documentary focusing on Jaci as victim and the person she'd been. This included her Welsh upbringing.'

'And what did you say to him?' asked Harri, opening the drawer of his desk. He noticed Eleri's voice had turned raspy and he handed her a small bottle of water. 'Drink this.'

She took a swig from the bottle. 'Thanks. I told Mr Cowan I wasn't interested, and I'm not. It's not been easy being known in a small town as the sister of a murdered woman. I tried to shield Gwennie from all that, but I know there were comments at school. I made Jaci a three-dimensional person to her, showing her photos of when we were young and talking about the good times.'

'What about your mother, Marion?'

Eleri grimaced. 'Mum's very bitter, but I told her early on, no speaking in that way in front of Gwennie. To be fair, she didn't really mention Jaci in Gwennie's presence.' Eleri stopped. 'It's terrible to talk about your daughter in the past tense. Do you have kids?'

Harri nodded. 'Two.'

'The thing is, I know Gwennie was contacted by the TV company, which is why I rang you this morning. But there are other things too.'

Harri wished Siân was in the room, taking notes, but the connection with Eleri was fragile. This felt an important moment. 'Go on. What happened?'

'This Beck Cowan somehow got hold of her phone number and said he wanted to talk to her. I put my foot down. Gwennie is seventeen and still a minor, but she wasn't best happy. We had an awful row and she screamed at me that I was ruining her life. So when I rang you, I just wanted to say the TV company had been sniffing around her.'

'You think she might have been meeting the contact on Thursday? It's an odd time to meet, the night of a busy festival, and if it's a professional company, they'd surely not have made a lone female stand in the street.'

Eleri turned her head, regarding the CID offices where the team were busy looking into her daughter's death. 'There are other things. The orange coat she was wearing when she died was new. She said she'd got it from a charity shop, but I didn't believe her. Even a new coat like that would have been twenty or thirty pounds second hand, more like a hundred new. She didn't have that kind of cash. The same with her bag.'

'The one with the silver strap. Has someone asked you about that?'

'The detective who brought me up here called last night to ask me about it. It's missing, all right, but what I didn't tell her was that it was new too.'

'Did you ask her where she got it from?'

Eleri shrugged. 'I'd have got more lies. But what if she was being paid by that TV company?'

Harri wasn't convinced by the logic, but it sounded as if Gwennie had got hold of cash recently. 'We'll speak to this Beck Cowan as soon as possible. Had you noticed any changes in Gwennie's demeanour? Some of her friends have said she withdrew over the Christmas period.'

Eleri shook her head. 'I hadn't noticed. You found that English boy she'd been seeing?'

'Yes. His name's Liam. He's thinking about paying you a visit but isn't sure of the welcome he'll get.'

Eleri crossed her arms. 'As long as he didn't kill Gwennie, he can come and see me.'

–

Harri had to rush from the meeting with Eleri to the scheduled press conference. Journalists made his blood boil. He brushed his unruly curly hair in the lavatory and Siân sponged a coffee stain off his suit collar ready to face the cameras. He was an old hand at these things and he'd got the impression the smattering of journalists had other fish to fry. They'd be heading out to Ceigwyn and pestering residents there, trying their best to link Gwennie's attack with the disappearance of her aunt more than a decade earlier. When the briefing was over, he looked at the information that had been gathered by Siân in relation to the proposed documentary.

The TV programme was being produced by a company called Black Stripe Productions based in London. The CEO was Beck Cowan and, as he claimed, the company had won a BAFTA for a documentary in 2019 and was responsible for a string of programmes. Harri opened the door and called out.

'Freddie come here, would you?'

DC Freddie Carr, a new-ish recruit to the team, unfolded himself from his chair, where he'd been glued to the screen, probably continuing to look at CCTV from shops in the Ceigwyn area. He was English and his wife had been pushing for a new start in Wales for reasons which Harri hadn't been able to fathom. He suspected Freddie was a reluctant relocator, but a couple of suspicious deaths since his arrival had convinced him that Carmarthenshire could be interesting enough when it came to his career.

'Fancy a call with a TV producer?' he asked. 'I've got someone called Beck Cowan who was in contact with Gwennie while preparing a programme on the Jaci Jones disappearance.'

'Sure.' Freddie's response was distracted, and his eyes strayed back to the computer.

'What is it?' asked Harri. 'Got something to show me?'

'Yes, although it's a bit weird. I'm reviewing the footage from The Feathers, the largest pub in Ceigwyn. There are a number of links to Gwennie in that we know she went for an unsuccessful job interview there, her current boyfriend Liam both worked and had accommodation at the pub, and it's where Gwennie's ex Huw claimed he spent most of the evening. But there's something strange. Do you ever feel that you're seeing double?'

Frequently, thought Harri. Especially after I've been overdoing the sugar.

'What's the matter?' he asked, starting towards the console. 'Has someone been messing with the tape?' He couldn't help but notice his subordinate's smirk. All right, he knew they didn't actually use tape any more, but it was just a saying, wasn't it? 'The recording I mean.'

Freddie shook his head. 'No, it's all time-stamped, and because of that, from what I can see, Huw's alibi checks out until twenty to seven. After that, he walks about, which coincides with the time Eleri saw him at the quay. I wondered if I should look again and see if anyone else was acting oddly. There are only two pubs in Ceigwyn: The Feathers and The Anchor, further out of town. I haven't got onto that one yet, but I keep seeing a man who appears to be hopping around the bar in an odd way. Dressed in a denim shirt and black trousers. Look.'

Freddie used the mouse to rewind the colour image on his screen by two minutes and he pointed out a tall man with wavy black hair that curled over his ears. At three minutes past four, he was standing at the bar ordering a pint, which the bar server passed over to him. He took the pint away with him and disappeared from view. A minute later, he was back at the bar, holding a glass with just froth at the bottom.

'A quick drinker,' said Harri. 'I had that talent once upon a time.'

'But look.' Freddie forwarded the image for another minute and on a different camera two men wearing identical shirts and trousers could be seen talking.

'Well, there's your answer,' he said. 'Two men dressed alike with similar haircuts on a night out. Why are you bothered?'

'I don't think it's just their clothes that are identical. Look at their faces when they turn towards the camera.' Freddie moved the video forward again and paused it.

Harri was beginning to lose patience. 'All right, twins then. We have them in Wales, you know. In any case, at four p.m. Gwennie was still alive.'

'I know she was. Because she's here on camera.'

Harri leant forward, frowning as a woman wearing an orange jacket walked up to the two men. She spoke briefly to one of them, then shoved him on the shoulder before storming out.

'Christ,' said Harri. 'Bloody well spotted. We need those IDed as soon as possible.'

## 13

'They're reasonable enough words,' said Cal to Mallory. '"Complicated and hidden" is an accurate reflection of Jaci Jones's private life. Her working days were as we'd expect. A good job as personal assistant to a female boss. That relationship was investigated and nothing was found to raise suspicion, even in relation to the two men she'd been seeing. She had a group of friends at work and one friend, Lizzie Carey, who she was particularly close to. All of these work colleagues said that Jaci was open about going away for mid-week breaks, but extremely coy about where she went and who accompanied her.'

Mallory scratched her arm, forcing herself to go back in time. 'Which is why I came up with the phrase "complicated and hidden". It expressed how we felt Jaci approached her private life, nothing more.'

Cal nodded. 'The issue is the context within which the words were used, on television, alongside perceived failings of the start of the investigation. Who approached *Crimewatch* to cover the case?'

'From memory, they approached us, but we were willing participants. Terry couldn't wait – all his mates down the pub and old colleagues would be able to see him after the reconstruction. That part was well done. We used the actual flat and got an actor to retrace Jaci's final movements.'

'Did you get a lot of calls afterwards?'

'Tonnes, but to be honest, I was then caught up in the fallout. Terry's interview after the segment showing the reconstruction was a disaster. He looked smug and patronising. It wasn't just Jaci's family who turned on us – women's groups, Jaci's colleagues, even Eddie Novak, her next-door neighbour, refused to speak to us afterwards.'

Cal regarded Mallory. 'The memory clearly stings, but sometimes these things take on a momentum. If it's any consolation, I think I too would have assumed Jaci had gone on one of her jaunts. And with the exception of her two colleagues, not one of her other lovers came forward?'

'None. That's why I came up with "hidden", because the allegations of her love life were impossible to corroborate. She didn't mention anything to her work colleagues beyond stating she'd be going away for the weekend. They had no idea with whom. No first names, no last names.'

Cal nodded. 'What you've told me is pretty much what was in the file. I'll probably have some more questions for you in due course. How about I tell you where we are in relation to the missing persons inquiry?'

Mallory nodded. 'I've wondered over the years, but there have been no reports of an arrest.'

'And that sums it up really. The original investigation team, which included you and I believe your ex-husband, found no convincing suspect and that has remained the case. There was a review of the investigation in 2018 with another scheduled for next year. The 2018 review found no new suspect but agreed with your initial conclusion that Jaci had come to harm and that her attacker was almost certainly known to her. The review also reassessed the methodology and assumptions of the first investigation, and I have to say you came out with flying colours.'

'It would have been nice to know that.'

Cal met her gaze. 'You know how things work. You were still a serving officer then. You'd have heard from us if you'd needed to be interviewed.'

'What about Terry Foster?'

'Terry was spoken to, I believe. He'd retired but volunteered all he could remember.'

'Is he still alive?' asked Mallory.

'I believe so. Why? Thinking of paying him a visit? This is still an active investigation, Mallory. I don't want you going to see him without speaking to me first. All leads come through me.'

'All right.' Mallory was prepared to let that one go, for the moment. She still had Terry's home number on her phone. 'I do need to speak to some of the original witnesses – Karen, her landlord, Eddie, her neighbour. Maybe one of her colleagues. Lizzie for example.'

'Lizzie unfortunately died a few years ago from an asthma attack. I've looked at the death and it was ruled as being from natural causes, and I've no reason to dispute it. I can give you the contact details for Jaci's boss, Julie Edge. But any contact must be strictly about the investigation into a link to Gwennie Jones's murder. Please don't interfere with my job.'

'Were you aware that a TV company is making a documentary about Jaci's disappearance? Have they been in contact with you?'

Cal sighed. 'I've heard something, but no one's been in touch with me. Have they contacted the family?'

'I believe so. The feeling is Gwennie thought she might have a starring role.'

Cal groaned. 'Great. I can't imagine anyone else in the family wanting to participate in a documentary.'

'What about Marion? Was she spoken to at all for the 2018 review?'

'The team told her that we were having a fresh look at Jaci's disappearance and informed her at the end that we had no new information in relation to suspects.'

'And how did she take it?'

'Not well, according to the file. It was before my time but, as I mentioned, I have since spoken to Marion.'

'And how did that go?'

'Again, not well.' Marion clearly still had a problem with the investigating team, an attitude inherited by her daughter Eleri. 'But…'

'But what?' Mallory's phone pinged with a message.

'I think Marion knew a little more than she was prepared to share with us. She made a mistake, and this is what I've driven all the way from London to tell you. If you look at the files, you won't find anything there that will help you find a connection with the death of Gwennie Jones. There's nothing new that you don't already know.'

'Marion made a mistake. What do you mean?'

Cal signalled to the waiter for the bill. 'I get the impression Marion isn't the person she once was. Reading the files, she comes across as a Rottweiler.'

'Yes, that's about it.' Mallory swallowed, remembering some of the woman's worst taunts. 'What's she like now?'

'More faded than suggested by the files. The last ten years have taken it out of her. But her memory also seemed to be going. She called her daughter Eleri by Jaci's name twice, as if she was getting the two mixed up.'

'She can't have mellowed towards the police.'

'Absolutely not, but I suspect age is catching up with her. Possibly some kind of dementia, although God knows

I'm no expert. The thing is, when I was getting ready to hang up, she mentioned someone called David. It was a very casual reference, as if she'd forgotten I was there.'

'David? I don't remember a David. What did she say about him?'

'She said, almost absent-mindedly, "It's a shame Jaci didn't marry David." I asked her who David was and she snapped and said it was a childhood boyfriend. Nothing of any importance. She couldn't get off the phone quick enough.'

'And you think it significant?'

Cal shrugged. 'I have nothing else, so I went back to the office and did a bit of digging around the name. As you say, there's no mention of David in any of the files. So I picked up the phone and called Eleri, Marion's daughter. She wasn't best pleased to hear from me, but she answered my questions clearly enough. Then, when I asked about a "David", she went all funny on me.'

'In what way?'

'Asked why I was asking, so I mentioned that Marion had made the comment.'

'She snapped that David was dead and her mother wasn't well at the moment.'

'She said that David was dead?' Mallory's hopes fell. A lead that went nowhere. 'Why do you think it's helpful for me?'

'Because,' said Cal, gathering her things, 'if I were the betting kind, I'd say David is someone missed by the original investigation. Maybe start there.'

## 14

Harri decided to accompany Freddie on his visit to The Feathers as it was years since he'd been inside the building. Back when he'd been a new recruit, they'd raided the place after a tip that stolen goods were being fenced on the premises, and it had resulted in a face-off between locals and uniformed officers. Since then, he heard the place had cleaned up and was geared for the tourist trade, with the emphasis on good dining. Freddie had been correct that the pub linked two of the suspects – Huw and Liam – and he wanted a feel of the place, given the air of menace in the interaction with the mystery twins, a young girl up against two strapping blokes. On the trip up, he managed to contact Mallory and give her more information on the TV company looking at Jaci's death. The weather had warmed up a little, just the constant drip of rain on the windscreen as he updated her on the progress.

'The guy's name is Beck Cowan and we need to check if he's been giving Gwennie money. Eleri's sure she'd been getting extra cash from somewhere.' In the background, Harri could hear the noise of the road. 'Where are you?'

'I've just finished speaking to Cal Bentley from the cold case team. I've one lead that I need to follow, but I might make a trip to London to check out some of the witnesses from 2008.'

'What, now?' He'd forgotten how Mallory made these impulsive decisions.

'Why not? Will the budget stretch to that?'

Harri grunted. 'Make sure you get receipts.'

'Will do. Is this Beck Cowan based there?'

'Siân said the company has a London address. You going to pay him a visit? I was going to ask Siân to give him a call.'

'I can take this. I'll report back on anything interesting.'

Harri cut the call as they drove under the arch of the old coaching inn and parked up beside a van that offered Aga servicing. In fact, most of the lunchtime custom appeared to be tradespeople, which suggested it had a strong local clientele. When they walked into the bar, a few people peeled away; their appearance must have shouted 'Old Bill'. Harri noticed with amusement that Freddie looked put out. He'd learn that they carried the aura of law enforcement wherever they went. There was a lone woman behind the bar in her mid-forties, glamorous like the old-style bar staff that you rarely saw any more. Freddie, after a glance at his boss, showed her his warrant card.

'We're investigating the death of Gwennie Jones. Are you in charge?'

The woman nodded. 'Jo Price. I run the place with help from my staff, including Liam, who was Gwennie's boyfriend. He mentioned to me that you'd spoken to him. I couldn't believe it when I heard the news. That family has been through enough.'

'You know Eleri personally?'

'She comes into the bar occasionally. Gwennie tried to get a job in the kitchen, but really I wanted someone over eighteen, so I had to turn her down.'

'Were you working here on Thursday night?' Freddie glanced around the bar.

'Of course. It was all hands to the pump for the festival. Literally.' She seemed pleased at the joke, especially when Freddie smiled. Harri guessed women would find him attractive, with his pale leanness. 'I've already given a statement to the police. I've not been able to help at all.'

'Is there anywhere private we could speak?' asked Freddie. Like Harri, he had probably spotted one of the customers perched on a stool at the end of the bar who hadn't made a quick exit. In fact, he was regarding his pint with a studied indifference.

'Of course. Come into the back.' Jo lifted the hatch. 'Ben, could you watch the bar for me for a sec?'

Ben stiffened at the use of his name but nodded; he rose but left his pint behind.

Jo took them to the back office where a modern MacBook blinked at them. She didn't offer them a seat but watched as Freddie took out his tablet.

'Tell me about Liam Ball. Is he a reliable employee?'

'Liam? He wouldn't say boo to a goose. He had to rush away when his dad was taken ill, and that was before Gwennie was attacked. I didn't mention him when I spoke to the officers as he was a long way from here. They did ask me about Huw Roberts's movements when I handed over the CCTV footage we have from the evening. I saw him a couple of times that night but can't pinpoint the exact times.'

Freddie nodded. 'I've not yet seen your statement, but did you mention that Gwennie Jones was in the bar on Thursday afternoon?'

'Gwennie? Here?' Jo shook her head. 'No way. I'm strict about keeping my licence and I know for a fact that

Gwennie was still seventeen. My nephew was in the same class as her.'

'I'd like to show you something.' Freddie played the video for her as Jo frowned.

'That is Gwennie. What the hell was she doing in here? There's no way she'd have got served. Do you have footage of her leaving?'

Freddie nodded. 'She came and left within two minutes at ten past four. You never saw her? I can see it's not you serving behind the bar.'

Jo shook her head. 'That's Sally, one of my afternoon employees. I might have been out back. It was busy all afternoon that day and I had to change the barrel a few times, plus some of the overnight guests from the rooms I rent out above arrived about that time.'

'Who were the two men Gwennie was talking to?'

Jo only hesitated for a fraction of a second, but it was there. 'It's the Bethel boys, Dylan and Tomos.'

'Are they twins?' asked Freddie.

Jo shook her head. 'Just a year between them, and they often dress alike. Not sure what that's all about. They usually come in together.'

'Local, are they?' asked Harri. The name Tomos Bethel was ringing a bell, and not because their names together were uncannily similar to the poet Dylan Thomas. A quick search on the computer would show if he had a criminal record.

'Dylan lives down by the quay,' said Jo. 'Once upon a time, you'd have called him a yuppie. He's got a young baby with his girlfriend. Tomos still lives at home in Felinfach with his mam.'

'All right,' said Freddie, writing down the names. 'Anything else you can tell us about Dylan and Tomos Bethel? Are they good customers?'

Harry could tell she felt on safer ground. 'Very. Never had any trouble with either of them.'

And yet I know the name Tomos Bethel, thought Harri. 'Which of the two is Gwennie having an argument with?' he asked.

'Argument is a bit strong, isn't it?' asked Jo. She coloured at their silence and made a show of squinting at the screen. 'I think that's Tomos.'

'Think?' asked Freddie.

'I'm pretty sure,' said Jo.

'OK. Can you remember if the brothers were in all night?' Harri knew they'd be able to verify it through CCTV, but he wanted to see what this woman had to offer.

She shrugged. 'Not all night. At some point they must have left, but I can't tell you when.'

Harri nodded, a memory stirring. Tomos Bethel. I remember you.

# 15

The name David and permission to interview some witnesses from 2008 was all she'd gained from meeting with Cal Bentley, and yet Mallory couldn't shake the feeling that she'd been vindicated by the 2018 review of the case. The memory still stung – it would take more than the reassuring words of a DCI to wipe out old hurts – but Mallory felt invigorated, her mind on the job at hand. She needed, however, to move fast before Marion and Eleri Jones discovered her presence in the investigation. The station was out of bounds and there was very little she could do twiddling her thumbs in Wales. Her role was to assess the relevance of Jaci's disappearance to her niece's death, so she needed to go back to the start. And the start was her, Joe and Terry Foster. Terry's phone was answered on the first ring. He sounded exactly as she remembered: London estuary accent, higher pitched than most men.

'It's me, Mallory Dawson, your old colleague.'

There was a brief silence. 'Mallory Dawson. Well, well, well. I thought I'd be hearing from you, given the news this morning. Wanting to chat about old times?'

Mallory wondered if she detected a note of bitterness, which was unlike him.

'I'm actually calling in an official capacity. I'm working for Dyfed Powys police as a civilian investigator. You know how it is these days – contractors, short-term assignments.'

'So I'd heard.'

'You had?'

'I saw Joe at a retirement do last year. He told me you were working in Wales on an ad-hoc basis. Can't say I'm surprised; you were never one to sit there doing nothing. Enjoying it?'

'I suppose. It's what I'm trained for.' She didn't mention Harri and the relationship they'd developed. Not that Terry would mind. He wasn't the lewd type, but he'd liked it when coppers married each other. Saved the hassle of dissatisfied spouses complaining about the burden of the job, he'd once told her.

'You heard about my attack?' she asked, rubbing her thigh. 'I was medically retired from service.'

'I heard, and I was sorry about that.' Another pause. 'You're seriously telling me they're asking you to be involved in the investigation into the killing of that young lass. Does Marion Jones know?'

'Not yet. Not ever, hopefully, although I spoke to DCI Cal Bentley just now, who I believe you've met. She thinks Marion isn't the woman she once was.'

'None of us are the people we once were.' Terrence gave a deep cough. Mallory remembered him being a former heavy smoker, and she wondered if his past was catching up with him. 'Coming to visit me?' he asked hopefully.

'I might, but not immediately. I've been warned off speaking to you.'

Terry gave another raspy laugh. 'And yet here we are.'

'Here we are,' agreed Mallory. 'I'm still feeling my way, deciding what avenues to take. You know our investigation was exonerated in 2018.'

'I heard.'

'You never thought about calling me to let me know?'

'I wasn't sure you'd want to rake all that stuff up. You were climbing the ranks. Anyway, I was on the way to retirement. We all have our priorities.'

Mallory decided to let it go as she needed Terry's help. 'Look, there's something I want to ask you.'

'Go on.'

'When she took up the post on the cold case team, Cal Bentley made a courtesy call to Marion Jones as Jaci's next of kin. That's where I've got the intel that Marion's not the woman she once was. Cal thinks it could be the start of dementia.'

'Ouch,' said Terry. 'Don't mention the D word. Every time I lose my glasses I think I'm on that slippery slope.'

'Cal comes across as a shrewd judge of character, but she also had a tiny nugget of information. Apparently, Marion said that Jaci would have been better off if she'd married David. Do you remember any mention of a David in her life?'

Terry took a sharp intake of breath. 'Bloody hell, Mallory, I can't be expected to remember anything like that. All I can say for certain was that if a name had been mentioned, then we would have followed it up.'

'Well I can tell you the name was news to me, and Cal's checked the files too. There's no mention of any David.'

'So there was a boyfriend at home called David who Jaci didn't marry. Is it important? We weren't looking for anyone from Wales, were we? Jaci was thirty-one so it was only natural that she had boyfriends in the past. She'd been living in the flat for six years, so we're talking about an old, old relationship.'

'I guess so, but Cal followed it up with Jaci's sister, who went on the defensive.'

'Eleri? She was a chip off the old block, so you need to be careful there. Marion might not be the woman she once was, but I bet Eleri's still all there.'

'I know, but I've been asked to look into a connection with the cases and where do I start? I'm running with any information I can get. Eleri told Cal that David had died, but it sounded to the DCI like a fib. It's something I can follow up at least.'

'Possibly. I always thought the family knew more than they were telling, but after that TV programme, that was the end of their cooperation with the investigation. I still think the answer lies with one of her London-based boyfriends, maybe one of her work colleagues.'

'But we never found any, did we? Suppose we missed the Welsh connection. Can you remember who visited Jaci from Wales apart from Marion and Eleri?'

'Eleri said she'd never been to Jaci's flat, so just Marion. We never pursued a Welsh connection because we never found one, although I did send officers to Ceigwyn to ask around. They came back with nothing.'

'Maybe one of us should have gone to Ceigwyn after Marion and Eleri cut all ties with us. Perhaps they were hiding something and attack was a form of defence.'

'Maybe,' said Terry, coughing again. 'But I'm not living out my retirement on maybes. You were always a good investigator, so here's your chance.'

'But we still think Jaci came to harm, don't we? There were rumours of her living in Ibiza with one of her boyfriends or maybe travelling to Australia to escape an overkeen admirer.'

'Her passport was still in the flat, remember. She'd have had to source a new one and siphon off money to pay for a new life. The financial team saw no evidence of this. There was evidence of small amounts of money coming in that we never got to the bottom of, but it was pocket money. We're not talking about dealing or sex work. She might have knitted baby blankets as a sideline for all we know but she didn't go abroad. I can't see how.'

Mallory sighed. Terry hadn't changed at all, which was a shame because he didn't sound as if he was enjoying the best of health. 'She's dead, isn't she?'

'Definitely dead,' said Terry. 'We can at least agree on that.'

–

Cal had given Mallory three contact numbers for the witnesses she was allowed to speak to. Karen Overton, Jaci's old landlord, must have changed her mobile as a recorded message told her the number was unavailable. The number for Eddie Novak, Jaci's neighbour, at least rang out, but switched to voicemail. After a moment's hesitation, Mallory left a message. He must be well into his eighties now and unlikely to welcome the dredging up of old memories, but of all the witnesses back in 2008, he had been the most willing to talk. Julie Edge, Jaci's old boss answered on the first ring and sighed down the line.

'I saw the news. It ruined my evening. Not a week goes by when I don't think about Jaci. I was only her boss – we weren't close at all – but I can't help thinking I should have, I don't know, engaged with her more. Maybe asked her a bit more about her life.'

'You were her boss; that's not how it works.' Mallory got out her paper diary and started to scribble in it. 'Are you still employed by Squire Insurance?'

'I'm one of the directors now but we're no longer based in Wimbledon.'

'Shame. I was thinking of making a trip to London this afternoon. I don't suppose you'll have any free time tomorrow?'

'I'll make time. I still live in Battersea Park – I'm a city girl who commutes out. I could meet you around ten thirty tomorrow morning. It's one of the perks of seniority. I'll work from home to clear some emails and then we can get together. How does that sound?'

'That would be great.'

Mallory could hear a tapping down the line. Julie at her desk using the tip of her pen against the wooden surface. 'Are the cases connected? You know, the disappearance of Jaci and her niece's death. Is it the same person?'

'At the moment,' said Mallory, aware of the enormous task ahead of her, 'I have no idea.'

# 16

Harri remembered Tomos Bethel with startling clarity. It was as if his memory had been shaken awake after a long sleep. That's what going on holiday did for you, he thought. Addled the brain. Mallory had been funny with him too since the holiday, and he didn't think it was just preoccupation with the case. While the trip to Ireland had been wonderful, it had thrown up questions about their future that neither had been able to articulate. Perhaps when the killer of Gwennie Jones had been identified they could have that long-needed chat. Which brought him back to Tomos Bethel.

Harri had received a religious upbringing like most of his generation in Wales. His parents had both attended the local independent, or *annibynwyr*, chapel, a huge building that had already seen a sizeable decrease in its congregation by the early 1980s. His grandmother had talked about the days when all the seats downstairs and in the U-shaped balcony on the first floor would be packed out every Sunday. Now, according to his sister Fran, the chapel was at threat of closure, attendance down to thirty regulars, most over the age of sixty. Harri hadn't been inside the place or any chapel since his wife Paula's funeral, held on a miserable March day. He'd dropped his kids off at his parents, not wishing to inflict the bleak service on a couple of toddlers. Some religions liked children at the funerals, but chapels were more circumspect, and he'd wanted to grieve alone. The point was that Harri and religion didn't really mix, although he liked singing to hymns and had fond memories of Sunday school, and the stories of Saul being lowered in a basket and Jonah inside the whale.

About five years ago, though, Harri had been called to a case so bizarre that he'd filed it under 'a potential chapter for my memoir', not that he actually had any intention of ever writing one. He'd been called by uniformed officers to the tiny chapel of St Dwynwen in the tiny hamlet of Court Isaac. The chapel had been decommissioned by the Church in Wales, but the Friendless Churches Trust had taken ownership of the building and opened it for services at Easter, Christmas and Harvest Festival. It had no electricity or running water, and you could forget about heating, but light was provided through a small generator. It was in relation to this chapel that Harri had heard the name Tomos Bethel.

They were driving towards Felinfach as Harri told Freddie about his encounter with Tomos Bethel. It had begun to sleet and there was something wrong with the wipers on the car, the rubber on the blades snagging against the glass.

'Back in 2019, I think it was, certainly before the pandemic, which is how I measure my memories, I was called to a burglary at a church called St Dwynwen. A door had been forced and two brass candlesticks and a plate had been taken from a locked cupboard. I was still a DS then and I turned up to take a statement from the church warden, a woman named Jane Callander.'

'Church robberies were a thing in the north-west of England when I lived there,' said Freddie. 'Lead from the roof was the most common, but sometimes artefacts from inside too.'

'People largely leave the places alone around here, but this was an exception. Anyway, Jane said the person she thought responsible for the crime was Tomos Bethel, who had come to do some carpentry on one of the beams. She'd caught him sniffing around the cupboards and thought him the most likely culprit.'

'Did you interview him?'

'I met his mother when I visited the address on his invoice in Felinfach, which is where we're going now, and she directed me to a farm down the valley where he was fitting a new kitchen. I went to see him and when I told him about the candlesticks he laughed. Said something along the lines that they'd fetch a tenner in the local pub and he wasn't that desperate.'

'Sounds about right,' said Freddie. 'Did he seem credible?'

'Very, I would have said.'

'So, is there a reason his name stuck with you?'

'I had reason to interview him two weeks later after Jane was attacked as she was leaving her house. She lived in a lane near the church, and someone was waiting for her as she drove up in her car after a shopping trip. It was a dark evening and her entrance to her house was poorly lit, but she had no reason to feel under threat. The perpetrator hit her over the head and disappeared, probably in a vehicle parked elsewhere in the village.'

'And you connected it to the break-in at the church?'

'We talked to anyone who might have had a grudge against Jane. An assault is significantly more serious than a couple of missing candlesticks and we treated the crime as such. I visited Tomos, who was working on a different project, and he said he knew nothing about the incident. His mother said he was at home all evening, and his van didn't come up on any cameras at that time of the evening.'

'Did you realise he had a brother who lived nearby?'

'No, but then so what if I'd known that?'

'You could have seen if his vehicle was spotted around the victim's property. Wouldn't be the first time a brother has helped out a sibling with a grudge.'

Harri suppressed his irritation. Freddie was right of course, but he remembered laughing along with Tomos when he'd mentioned the low value of the stolen goods. He'd believed the good-looking carpenter, with his calloused hands and easy manner.

'Did she survive the attack? The church warden, I mean.'

'She did,' said Harri, turning his head to look out of the window. Freddie was a good driver, but Harri wasn't the world's best passenger, and the lack of sleep had made him queasy. 'I haven't been in touch with her for years, but I can't imagine her life returned to normal afterwards. Whose would?'

'Head injury,' said Freddie, turning down the lane towards the Bethel cottage and coming to a halt outside a stone cottage. 'That's a connection between Ms Callander's assault and Gwennie's attack. I wonder what the psychologists would have to say about men who attack women about the head. I mean, obviously a physical assault is terrible, but I wonder why some focus on the head?'

Harri thought of the photo of Gwennie they were using in the appeals and her youthful freshness. 'Could be an attempt to obliterate her beauty in Gwennie's case. I wonder, though, if it's not about control. There's going to be more psychological and physical damage from a head injury. Right, let's see what Mr Bethel has to say for himself today.'

## 17

Mallory was looking up train timetables on her phone when it rang and an unfamiliar number flashed onto the screen. She answered it, prepared for the silence of an automated spam call. Toby had told her she shouldn't answer any unfamiliar numbers, but apart from her son, Joe and Harri, no one ever called her, so she was hardly likely to give out her bank details to a random number.

'Am I speaking to Mallory Dawson?' The voice was Welsh, educated and slightly pushy. It still might yet be spam.

'If you're selling me something, I don't have any money.'

The man laughed. 'Not selling, but there might be some money in it for you. My name's Beck Cowan and I'm the CEO and owner of a TV company making a documentary on the disappearance of Jaci Jones. I believe you were one of the original investigating officers.'

'How did you get my number?' asked Mallory, thinking rapidly. Perhaps Beck Cowan had joined the dots and realised she was working for the police. If so, her name had got out there quickly and she'd need to get to London fast.

'It's the same one that you used back in 2008; I got it from an old journalist contact. Were you aware that Jaci's niece was killed on Thursday evening? It's been in some of the national papers.'

Mallory allowed herself to relax a little. For Beck to ask the question, he clearly had no idea of her current status, although, to be fair, Mallory didn't exactly know what her status was either.

'I saw a newspaper article,' said Mallory, neutrally. 'I'm not sure I'm going to be able to help you with the documentary.' Terry hadn't mentioned the TV show, which suggested they hadn't contacted him yet. 'Have you been in touch with the SIO, Terrence Foster? He's the best person to talk to.'

'Mr Foster's number has changed. I sent an email to the Comms team in the Met, asking them to forward my enquiry, but I've yet to get a reply.'

I bet, thought Mallory. First of all, they wouldn't want a TV company interfering in a still-live investigation, and even if they had forwarded the message on, Terry hadn't liked technology back in the day and she doubted he'd be spending his retirement refreshing his smart phone. She needed to plead ignorance about the documentary, which shouldn't be too difficult, given that she only knew the little Siân had told her.

'You want to talk to me about the investigation back in 2008?'

'We do, and on camera if that's possible. We feel that the team was unfairly treated, given Jaci's concealed personal life, and we'd like to hear your side of the story.'

'Are the family taking part?'

Beck hesitated. 'Eleri Jones, Jaci's sister, declined to be involved, but Gwennie expressed an interest in appearing. Her mother said it was up to her daughter. We're obviously not contacting the family at present, given

Gwennie's death, although we will need to at some time in the future.'

'So you're contacting others to get their take on it?'

'Something like that.'

Mallory paused. 'You mentioned money. Are you paying all the participants?'

Beck laughed. 'Getting down to brass tacks, eh? Yes, everyone is getting paid on a scale according to the amount of proposed screen time that they'll have.'

Interesting, thought Mallory. So even Gwennie was likely to be getting some money. She wondered how that sat with Eleri and Marion.

'I'm intrigued,' said Mallory, 'but why don't we meet up first to discuss terms? Where are you based?'

'In London. Are you still living here?'

So he didn't know she was in Wales. This was a good thing. 'Tell you what. How about I meet you at the Regency Cafe in Pimlico at nine a.m. tomorrow morning for breakfast? I'll see you then.'

-

Two hours later, Mallory was on an early afternoon train to London. There had been no time to return to her cottage, so she'd bought the bare essentials from Primark in Swansea and left her car on a side street. It was the first time she'd been back to London since she'd left to take up the job as night manager on Eldey Island. That had brought her into contact with Harri and marked the beginning of a new career when she thought her working days were over. Strange that it felt like a time of change once more, and she thought about the job advert she'd seen on Indeed that morning. She'd begun to think that maybe a career as a civilian investigator wasn't a permanent solution to her professional future and its impact on her relationship with Harri. There were decisions to be made which began with giving herself other employment options.

She spent the time on the train jotting down everything she'd known back in 2008 about Jaci's Welsh connections, which wasn't much. It had only been Eleri who'd remained in Wales, and those who knew Jaci said her accent was hardly noticeable. There was the terrible possibility that they'd completely overlooked the importance of Jaci's old life, but there was also the chance that the documentary had stirred up something that had resulted in a London-based killer going to Wales to attack Gwennie. For the life of her, Mallory couldn't think what that might be, and part of her hoped Harri might discover a conflict unrelated to Jaci's disappearance. However tragic two violent deaths in the Jones family might be, it would at least have given Mallory the satisfaction that nothing she'd missed in 2008 had come back to haunt her.

–

Paddington station looked much the same as she remembered it, albeit with a few new shops thrown in. The place smelt different to Wales, with not even a cold wind to blow away the acrid smell of the city. She decided against messaging Toby to say she'd followed him to London. There was no reason to meet up, although she did want to speak to his father, which she'd try to do away from his home.

She'd forgotten the layout of the Tube network, which had once been so familiar to her, but found her way to Wimbledon. It was warmer there than Wales, with weak sunshine trying to break through. She'd need to find somewhere to stay, preferably a cheap B and B, and thought she'd try her luck outside the centre. First though, she needed to see the flat as she'd first glimpsed it in 2008.

Christine Truman House was a Sixties-built concrete block whose harsh profile had been softened by window boxes and a mural on one side. Mallory doubted any of the flats were still in local authority ownership; they were probably worth well over £500,000 each now. Number eighteen had a different door from the one in 2008, now solidly constructed out of uPVC. She remembered a large window with opaque glass that would have shown the outline of the person in the lit hallway. According to Eddie Novak, Jaci had repeatedly asked the landlord for a new door but had been fobbed off.

The flat to the right had a child's bike outside and there was the sound of a baby crying inside. Eddie Novak was long gone.

'I've told you before, no journalists.' Mallory spun round as a woman wearing an Afghan coat came along the walkway carrying a Prufrock coffee cup. 'Where are you from? The *Sun*? You've no camera crew, so you can't be on TV.'

'I'm...' Mallory stopped and looked at the woman closer. There was something about her auburn hair and round face that looked familiar. 'Is it Karen?'

'So what if it is? I've told you, I'm not interested.'

'You don't remember me. I'm Mallory Dawson. I was one of the detectives on the original investigation. I was a DC then. We spoke that first day when you came over with your set of keys. I did the interview.'

Karen Overton squinted at Mallory with myopic eyes. 'I do remember you. You've not changed, except maybe got a little thinner. Lucky you. What are you doing here?'

Mallory shrugged. 'I need to speak to you about the past. I'm sorry – I know you must have been pestered over the years and now I'm here intruding on your afternoon. But there are some questions I need to ask you.'

To Mallory's horror, her voice cracked. Christ, what was wrong with her? She hadn't been like this back in the day. The year Jaci had disappeared had been a time of hope and courage, but she'd lost both somewhere along the way. Karen's expression changed to one of concern. 'You must be freezing standing there. Come inside and I'll put the heating on. We can share this latte. I always get large. God knows why; I never finish it.'

Karen pulled out a large set of keys from her pocket and opened the door. The hallway was much the same as Mallory remembered except for a large Georgia O'Keeffe print dominating the wall and a tall lamp in the corner.

'Remember where the kitchen was?' Karen steered Mallory into the square room, which had been refitted with shiny black units. Mallory had forgotten how large the rooms were – the benefits of a purpose-built block – and she sat at the glass table pushed up against the wall.

'When did you move back in?' asked Mallory, looking around her. Karen had been largely absent as a landlord back in the day, renting out her flat after moving in with her partner and ignoring Jaci's pleas for a new front door.

'Around 2010, when my relationship broke down. I didn't rent it out after Jaci went missing. The weird thing was for the first year, she continued to pay the rent. The company put her on sick pay, which lasted 12 months and, in agreement with Marion, I continued to charge rent and the flat was left exactly as it had been. Marion genuinely thought Jaci was coming back.'

'But you didn't?'

'Not really. I agreed with the police that she'd come to harm but I had no insights into her private life. I only met her twice, both times when I came to do an inspection, as I didn't trust the managing agents to do it properly.'

'How did you find her?'

'Quiet and unassuming. She had difficulty looking you in the eye, but she was nice enough and kept this place immaculate. I had no complaints about her as a tenant.'

'What happened in 2009, when the rent stopped being paid?'

'Marion and Jaci's sister came over and cleared the place. They brought a van from Wales, I think, and removed all Jaci's things. I was in Spain at the time on holiday with my ratbag ex, so wasn't here to oversee things. When I came back, I saw they'd taken a few things that belonged to me, as the flat had been offered semi-furnished.'

'Did you ask for them back?'

Karen shrugged. 'It was piffling things. A bedside lamp, the toaster. The women obviously thought they were Jaci's, so I let it go. I did try to contact them to say they'd missed a cupboard but the number I had for Marion didn't have voicemail and she ignored my calls. Maybe she'd had enough of the flat and its memories by then.'

Mallory frowned. 'They forgot to clear out a cupboard?'

'Sure. The one in the nook between the bathroom and bedroom. It was easily missed as the doors were flush with the walls. You pressed them to open. There was nothing exciting in there, but I boxed it all up and shoved it at the back of my wardrobe waiting for Marion to claim it.'

'What?' Mallory put her coffee down on the table. 'Do you mean to say you still have it?'

'Pretty sure it's still there. Do you want to see?'

'Of course. Can you show me the cupboard you mean?'

Mallory and Terry had executed a second search of the flat after that of the uniformed officers. It was the first pass that had found Jaci's bag which contained her purse, and her passport had been discovered in the bedside drawers. Mallory and Terry had taken Jaci's laptop and bank statements. There had been little else to inspect.

Karen showed Mallory the cupboard, pressing the doors to open it while Mallory wracked her brains trying to remember if she'd searched the space before. Christ, what had they missed?

# *18*

*November 2008*

Mallory followed her boss into the flat. He had one of those spiv coats that she associated with the dealers down the market, but unlike some members of the CID team she'd just joined, he had taken a shine to her and was keen to show her the ropes. He'd briefed her on the drive down. A thirty-one-year-old woman had gone missing and possibly hadn't gone away for a dirty weekend like initially thought. Mallory had winced at that phrase. She associated it with clandestine trips to seedy seaside resorts. Jaci Jones was a grown woman and single. What she did with her days off shouldn't be of any interest to them. Except, of course, now she was missing it was definitely something they'd be looking at.

The flat was a little like Mallory's rented accommodation: boxy and rather impersonal, the walls painted beige and adorned with floral prints.

Terry made straight for the bedroom where a forensic team was in the process of stripping the sheets. 'This room is where all the secrets are.'

Mallory watched an overalled woman photograph the contents of Jaci's bag, a purse and a white iPod. A compact laptop, the kind that could fit in a small bag, was on the table. 'Can you access that?' asked Mallory.

The woman looked across at her and nodded. 'I can't find the lead at the moment but it's still got twenty per cent battery. The pass number is sellotaped on the back. Do you want to take a look at her Hotmail account? There doesn't seem to be much in the documents folder.'

'Sure.' Mallory looked to Terry, who shrugged. She looked first at Jaci's read emails: Mum, Eleri, Lizzie and 'B', who had arranged a get-together the previous week. 'Usual place.' She looked across at Terry. 'We've got an email arranging a meeting last month,' she said.

'She didn't go missing in October, did she?' Terry scratched his neck. 'Who's it from?'

'It's signed "B". The address looks generic. A bunch of numbers on a Hotmail account.'

'Forensics might be able to do something.' Technology wasn't his thing, and Terry wasn't going to show himself up in front of her, she guessed.

Mallory didn't want to tamper with the computer but saw that Jaci had thirteen unread messages in the last twenty-four hours, probably from anxious work colleagues, family and friends. 'She's not read any emails since she disappeared.'

'If her laptop's here, she's not going to be able to.'

Mallory had heard of a new phone where you could read your emails on the screen, a little like a Blackberry. It was out of her price range, though, and she guessed Jaci's too.

'We ought to find out who "B" is in any case.'

'Who the bloody hell signs themselves off with an initial?' asked Terry, suddenly irritated.

Someone who wants to keep their identity secret, thought Mallory. She caught the photographer's eye. 'Could you take a photo of that email for me?'

'Sure thing.'

Mallory looked around the bedroom, but it looked as uninteresting as hers.

'Any signs of contraception?' she asked one of the forensic team.

'Packet of Microgynon in the bathroom. Combined oral contraceptive pill.'

Mallory looked across to see Terry's reaction, but he'd got bored of the bedroom and was lifting up sofa cushions in the lounge, presumably hoping the forensic team had missed something. There was a small balcony off the room that overlooked the square quad. Mallory slid back the door and stepped out, walking up to the concrete parapet. Jaci had tried to grow some geraniums over the summer, which now sat shrivelled in glazed pots.

'Not much out there, guv,' said Mallory, knowing Terry liked the old-fashioned address.

'Hm. This flat is like my wife's Sunday chicken. Picked clean. Reckon someone's been in here before us?'

Mallory felt she was being tested. 'Perhaps. It's quite sterile, and Jaci's been here six years. You'd expect more personal possessions.' She looked up at the ceiling. No loft space and no outside locker either. What you saw was what you got. The case was going to be a difficult one.

# 19

Mallory stared at the space in dismay, pretty sure neither she nor the forensics team had spotted the doors flush with the wall. Police searches were a particular issue for many investigation teams. Undiscovered attics, old septic tanks, wall cavities and other hidden places could conceal a multitude of secrets. Mallory suspected that someone in the team might have opened the cupboard at some point, rifled through it and dismissed its contents. But it hadn't been her. During the search of the house, she'd walked from bedroom to living room without once looking at the wall to the right.

Karen opened the cupboard doors wide to reveal five shelves from floor to ceiling which held an assortment of items, including a sewing machine, wool, paperback books, a yoga mat, a plastic box marked '*Photos*' and wrapping paper.

'It holds a lot, as you can see, and it's basically the only built-in storage in the flat. Jaci didn't have as much stuff as this. You'd never get this lot in a cardboard box.'

They moved into Jaci's old bedroom and Karen knelt in front of the wardrobe. She'd gone for the glitz in this room, with mirrored cupboards and a bed with a high cushioned headboard, not the decor you'd choose for a rental. She'd reclaimed the flat as hers.

'I've thought about getting rid of this box a lot over the years, but Marion was such a Rottweiler I had nightmares about her coming to see me and demanding its contents. It's also – I don't know – the last reminder of Jaci in this flat. I've just put off dealing with it.'

'But surely Marion didn't know about the existence of the cupboard.'

'Not the cupboard, no, but take a look at what was there. Marion must have realised that this stuff was being held somewhere.'

Karen pulled out a small square box emblazoned with the Harrods name. She shot an embarrassed look. 'The box is mine, not Jaci's. A former boyfriend gave me a bloody awful handbag that would have better suited his mother. I kept the box though.' She lifted the lid and Mallory glanced over at the contents, her initial reaction one of disappointment. She took the box off Karen and shook the items onto the bed. There was an envelope of certificates which Mallory rifled through, mainly Jaci's GCSE results and a typing commendation. Next was a photo album, about six inches by four, but containing only three photos, all of Jaci. The clothes she was wearing looked dated, far older than 2008, but Mallory's focus was on the woman's hair. She put it to one side; she'd study the image again when she was on her own.

She picked up a thin book with a picture of a huge sunflower on the cover and saw it was a diary dated 2007. It was sparsely filled with comments such as 'hair' and 'eyebrows'. Next to it was a shiny black make-up bag smelling of powder and perfume. Mallory briefly unzipped it, but there was nothing but old tubes of foundation and some half-used lipsticks. The final item of significance was something that might, might have helped the investigation back in 2007: a small Dictaphone containing a tiny tape. Shit, how did they work? She looked to Karen, who shrugged.

'Just an MP3 player, right?'

'Hmm.' Mallory's eyes swept the detritus left at the bottom of the box: three used pencils, one little more than a stub, and a plain notepad, so tiny it could fit in the palm of your hand. Two of the pencils were unbranded HB, but the third had the name of The Cedar Tree hotel. Jesus, Mallory repressed a gasp. Where the hell was The Cedar Tree hotel? This was a seemingly unimportant item that gave them a name when before they'd had nothing. Mallory was so absorbed looking at the pencil that she almost dismissed the small notepad. She idly picked it up and flicked through it. On a page near the middle was written the name '*Gemma*' inside a heart. Mallory stared at it in dismay as Karen, looking over her shoulder, saw the name.

'Gemma? Do you think Jaci was gay?'

Mallory traced the heart with her finger. 'We kept an open mind in terms of Jaci's sexuality, but there was no evidence that she'd had relationships with women.' God, she felt like a complete incompetent. There was so much here that looked inconsequential but gave them leads that had been conspicuously missing in 2008. With a pounding heart, she put everything back into the box and shut the lid. 'Can I take this?'

Karen hesitated. 'I heard you'd been in an accident and had left the police. You're not working for some TV company, are you?'

Mallory thought of her meeting the following morning. 'I'm employed by Dyfed Powys police, but I'd appreciate it if you didn't mention it to anyone. If you want to check my credentials, you can ring DI Harri Evans.'

Mallory could see Karen loved the secrecy of everything. 'Of course I won't say anything. I mean, I've not told anyone about Jaci's things stuck here, except for that policeman.'

Mallory frowned. 'What policeman?'

'The man who was with you the time we met – Joe, I think his name was. I bumped into him at a bar a couple of years ago and told him I had a few of Jaci's things.'

'And what was his reaction?'

'He didn't want to know. Suggested I get in touch with the family, which, as you know, I'd already done.'

'Well, as you say, there's nothing much here is there? No harm.'

Karen smiled in relief. 'Still, I'm glad to finally get rid of it, you know? It's good to see you again. I didn't mean to be rude when I said you were looking thinner. You actually look good.'

'I do?' asked Mallory, desperate to get away and relook at the contents of the box.

'Definitely.'

Mallory placed the box on the bed and looked at Karen. 'What do you think happened to Jaci?'

Karen ran her hands through her hair. 'I think she was taken from this flat by someone she knew and trusted. When I came here after her disappearance, despite the police search, I was struck once again by how neat everything looked. Yet on the TV it said she had lots of secret affairs. How did you know this?'

'Well,' said Mallory, 'she implied to work friends that there was someone she liked to go away with during the week but was cagey about his identity. So there was that, but she also had a history of this sort of behaviour. She dated two men in her workplace, for example, and was open about that, but was keen to stress it wasn't an exclusive relationship.'

'Sounds quite progressive to me,' said Karen. 'She was wilder than me, I'd say, but you'd never have thought it, looking at us both.'

'That's why we thought her relationship was both complicated and hidden. We never meant to do a disservice to Jaci.'

'It depends who's saying it and the tone they're using though, doesn't it?'

Mallory thought of Terrence Foster and nodded. 'Yep. It really does depend on those things.'

Karen glanced across at Mallory. 'I saw Marion once after the TV appeal and she was raging. She was particularly vocal about your role. Why did she focus on you? I mean it was your boss on TV, wasn't it?'

The events of the day caught up with Mallory, and she experienced a wave of exhaustion. 'I think the issue was that Marion and I clicked to begin with. I was young, younger than Jaci, and I guess Marion felt some affinity with me. She then rang me straight after the TV appearance full of fury and I guess in my inexperience I didn't say the right thing.'

'What did you say?'

Mallory sighed. 'I said that Jaci did have a hidden love life, and she put the phone down on me.'

'Odd,' said Karen. 'I mean, it's not the worst thing in the world, is it?'

Mallory thought of the small community from which Jaci had sprung, where she now found herself living. The aftermath of the TV appearance there, watched by millions, would have been profound, even if Marion had also left the community.

'I failed the Jones family,' said Mallory, finally, her focus back on the pencil. 'And I'm not going to do it again.'

## 20

Tomos Bethel wasn't home, but his mother was standing in the doorway as three Welsh corgis waddled over to greet Harri and Freddie as they got out of their car. Harri had once been nipped on the ankles by his mother's dog, which had given him an enduring wariness with the breed. He allowed all three to sniff at his trouser leg while Freddie bent down to pat one of them. The well-lit yard was neat as a pin, something Harri remembered from last time. There was no rusting machinery or rotting piles of wood. Given that Dylan lived in Ceigwyn with his new family, it must be Tomos who kept the place so tidy.

'Mrs Bethel?' he called over to the woman waiting for them without expression. 'Is Tomos around?'

'He's working,' she said. Fflu Bethel spoke Welsh but responded to Harri in English. 'He'll be back around five.'

Harri looked at his watch. 'It's ten to now. Can we wait?'

Fflu nodded and opened the door. The farmhouse interior was as clean as the outside, with the smell of lavender polish overlaid with wet dog. She took them into the kitchen and motioned to two chairs beside the Aga. 'It's a cold night. I haven't lit a fire in the living room yet.'

She placed an old kettle on the plate. The house might have been immaculate, but all the furnishings had a lived-in feel to them. The dogs settled in a huge basket in front of the flames, nestling up to each other for warmth. Harri remembered Fflu Bethel wasn't one for small talk, but luckily, as the kettle began to hiss, there came the sound of a van pulling up to the yard. Footsteps crunched over the gravel, causing the dogs to bark, and the front door opened. Tomos Bethel entered the kitchen, taking in the two of them, his eyes settling on Harri.

'DS Evans?'

'Harri. And it's DI now.'

Tomos nodded. 'You're here about the row with Gwennie Jones.'

So he'd been expecting them. 'Did Jo from The Feathers call you?' asked Harri.

Tomos shook his head. 'There are cameras in the pub; I helped install them as a favour to Jo after a fight between customers. I was pretty sure the altercation with Gwennie would come to light.'

'You didn't think of coming forward with the information?' asked Freddie. Harri could tell he'd taken an instant dislike to Tomos, two good-looking men scenting each other out.

Tomos shook his head. 'I have history with the police. I was falsely accused of a crime five years back and I don't forget things in a hurry.' Tomos perhaps realised this was the wrong thing to say, given that he'd been accused of an act of revenge at the time. He bit his lip and regarded Harri with defiance. 'I was being fitted up.'

'You were interviewed as part of the inquiry and were ruled out after your mother gave you an alibi.'

Tomos glanced across at Fflu. 'It wasn't just the alibi – you had no evidence at all that I'd stolen a brass plate except an injured woman's fantasies.' Tomos flung his arm around the room. 'I have all I need here and live a simple life. Can you see me risking jail time for that tat?'

Harri shrugged. Thieves were thieves, regardless of what they might materially own.

'He's been doing some preaching,' said Fflu. 'In our chapel and around Carmarthenshire. He lives by our Lord's Word and the commandments in the holy book.'

Harri frowned. 'You're a lay preacher?'

Tomos inspected the back of his hand. 'Like my father and *dadcu* before me. What of it?'

'I don't remember you mentioning it last time we met, that's all.'

'He's new to it,' said Fflu, unable to keep the note of pride from her voice.

Harri nodded. He could see why it would be a big deal to Fflu, but he hadn't had Tomos pegged as the religious type. 'Can we get back to Gwennie Jones? Care to tell us why she was so upset with you?'

Tomos crossed to the kitchen sink and washed his hands using a bottle of liquid soap. 'She'd been talking to some TV guy who was going to make a programme about Jaci Jones's disappearance. Waste of time if you ask me, but because they had nothing else to go on, they decided to focus on the Welsh angle.'

'And where do you come in?' asked Harri, noticing that Fflu had become still, her watchful eyes on her son.

'I don't come in at all. I know Eleri from school days and in my opinion that family's been through enough. Gwennie was doing some babysitting for my brother, Dylan. The baby's a bit young to be left but Gwennie was sensible enough, and it was only for an hour or so. Anyway, while Dylan and his partner were out, I dropped by and Gwennie was there. She asked me if I remembered Jaci.'

'And?' asked Harri, noticing Freddie had stopped writing.

'I said I knew her a bit and that she was a nice girl, which was true. She then told me that she was going to take part in a documentary about Jaci's disappearance, and I told her she was an idiot.'

'Why was she an idiot?'

'Because she wasn't even born when Jaci went missing. What's she going to add to a TV programme except a pretty face?'

Fflu snorted. 'They're all pretty faces, the Jones girls. Not that it's done them any good.'

Freddie coloured in outrage and Harri shot him a warning look. 'How did Gwennie take it?'

Tomos shrugged. 'She slammed the door in my face. I don't care, but I went onto the town's Facebook group on Thursday and said that if any TV companies came calling, they were just looking to make a quick buck at our expense. Gwennie must have seen it somehow; I didn't think she'd have a Facebook profile. Maybe her mam showed it to her. The next minute, she's flying at me at the bar.'

'How did she know you'd be in The Feathers?'

'It's where he is most Saturday afternoons,' said Fflu. 'Him and Dylan both. The whole town would look there if they wanted to speak to him.'

'Can you tell us the nature of the conversation?' asked Harri.

Tomos laughed and wiped his hands on a towel. 'Conversation? I was having a pint and she came storming in like a dervish. Started poking me in the chest and saying I knew nothing and that there was a Welsh connection.'

'She said that?' asked Harri. 'What else did she say?'

'I asked her what she was talking about and she went all quiet on me saying I'd have to wait for the TV programme, but it would all come out about Jaci.'

'Did you think she was telling the truth?' asked Freddie.

Tomos shrugged. 'I dunno. I told her she was too young to be in the pub and to get out. I was in my twenties when Jaci went missing and I've nothing to add to the story. I've never been to London, never been to Wimbledon.'

Just like you've never been to Jane Callander's cottage, thought Harri.

'What did your brother have to say about it? I mean, he was in the bar with you. Had he seen your Facebook post?'

'Dylan thought it was funny. Poor little Gwennie, she was just like Jaci. Desperate to get out of this place. At least Jaci made it to London.'

'But you never visited her there. What about Dylan?'

Tomos laughed. 'Not him. He likes them—' Tomos stopped.

'Likes them what?' asked Freddie.

Tomos picked at his thumbnail. 'He likes them blonde.'

-

When he got back into the car, Harri saw that he'd missed three calls from Siân.

'What's up?' he asked her. Freddie hadn't started up the car and was looking back at the house in the rear-view mirror.

'Eleri Jones's house was broken into this afternoon. She was in town doing some shopping – she was only out for about three quarters of an hour, so someone was clearly watching the place.'

'Christ. Do we think it's related to the case or opportunists? Home security isn't a top priority for grieving people, and we've seen this kind of thing before.'

'I think they were looking for something, boss. I'm here at the house and it looks like a systematic search has taken place.'

–

Harri and Freddie arrived twenty minutes later. Eleri was standing dry-eyed in the kitchen, her arms folded.

'Is the killer after me now?' she asked Harri.

'I doubt it if they waited for you to leave the house. It sounds like they wanted you out of the way. Do you have any idea what they might have been looking for?'

Eleri shook her head. 'I don't know. They've gone through everywhere, including mine and Gwennie's bedrooms. I can't see anything taken.'

'Money? Jewellery?' asked Freddie.

'I don't keep money in the house. My jewellery is all there but there's nothing valuable you'd want to take anyhow.'

Harri looked around the room. The search was superficial and non-malicious in that there was no apparent damage to property. They had been looking for something specific and either they'd failed to find it or had been successful.

'I'd like a family liaison officer to come and stay with you. These things are frightening, and we can't rule out the possibility the thief didn't find what they were looking for.'

Eleri shook her head. 'There's no need. My mam is on her way here. She'll be company at least.'

It was an odd comment. What did Eleri mean by 'at least'? Harri studied Eleri and noticed her hands were shaking. The break-in had unsettled her, which was entirely natural, but she still refused to have an officer on the premises. It rang alarm bells, but he couldn't yet see the significance of the break-in. It wouldn't be the first time a grieving family had been targeted by a low life. Marion's imminent arrival, although expected, was another complication. He needed to warn Mallory to keep a low profile in the town when she returned from London. It was the best place for her at the moment, as a showdown with Marion was definitely not what he wanted right now.

# 21

Leaving Jaci's old home, Mallory knocked on the front door of the adjacent flat and a woman answered, carrying a newborn baby. Mallory forgot what she was about to say and stared at the child in wonder. She'd forgotten they came so small, the doll-like baby's slate-coloured eyes unfocused.

'Goodness, how old are they?'

'Josh was born yesterday. And before you say anything, yes, he has a fine pair of lungs on him. Are you the health visitor?' She looked dubiously at the Harrods box that Mallory was carrying.

'Oh God, no. Sorry, it's that shock of dark hair; your son looks just like mine did when he was born. I'd kinda been expecting a bald baby and I got one looking like a member of the Hair Bear Bunch.'

She saw the reference was lost on the woman. Mallory stepped back, as a blast of warm air shot out of the flat. 'I don't want to keep you, but I'm looking for the whereabouts of a man who used to live here. He was called Eddie Novak?' She'd already discovered from Karen that he'd left years earlier with no forwarding address.

The woman shook her head. 'We bought this flat three months ago and that wasn't the name of the sellers.'

'It doesn't matter. Enjoy your time with your son. Mine's seventeen now and it all feels a long time ago.'

The woman nodded and closed the door. Mallory wondered what else she could do to find Eddie. To come this far and not meet him felt like a failure. Although perhaps not a friend of Jaci's, they'd developed a series of knocks to communicate with each other, which suggested Jaci might have been worried about the attentions of someone. Terry had dismissed the tapping as an old man's fancy, but Mallory hadn't been so sure. She messaged Cal to check Eddie's contact number and took refuge in a small cafe to book a hotel room for the night.

Finding somewhere cheap-ish proved a nightmare. She was wary of Airbnb and wanted the anonymity of a chain. She finally found a room at the local Premier Inn, and she booked a night's stay. While she was finalising the reservation, Cal messaged to say she'd spoken to Eddie's son. Eddie had left the flat in 2012 and moved first to his son's and then to a nursing home. Cal had asked for permission for Mallory to visit him in the nursing home and his son had grudgingly agreed. 'The old guy lives in the past, so go easy on him,' Cal had written.

Checking the postcode, Mallory saw that the nursing home was in Wimbledon, a stone's throw from where Eddie had once resided. With the box under one arm and pulling the suitcase with the other, she tracked down the location of Pallion House and headed through the crowded streets. Even in the height of summer, Wales wasn't this kind of busy, and she was bad-tempered by the time she got to the home. She thought she'd have to navigate a barrage of officialdom, but a harassed care worker asked her to sign in and pointed her towards Eddie's room on the ground floor. Mallory knocked on the door and walked into a cosy space with a high bed in the centre, made up with a Welsh blanket covering the bed. At the side, in a high-backed chair, sat a tiny man, dressed in a Pringle jumper and corduroy slacks, his thin feet stuck into a pair of slippers.

'Mr Novak?'

He fumbled for his glasses and found them on the top of his head. 'You the policewoman my son was talking about?'

'I am. I wanted to talk to you about Jaci Jones. I won't take up much of your time.'

'It's been a long time since anyone spoke to me about Jaci. You can take as long as you want. No one's wanted to talk about her for years; I thought it had all been forgotten about.'

'Nothing could be further from the truth.' Mallory remembered the warning about spending too long in the past. 'It's just that there's been no fresh news for such a long time.'

His expression changed, the look of hope unbearable. 'You have news for us now?'

Mallory hesitated. The news of Gwennie's death hadn't made it to him. She looked across at the TV, which was tuned into an episode of *Bargain Hunt*. She guessed nursing homes weren't places where residents kept up with the news, but perhaps that was a misconception. 'I'm involved in a case in Wales that might help us with Jaci's disappearance.'

'Wales? You mean Ceigwyn? That's where Jaci was from.'

Mallory swallowed. 'That's right. Did she talk about her hometown much to you?'

Eddie shook his head. 'Not much. I think she was glad to get away. She said it was too small for her, a place where nothing ever happened.'

'But you remembered the town's name. She must have talked about it sometimes.'

Eddie frowned. 'She told me what its name meant. *Cei* means quay and *gwyn* is Welsh for white. Ceigwyn. The white quay.'

Mallory had a stab of longing to be out of this hot building in the filthy city and down on the Welsh quay eating an ice cream. 'Did she tell you anything else about Wales? What friends she had, for example?'

Eddie reached for a glass with shaking hands. 'I don't remember. I think she had a sister there who was a bit straightlaced. Not like Jaci, who liked a laugh.'

'What about boyfriends?'

Eddie slapped his hands on the table. 'You were always asking me about men. Jaci didn't have anyone in particular. She liked being single and doing what she wanted. There's no one she wanted to settle down with.'

'I didn't mention settling down. I'm talking about having fun.'

There was a silence as Eddie thought. 'There might have been someone. I don't know who. I came into her flat once and she had someone on speaker phone. He had a Welsh accent.'

'Do you know what they were talking about?' asked Mallory.

'Of course not. I heard her say she had to go and she switched off her phone.'

'But it was a Welsh man?'

'Yes.'

'Do you think his name might have been David? We think she knew someone by that name when she was younger. Does David mean anything to you?'

Eddie considered for a moment and shook his head. 'I don't recognise the name.'

'What about the name Gemma? Did she mention a friend by that name?'

Eddie considered. 'Maybe, I don't know. Gemma rings a bell, so maybe we talked about her. You know, she didn't like her own name.'

'Jaci? I didn't know that. Did she tell you that sometime?'

Eddie nodded, scratching his chin. 'She said it sounded too ordinary. Maybe that's when she mentioned the name Gemma. She said it sounded more romantic.'

'OK.' Mallory took a deep breath. Maybe Gemma wasn't another person but an alias that Jaci used. 'Did she mention a last name she might have liked? I mean, Jones is an ordinary Welsh name, isn't it?'

'Oh no. She liked Jones. Gemma Jones goes well together, doesn't it?'

'It does,' said Mallory. 'Did she say that? Perhaps she used that name sometimes.'

'I don't know.' Eddie was cross, perhaps aware that he'd revealed too much. 'It's all a long time ago.'

'Eddie, going back to the man with the Welsh voice, did you mention the phone call you overheard when we spoke to you back in 2008?'

'I never spoke to you, only that DI.'

'Terry Foster. He's retired now, but he never mentioned you telling him about a Welsh man.'

'I might not have told him.'

'Why would you do that?' asked Mallory, beginning to feel depressed. What else had they missed back in 2008?

'Because he was asking me about men Jaci went away with and I'm telling you she liked to go away on her own to chill out. There was no man involved.'

'You can't be sure of that though, Eddie, can you?'

Eddie shook his head. 'Jaci always went alone. She said, "this is me time, where I'm truly myself".'

–

Eddie tired soon after and Mallory escaped to her hotel room. It was a relief to get into the shower and wash away the grime of the train and the South while she thought about her day. She was inclined to believe Karen's account of what she knew. She hadn't had to invite Mallory into her flat, or reveal the presence of Jaci's things. A cooperative witness would be Mallory's assessment of her. Eddie was now well into his eighties, and although happy to talk, he presented a different picture of Jaci to the one Mallory had fixed in her mind. Jaci's friends and colleagues had mentioned that she was sociable but reserved, giving little away about herself. Eddie, however, had described her as fun. It struck Mallory suddenly that his was one of the few testimonies they had from a male perspective. Even if he'd been older and his relationship with her paternal, Eddie had been keen to emphasise how fun Jaci had been.

Before getting into the shower, Mallory texted Joe, telling him she was in London for work and asking for a meetup. If he was with Toby this evening – likely, given he hadn't seen his son for a week – he might not be glued to his phone, and she saw when she returned to the bedroom that Joe hadn't yet read the message. Instead, Mallory opened the Harrods box and looked once more through the contents. She used her mobile to search for the make of Dictaphone. She'd promised Cal that she'd share any information, but first she had to check whether she actually had anything to share, which meant listening to any information stored on the device. On the way to the hotel, she'd picked up some triple A batteries and replaced the old ones. There was a YouTube video that showed you how to use the machine, which Mallory watched twice before she picked up the device. She pressed the play button, which immediately clicked off, suggesting that the tape was at the end. She found the rewind button and listened as the tape spooled to the beginning. Toby had told her that tapes were back in fashion, the 'cassette revival', as he'd put it. Mallory had no idea why. They'd been out of fashion by the time she was a teenager, and she could see no benefit of a piece of plastic that produced a hissing sound when played.

The same hiss came at the start of the tape and continued as Mallory listened, holding her breath. There was nothing there, just white noise. Mallory put the device down and dressed in the jeans and jumper she'd bought in Swansea. Propping herself up on the pillows, she leant back on her bed and continued to listen to the wheeze of the tape. It was just as well she hadn't called Cal or Harri in her excitement. There was absolutely nothing to tell.

While the tape stuttered on, she picked up the 2007 diary and started on the week of the first entry. Jaci had been a spare writer, with a corporate feel to her notes. On the first week of February, she had taken a mid-week holiday and marked each day as 'annual leave'. Some weeks had no entry whatsoever. She didn't record trips to the pub, meetings with friends and absolutely nothing about trips to hotel rooms with strange men.

They never found Jaci's 2008 diary. It had felt like a missing piece of evidence, and Joe had thought its discovery would crack the case wide open. If the diary was written along similar lines to this one, however, they weren't missing much. Mallory reached December despairing of the find before flinging it on the bed. A minute later, the tape clicked off. Mallory looked at the clock: a whole thirty minutes of nothingness. She couldn't work out if the tape had never been used or if it had been wiped. Forensics would have a good idea, but she doubted they'd be able to recover anything meaningful. Before turning to the photos, Mallory ejected the tape and switched sides. She remembered her mother playing her Fleetwood Mac tape, saying she preferred side B to the A side. Bloody hell. Toby wouldn't have a clue what she was talking about.

She was about to pick up the photo album when she heard a voice come to life on the Dictaphone. 'If you ever looked at me once with what I know is in you, I would be your slave.' There was a moment of silence and then Jaci's voice again. 'I have dreamt in my life, dreams that have stayed with me ever after, and changed my ideas; they have gone through and through me, like wine through water, and altered the colour of my mind. And this is one: I'm going to tell it – but take care not to smile at any part of it.' Another silence and then the return of the infernal hiss.

'Fuck.' She played the extracts again, putting the words into the internet search on her phone. They were quotes from *Wuthering Heights* by Emily Brontë. It seemed Jaci had been reading extracts from the book and recording herself on Dictaphone. Perhaps these had been messages for her lover, recorded rather than sent by letter or email.

Mallory listened to the rest of the tape, but it had nothing else to offer up.

She rang Harri's phone, which was switched off. Cal, however, answered on the first ring and listened to Mallory's update. 'I don't know anything about the significance of Emily Brontë or *Wuthering Heights*, but I think I might be able to explain the Dictaphone. I don't know if you remember, but according to one statement, about a year earlier, her boss, Julie Edge, thought she saw Jaci slip something into her bag.'

'Of course.' Mallory did remember the detail, but it had been another unexplained action. She'd thought that perhaps Jaci had been taking home a notepad or some other piece of stationery. Part of the exodus of office supplies to workers' homes. She still had some Met Police pens from a conference herself. 'I remember. Julie mentioned it only because the team was looking for any suspicious activity. We thought it might have been anything from an office file to a pen she was filching from her desk. I'm pretty sure a Dictaphone was listed amongst her work things, so she probably slipped a spare into her bag.'

'You've checked the whole tape?'

'Yep. Listened to endless white noise. The first side of the tape was missing, almost certainly wiped. I can't decide why the second side still had these extracts. It surely can't have been Jaci's killer who wiped the content because they could just have easily removed the tape or the device itself.'

'I don't know,' said Cal. 'Jaci might have had second thoughts about what she'd been recording and wiped it herself. You say there's nothing in the diary? I still want to see it and the photo album.'

'There's a couple of things that are potentially more significant. At the bottom of the box there was a pencil with the name The Cedar Tree hotel embossed on one end. It's the first time we have something in Jaci's possession that links her to a hotel. I've done a quick search and there are three hotels by that name in the UK – in Staffordshire, Northumberland and on the Welsh borders.'

'The Welsh one is a possibility, isn't it, given Jaci's background?'

'Are you OK with me following that up? It's a link to Wales and the Gwennie Jones killing.'

Cal sighed down the line. 'All right. Anything else?'

Mallory told her about the pad and Jaci's possible use of the name Gemma.

'Bloody hell, you have been busy. I don't remember that name coming up in the files, but I can run another search. It's news to you, I take it?'

'Definitely, but we considered the possibility that Jaci was using an alias when she checked in to hotels. There's something else I wanted to talk to you about.' Mallory flipped open the photo album and pulled out the three photos, checking there wasn't anything written on the back. 'I'll describe them to you. The first is time-stamped the twelfth of July 2008. I'm wondering if it was maybe taken with a digital camera and printed out, like we did back in the day.'

'I'll take your word for it,' said Cal. 'It's just Jaci in the picture?'

'Yes, and she's definitely not in this country. I'm guessing somewhere in the Med. She's got a decent tan and is laughing at whoever is taking the photo. Jaci took a holiday with Marion around that time, didn't she?'

'Correct,' said Cal. 'A week in Portugal between the tenth and eighteenth of July.'

'One of the other two are from the same holiday, later in the week. Marion presumably took the pictures and gave the two photos to Jaci, who began a photo album with them.'

'Sounds a sensible assumption. What's your problem?'

'My problem is that Jaci has blonde hair.'

'What?' There came the sound of Cal dropping something. 'Sorry, are you sure? The photo distributed at the time of the disappearance shows Jaci with light brown hair.'

'The image was given to the team by Marion. We asked for a recent photo and that's what she gave us. She specifically said it had been taken in Wales when Jaci had returned for a couple of days. We took Marion's word that it was the most recent one she had.'

'Maybe she forgot about the holiday snaps. She didn't think it would matter.'

'But what about the change in hair colour?' said Mallory.

'Do we know she was blonde when she went missing? Maybe she was experimenting with the colour for her holidays and reverted to type when she got home. That would explain why Marion gave you the Christmas photo as the most representative of her missing daughter.'

'Is there any way of checking?' asked Mallory, knowing well what that entailed.

Cal sighed again. 'I'll ring Marion now. What's the third photo, by the way?'

Mallory studied the image. 'Jaci's got light brown hair and is standing next to a large tree. She's got her arm around the trunk, as far as it will go, anyway, and is resting her head against the bark.'

'Nothing to identify where it might have been taken?'

'Nothing at all. It's on a separate page to the other two. What's interesting about this one is that the other photos show Jaci in clothes from 2008 – jeans, off-the-shoulder T-shirts, halter-neck dresses. In this one she looks like she's raided a Laura Ashley shop.' Mallory stopped. 'Do I need to explain what Laura Ashley is?'

'I'll ignore that,' said Cal. 'So she's gone full on *Wuthering Heights*, then.'

Mallory frowned. 'You know, a little, maybe. It's odd, but her hair straighteners went missing, didn't they? In this image her hair is slightly wavy. It's as if she'd taken on a different persona for this trip away.'

Cal sucked in her breath. 'Complicated and hidden. You weren't wrong, Mallory.'

Mallory piled everything back into the cardboard box. When she picked up the make-up bag, it released a waft of the perfume she'd identified earlier. A powdery smell and that elusive scent that struck a memory long buried. She fumbled for the zip and this time examined each item. Three lipsticks, all in shades of pale pink, brown mascara, its wand clogged up, a tube of foundation which still oozed a light pink cream liquid, and finally, the source of that powdery smell. An empty bottle of scent.

Of course, thought Mallory. The perfume.

# 22

*December 2008*

They were running out of leads and Terry was taking it out on the team. Following his disastrous *Crimewatch* appearance, he was hanging onto his job by the skin of his teeth and scattering his team far and wide in the pursuit of leads that felt to Mallory tenuous and disjointed. Terry Foster had got her on the hunt for a scent bottle because, apart from her phone and hair straighteners, it was the only item of Jaci's that seemed to be missing. Mallory, never one for scent, was having to become acquainted with various brands, some of which would cost her a week's salary. Jaci had purchased a bottle of perfume the day before she'd disappeared and it could not be found. Lizzie Cates, her colleague and friend, was adamant Jaci had bought it for herself and no one else.

'Jaci was upset that she'd run out of her perfume. She carried a little bottle in her handbag and used to spray it at her desk. It'd stink out the office, but we didn't mind.'

Lizzie Cates also stank of perfume, a floral smell that brought to Mallory's mind gardenias, although she didn't actually know their perfume. They were blowy, ostentatious flowers and that was how Lizzie smelt.

Terry thought it significant that they couldn't find the bottle, while Mallory considered it another dead end. The investigation was full of them – boyfriends that had failed to materialise, a phone switched off around the time Jaci went missing, a set of hair straighteners that had been taken when Jaci left the flat, and the remains of a fish pie for one thrown into the bin.

There was evidence that Jaci might have got dressed in a hurry. The flat was immaculate, and in the same bin as the fish pie was the wrapping for both the perfume bottle and a set of pyjamas from Next. The pyjamas had been hastily thrown onto a chair. Given there was nothing else in the rubbish bin, which was collected every Monday, this suggested that Jaci had eaten the fish pie and unwrapped both the pyjamas and perfume that evening. The pyjamas had been found, but where was the scent bottle?

'Can you remember what it was called?' she asked, still wondering why it mattered.

Lizzie shook her head. 'It was in a little round bottle. She said it reminded her of being a teenager. I tell you what I do have, though. I sprayed some on myself last week because I'd forgotten to put any on that morning. I was going to go to the perfume counter at Elys, but Jaci said I could have some of hers, even though there was only a little left. Here.' Lizzie rummaged around in her bag. 'Smell it.'

Mallory was still overwhelmed by the scent of gardenia but gamely smelt the scarf. There was a scent she couldn't identify, neither citrusy nor floral. 'Can I take this? It might be important. We need to identify the perfume bottle that's missing.'

Lizzy shrugged. 'If you like. I want the scarf back, though.'

–

Mallory had taken the flimsy piece of material and steeled herself for a trudge around the counters of Elys department store. The first woman at an Estee Lauder stand didn't recognise the smell. 'It smells like something my nan would wear. Hold on, I'll ask Brenda.'

Brenda was a woman in her late fifties with dyed blonde hair set like a helmet. She took the scarf from Mallory and sniffed it deeply.

'It's Je Reviens by Worth. Takes me back, to be honest. You won't find it stocked here. It used to be a fashion brand in the Fifties and Sixties, but it's fallen out of favour. They probably sell it in discount perfume stores.'

'Like the one in the shopping centre.'

'Exactly.' Brenda handed the scarf back to Mallory. 'It's nice to smell it again. It's got a nice history. In the 1940s it was the perfume of choice for soldiers to send to their girlfriends. Can I ask why you're asking?'

'I'm investigating the disappearance of Jaci Jones, which is now being treated as a murder. There are a number of items missing, which suggests Jaci may have initially gone willingly with her abductor. One of them is the perfume bottle. If we know what we're looking for, we can ask the public to look out for it.'

Brenda grimaced. 'That poor girl. I recognised her, you know. She came in here to browse. She was always immaculately made up, which is the sort of thing I notice.'

'Was she on her own?'

Brenda nodded. 'I'm afraid so. I never saw her with a man, if that's what you mean. She seemed, I don't know, otherworldly. Quiet, with her head in the clouds. Do you really think she's been killed?'

Mallory stuffed the scarf back into her bag to return to Lizzie. 'We think Jaci has come to harm and the inquiry is now a murder investigation.'

'God, what a time to be young. I saw the appeal on TV and I wasn't sure whether to call in.'

Mallory looked up from her bag. 'Oh? Why?'

'I don't know, it's just I did see her buy something, which might have been helpful. It was one of the nighties from the lingerie department. The man on the TV said he thought Jaci liked going for nights away. This was one of those types of nighties; you know, one you'd wear for a lover.' Brenda bit her lip. 'I feel stupid telling you, which is why I never rang in.'

'A lacy nightdress?' Mallory frowned, remembering the pair of plaid pyjamas on the bedside chair.

'Not, you know, revealing. It was long and just a bit lacy. Also expensive. I can show you, if you like.'

Mallory followed Brenda up the escalator. As someone who slept in a rank old T-shirt and bought her bras in Sainsbury's, she was a little overwhelmed by the world she found herself in. Everything was pastel and flimsy. Brenda went straight to a rail and pulled a nightdress out.

'This is it.'

It wasn't what Mallory had been expecting. It was more 1918 than 2008, the sort of thing you might wear with a nightcap, carrying a candle up to bed. She gasped when she saw the price tag. 'A hundred and twenty pounds?'

'I told you it was expensive. Strange, isn't it?'

Mallory touched the thick fabric. 'What's strange?'

'She wore expensive nightwear and cheap perfume.'

Mallory caught the whiff of censure in her voice. 'Maybe the perfume had a significance for her. Worth was once a quality brand, wasn't it?' This was happening more and more, Mallory defending Jaci – from the press, colleagues and even other women.

Brenda turned away. 'It's still a strange thing to do. Perhaps you should be looking for the nightie too.'

## 23

Freddie had sourced a takeaway pizza, the type full of cheese and not much else that Harri was pretty sure he should be avoiding. Even Siân had turned her nose up at the sight of its marbled surface. The three of them were in Harri's office, which now reeked of garlic as they ate their slices. He'd been called upstairs to give Steph an update with a focus on potential suspects and coming up with useful soundbites to appease the press. He had none. Huw and Daisy had been ruled out, as they appeared on camera at both The Feathers and down at the quay at the time of the murder. The second camera also ruled out Eleri as a suspect. Watching a clip of the footage had depressed Harri, with hundreds of visitors descending on the town for the festivities. Sometimes there were just too many potential witnesses.

'Tell me about Liam?' he asked Siân. 'There's no way he could have got back to Ceigwyn after seeing his father in Salford?'

'Nope,' said Siân, dabbing at the corners of her mouth with a tissue. 'Nurses have corroborated his presence by his father's side and CCTV at the entrance to the cardiac unit shows him exiting at regular intervals for a vape. Another victory for surveillance society.'

'So our current lead is Tomos and Dylan Bethel, who we know Gwennie had an altercation with on Thursday afternoon. Tomos says it was over a dismissive comment he made about Gwennie's involvement in a proposed TV documentary. That's not enough of a motive for murder so we need to dig deeper.'

'What about the connection to Jaci Jones?' asked Siân. 'Have we had any feedback from Mallory yet?'

'No, but she'd have only arrived in London late afternoon. I'll hopefully get an update from her later. It may well be that any evidence linking Gwennie and Jaci's murders is found here in Wales in the current investigation rather than in London, and I'd still like to keep an open mind. We do need to contact the film company and check whether there were any payments made to Gwennie, and Mallory is going to try to arrange a meeting.'

'It's the fact that she's standing on the street corner that gets me,' said Freddie, reaching for a third slice of pizza. 'She could have been killed in private, but instead, she's waiting on a street corner on one of the busiest nights of the year. Have we completely ruled out an opportunist thief? We've still not found her bag, and then there's the break-in at Eleri's house to consider.'

'One scenario is opportunism,' said Harri, 'and we're searching that area of the town extensively in case Gwennie's purse was taken and the bag discarded. Another possibility is that Gwennie was carrying something for whoever she was meeting, and that when she refused to hand it over, the bag was taken by force, but whatever her assailant was expecting to be inside was missing.'

'Drugs?' asked Siân. 'It's the most likely scenario around here.'

'Agreed,' said Freddie, 'which would also account for Gwennie's new coat and handbag, but the issue is she's not on anyone's radar. We've spoken to the known dealers and they say no way.'

'There's a first time for everything,' said Harri. 'She might have started using recently. However, I think it's too much of a coincidence that she's in contact with a TV company, suddenly starts buying new clothes and is killed waiting in a doorway to meet up with someone who steals her bag.'

'Then you *do* think there's a connection with Jaci Jones.'

Harri rubbed his aching head. 'We've a long way to go yet. Is there anything else?'

'Well,' said Siân, taking a swig from her can of Coke. 'I went back to interview Liam at his room in The Feathers. I wanted to see the setup there. It's a small place, but tidy. He seems a nice lad. As you know, he was convinced that Gwennie went cold on him over the Christmas period. She seemed keen in December, but by the holidays she was avoiding his calls.'

'This might coincide with the TV thing,' said Freddie.

'Which was what I thought, but when I pressed Liam, he thought there might be someone else. Someone Gwennie had subsequently met.'

'Does he know who? Are we looking for another teenager, for example, or an older man?'

'He didn't know, but he suspects an out-of-towner. Someone who came to Ceigwyn for the holidays. The problem is that they might have already left by now.'

'I wonder if there's a link with that TV company,' said Harri. 'How old is this Beck Cowan?'

'Mid-forties, according to the records at Companies House. Not sure it stacks up with Gwennie meeting him on a street corner.'

'So we might be looking for another boyfriend based in Ceigwyn?' Harri leant back in his chair, feeling more cheerful. He never liked having only one suspect, even if the Bethel brothers were technically a pair. The thought of someone they hadn't yet identified was an interesting line of investigation. 'All right,' he said. 'Let's focus on that tomorrow and in the meantime, I'll try to catch up with Mallory.'

# 24

Mallory never did find the nightgown, or 'nightie', as Brenda had called it. The phrase conjured up an image of Mallory's mother on summer mornings sitting doing the quick crossword at the kitchen table with a cigarette in her hand. Mallory was a pyjama girl, and it seemed, judging by the contents of her cupboards, Jaci had been one too. The nightwear might have been a present for Marion, although the price tag suggested otherwise. Mallory had tried to speak to Marion about the purchase, but relations had soured by then, and when another officer rang her to ask what Jaci had worn in bed, the phone had been slammed down on them. It probably didn't matter. Perhaps Jaci did have a nice night garment for special nights away and she'd taken it with her. It was likely with the rest of her missing things, probably never to be found.

Joe returned Mallory's call while she was bundling everything back into the box, ready to pass on to Cal. 'Is everything OK? Toby got back safely, if that's what you were worrying about.'

'That's good to hear. I did ask him to message me once he was home, but you know what kids are like. He'll probably remember tomorrow. That's not why I called. I've had to come to London in relation to the Jaci Jones case.'

'Oh God,' said Joe. 'I'm not sure I want to hear.'

'Look, I understand but I do need to talk to you. I'm staying at a hotel in Wimbledon and wondered if you were free for a quick chat. It doesn't have to be tonight, if you're busy. Tomorrow maybe.'

'Tomorrow is out for me,' said Joe, without much enthusiasm. 'I have a conference in Birmingham and I'm catching an early train. Can we do this over the phone?'

'Not really; there's something I want to show you.'

'Sounds intriguing.' Joe was thinking. 'How about we meet in Victoria? Perhaps in a hotel bar. Somewhere we can hear ourselves think.'

–

An hour later, Mallory was sharing a bottle of Pinot Noir with Joe. It was just like the early days of their relationship, when they'd meet up at Victoria before heading off to their respective flats for an early start the following morning. The conversation had fizzed back then, which included their assessment of the progress of the Jaci Jones investigation. Now, neither knew what to say to each other. The last time Mallory had seen Joe there had been a row over Toby's eating. Now he seemed more relaxed with her, if a little wary about her mission. Must be the new girlfriend.

'I'm glad this isn't about Toby,' said Joe, reading her mind, as ever. 'He seems to be settling down a little, although he was a bit wired when he got back home.'

'He's still too thin.' Mallory winced, remembering Karen's assessment of her own weight. 'But yes, he's less of a worry. Look, I need to talk to you about a few things. First up is this.'

Mallory had carted up the hatbox to the hotel, and placed it in front of Joe, watching his expression. He opened the diary and looked at Jaci's name on the front.

'Where did you get this?'

'Karen Overton discovered this lot in a cupboard at the flat. Seems we missed it during the search.'

'Not "we",' said Joe. 'The search had been completed by the time I joined the team.'

'We all missed it. You know what searches are like. Everything needs checking again and again. We didn't do that here.'

Joe shrugged. 'I was never asked to search the place. This one's nothing to do with me.'

'Karen says she saw you in a pub a long time after you'd left the investigation and mentioned she still had some of Jaci's things.'

'What?' Joe looked astonished. 'I don't remember this. When was this?'

'She didn't say.' And I didn't push her, thought Mallory.

'Anything of importance there?'

Mallory nodded. 'I finally have the name of a hotel stamped on a pencil. "The Cedar Tree". Mean anything to you?'

Joe shook his head. 'Where is it?'

'Could be one of three places, but the Welsh borders is the strongest possibility.'

'That's a decent lead. Anything else?'

'The name Gemma, which she might have been using as an alias.' Mallory glanced across at Joe, but he was frowning. The name meant nothing to him. 'There was also a Dictaphone with a tape that had largely been wiped. Have a listen.'

Joe held the tape to his ear, his eyes on her. 'What is it? A poem?'

'Quotes from *Wuthering Heights*, according to Professor Google.'

'That's a book, right?' Harri, Mallory reflected, would have at least heard of the Brontës.

'That's right, a book.'

'And the first side's been wiped?'

Mallory nodded. 'I don't know by who and why they stopped with one side. It feels kinda haphazard, so I'm guessing someone either did it in a rush or got distracted and decided the extracts didn't matter.'

'A killer would have simply taken the whole device.'

Mallory nodded. 'My guess is it was Jaci, but it doesn't make sense.'

'Nothing ever made sense, remember? It's why the case was deeply, deeply frustrating.'

'And you honestly don't remember Karen telling you about these contents.'

Joe touched his chest. 'Hand on heart, I don't. You know, there was a time just after we separated where I was drinking heavily. I have no memory of most of those evenings.'

Mallory nodded. 'It's fine. I just wanted to check with you.'

'What else do you have in the box?'

'Three photos in an album. There were probably more there once upon a time, but three are left. Take a look.'

She handed over the album to him and he saw the significance straight away. 'We were looking for a dark-haired woman and here is evidence that Jaci was blonde.' He squinted at the time stamp. 'Was she still blonde by the time she disappeared?'

'We don't know. I've spoken to the cold case team lead. I'm meeting her tomorrow to hand over this stuff as the case is her responsibility now. Just look at that final photo, though. Don't you think Jaci looks, well, different from the photo we used of her?'

Joe glanced at it. 'Very different I'd say. Bring the other one up.'

Mallory got out her phone, ignoring his presumptive tone, and together they studied the image. It had been given to them by Marion and showed a woman any mother would be proud of. Jaci had iron-straight dark hair and was wearing a checked navy-blue dress with a linen jacket over the top. The picture had a cropped feel to it because that's exactly what it was. The original image had contained both Jaci and Marion, and it had been this photo that Marion had insisted had been the closest likeness to her missing daughter.

'It's odd, but a phone call to Marion should answer some of your questions. She won't speak to you, but you could get one of the cold case team to look into it.'

'I'm already on it.' Mallory shut the album with a snap. 'Something doesn't feel right, and I haven't got Terry Foster with his outdated assumptions to deal with this time. What do you think Jaci was up to?'

Joe sighed and shrugged. 'Really, Mallory, I have no idea. What do *you* think? I'm not being difficult, it's just I really try not to think back to 2008. It's too painful, for a lot of reasons.'

Mallory took a deep breath. 'My brief is to find a connection between Jaci Jones going missing in 2008 and her niece Gwennie getting attacked. So far I've found nothing, and even this evidence doesn't give me anything beyond a confirmation that we always suspected – that

Jaci was a deeply private person who led a life that wasn't transparent to those who loved her.'

Joe looked at his nearly empty wine glass. 'I don't know what you want me to say. I've tried to put that case behind me. It's got so much history for me personally. It was where I realised CID wasn't for me, where I met you and we had all that shit afterwards because of that bastard Foster.'

'I came up with the description of Jaci's relationships being complicated and hidden. You can't blame everything on Terry.'

Joe drained his glass. 'Don't beat yourself up. Jaci's relations were complicated, even if we were desperately short on detail. They should never have put the guv in front of the cameras. It was bad optics and once the press began to run with the "who are the mystery men in Jaci's love life" angle, Marion turned on us.'

'Interestingly, according to Cal, the new SIO, Marion's got some issues that may be memory related. I'm hoping if my involvement in this new investigation gets out Marion doesn't kick off.'

'Hmm. Shall I get us another round?'

Mallory put her hand over her glass. 'Not for me. Get yourself one though.'

Joe hadn't been much of a drinker back in the day. He'd admitted that he'd turned to the booze post-divorce, and he must still have his own stresses with the bulk of Toby's care falling to him. He slid off his seat and went to the bar, using the opportunity to look at his phone. When he returned with another balloon glass full of wine, she leant back and tried to look casual.

'How's the new relationship going?'

Joe looked smug. 'Great. Jennifer is unattached, cheery and most importantly, Toby likes her.'

'That's the impression I got.'

'He also likes Harri. You two do have a thing going, don't you?'

Mallory nodded. 'Yes, but it's complicated. In cases like this he's effectively my boss, although there's been nothing really to declare, so we've just, I dunno, coasted. I think we need to finally start thinking about what the future might look like, which includes where I live and what I do.'

'You need to be careful. The Comms officer called me today to say they'd had a couple of press enquiries in relation to the whereabouts of the original investigating team. I'm going to be better protected as I'm a serving police officer. Both you and Terry Foster are more exposed as you're no longer on the payroll.'

Mallory felt sick. Perhaps she should have had that other drink. 'That's great.'

'I'm simply warning you, Mallory. You need to keep your powder dry. If the press gets a sniff you're involved in some way again they'll go digging, and that includes your relationships.'

Joe's obvious concern brought tears to Mallory's eyes, even if it was because she was the mother of his son. Once again, Joe read her thoughts.

'I do still care. We had some good times together, but we're better apart. I'm happier and, if you don't mind me saying, you are too. Wales suits you. You look kinda out of place back here.'

It was true. Mallory realised with a jolt that she missed Wales and Harri and her life there. Once the meetings were over and done with the following morning, she'd get back to her adopted country and make plans for the future. If only she could shrug off the feeling that it was all too good to be true.

# 25

The next morning, Mallory made her way to the Regency Cafe after failing to get hold of Harri. Her findings were exciting for her, as a former investigator into Jaci Jones's disappearance, but in terms of Gwennie's death, they still didn't amount to much. A potential lead on a hotel, a name with a heart around it, a Dictaphone with quotations from *Wuthering Heights*. Hardly earth-shattering, and Mallory needed to remember that she was employed to investigate the murder of Gwennie Jones, not her aunt.

The hatbox had given her a dilemma. She had to check out of her hotel, as there was no way she was going back to Wimbledon after a breakfast meeting in Victoria, but the Harrods box was conspicuous and a TV documentary maker was likely to spot anything out of the ordinary. In the end, on the way to the Tube, she'd bought a bag for life from Tesco and put the box at the bottom, stuffing a jumper on top. She'd hand everything over to Cal, who could assess if anything was worth examining for DNA. As far as Mallory was concerned, she'd extracted everything she could from the contents.

The Regency had apparently changed ownership since the days when she'd been living in London, but the busy atmosphere was much the same, with the addition of many more tourists. A man sitting at a table waved her over, clearly recognising her from the photos printed in the press seventeen years earlier.

'This one's on me,' said Beck Cowan. 'This has long been my favourite cafe. What will you have?'

Mallory had woken up with a thick head despite drinking only half the glass of wine the night before. The thought of a cooked breakfast made her feel sick, so she settled for poached eggs on toast with some orange juice and a black coffee.

'So,' said Beck, his eyes on Mallory's rucksack and large carrier bag. 'Where are you living now?'

Nice try, thought Mallory. He might not know she was now a civilian investigator, but she wasn't going to allow him to take control of the meeting. As far as he was concerned, once a cop… 'I believe you're producing a documentary on Jaci Jones's disappearance. Is there a particular reason why now? Jaci's been missing for decades.'

Beck sat back in his chair and folded his arms. 'Sure, but there is a group of women who've gone missing over the years whose cases have never been solved. I'm thinking of Suzy Lamplugh, Claudia Lawrence, Leah Croucher. There's an appetite for not only finding out where these women went but the personality behind the victim.'

'You've done documentaries on these women too?'

Beck hesitated. 'Not exactly.'

'But why Jaci as opposed to, say, one of the others? In a couple of years it'll be the twentieth anniversary of her disappearance. Why do it now?'

Beck looked uncomfortable, perhaps remembering he was speaking to a former Met officer. 'It feels the right time to look at the disappearance again. I know of the Jaci Jones case more than the others, as I'm Welsh too.'

Mallory took him in. He was a large man with shaggy hair and a beard that was neither hipster nor goatee. She liked that he didn't conform to her stereotype of a TV person, but she had to remind herself that he was persistent and driven. He was also holding something back, probably his approach to Gwennie Jones, another person in this perplexing case who was unwilling to show their hand.

'Why contact me now? It sounds as if this has been in production for a while.'

Beck grimaced. 'Like most TV companies, we wanted to bring something fresh to the case, so we decided to focus on Jaci's Welsh connections. We think her home life before she moved to London was never thoroughly investigated. Plus, to be upfront with you, although Jaci was supposed to have had, shall we say, a spicy love life here, no one was ever identified as being involved in these trips away.'

'So you thought you'd look at Wales.'

'Yes, exactly.'

And there I am, thought Mallory, living there and now involved in the investigation into the death of Jaci's niece. Not much of an investigator, are you?

'What exactly do you want from me?'

'As I mentioned on the phone, I'd like you on camera talking about your recollection of the investigation. It's not a stitch-up, I promise you. It's a programme of two halves. You'd be part of the background and then we'd switch to Wales and talk about the death of Gwennie Jones and any connection there might be.'

Mallory tried to hide the alarm she felt at this man blithely coming to Ceigwyn and turning her life upside down once more. She'd need to absent herself while that part was being filmed, not easy in a small Welsh town.

Moreover, she'd probably have to reveal her connection to Dyfed Powys police before the interview took place, otherwise she could be accused of railroading the programme. Mallory shook herself. This was hypothetical, given she had no intention of actually taking part in the programme. Overthinking was going to be her downfall in this case.

'When were you thinking of going to Wales?'

'Oh, later on in the year. We can't get near the investigation, so our plans are to let it run its course, unless, of course, DI Harri Evans gives us an interview. We're no armchair detectives – you know, the shows where everyone has a clipboard and they chuck images of evidence onto a large Perspex screen.'

'I know the type. So this is going to be a more reflective show, including how we messed things up.'

Beck stood and headed to the counter as their breakfasts were called. He brought back two hot plates and sat down. 'I don't think you messed up, but I do believe times have changed since 2008. I like to think policing has taken on board the messages from the #MeToo movement and the murder of Sarah Everard.'

Mallory tucked into her eggs, realising how hungry she was. It actually sounded like a decent enough TV show, but she doubted she would have agreed to participate, even if she wasn't living in Wales and involved in the new case. However, she needed some information from Beck Cowan before she left.

'I'm going to need some time to think over my involvement in the show,' said Mallory, aware that she was speaking with her mouth full. 'Are any of the family involved?'

'Um, well Gwennie had agreed to take part, but that's not going to happen now, obviously.'

'Were you going to pay Gwennie? She's only seventeen.'

'Of course, but I was going to wait until she became of age. Less ramifications about both her participation and any payments.'

It was as near Mallory could get to asking about Gwennie receiving cash. It didn't sound as if anything tangible had taken place yet, which suggested Beck wasn't the source of Gwennie's funds.

'Do you honestly think there's a relationship between the recent murder and Jaci's disappearance? Other than Marion, there was no evidence of anyone from Wales visiting Jaci in Wimbledon, although she made occasional trips back to her hometown. If someone there wished her harm, the most obvious place to do it was in Ceigwyn, not on her doorstep.'

Beck concentrated on buttering his toast while he considered the question. 'The problem with the work your team did, Mallory, if you don't mind me saying, was to concentrate on Jaci's love life. All right, there might have been men Jaci went away with, but there are other reasons for killing someone – money, revenge, hate, old hurts. That's more likely to happen in a place where a person grew up. Didn't you ever think of going there and checking?'

Mallory remembered interminable visits to the offices of Squire Insurance and interviewing the male employees. Terry Foster had been convinced Jaci had been having an affair with someone from work. It's where she'd spent most of the time, along with visits to the gym. The men at that club had also been interviewed and… nothing.

'Two members of the team were sent, but not me. People remembered Jaci as reserved and a little shy. The sexual predator that the press ran with didn't match the girl they knew, so they disengaged from the story. People clammed up and eventually that included the family.'

It would have been a good time to introduce the potential man called David that Marion had mentioned, but Mallory needed to keep the name from Beck. Despite his assurances that he was no armchair detective, that's exactly how she saw him.

'Have you come across any men in Jaci's past based in Wales?'

'I told you, we're not focusing necessarily on her love life.' For the first time, Mallory saw she'd riled him. 'The family are very sensitive about that and although they didn't want to be involved in the documentary, I see no need to upset them.'

Strange, thought Mallory. 'And yet you approached Gwennie.'

Beck made a face and put down his fork. 'We thought Gwennie would be a good match for our vision. She's significantly younger than the age Jaci was when she disappeared, but she's got the look of Jaci, long dark hair and petite. But with Gwennie gone, we'll struggle to get any family to appear. Eleri, who was Jaci's sister, wanted nothing to do with us from the start and that won't change now that Gwennie's dead.'

'Did you meet Gwennie?'

Beck shook his head. 'Not in person, but we spoke a few times via Teams. She was a nice girl, intense and confident, which wasn't how Jaci had been described. But, as I said, she looked like her aunt, and she'd have come across brilliantly on camera. I was going to look at generational trauma. That sort of thing.'

Beck's ruthless attitude was beginning to show. He might look like your big brother ready to give you a hug, but he was also a sharp TV maker whose goal was to get you to participate in his project.

'What about Marion, Jaci's mother?'

'Well, we had high hopes about Marion, but she's proved elusive. She doesn't answer calls and the emails I sent don't appear to have been opened. I don't suppose you're in touch with her?'

'Me?' Mallory nearly choked on her coffee. 'Marion had plenty to say about all of us, but most of her ire was directed at me. Why would I be in touch with her after all these years?'

Beck shrugged. 'Stranger things have happened. So you'll think about appearing on the show then?'

'I'll think about it,' agreed Mallory. 'I'm sure we'll be in touch again.'

# 26

Harri was sleep deprived and irritable. The two were, of course, connected. He missed Mallory and wondered if it was wise for her to revisit the past in this way. He had to admit that he had given her an impossible brief: work on a link between Jaci's and Gwennie's deaths but keep out of sight of the Jones family and press.

In some respects, Harri was now less concerned about print media. Back when he'd first joined the force, he'd been told to avoid talking about cases in the pub in case of a journalist lurking behind a pillar and beware of the odd bent copper who'd accept a bribe in exchange for some information. The press had changed beyond recognition in the intervening years, even if dishonest detectives hadn't. Although high-profile cases might warrant a journalist from London, the internet had resulted in a proliferation of newshounds, most of whom were happy to sit in their warm offices while trying to solve the cases. It was one of these who was most likely to spot Mallory's involvement in both investigations, and then all hell would break loose.

Harri took Siân with him to interview Dylan Bethel. He'd wanted to do it the previous evening, but according to Dylan's mother, her son was staying overnight in Liverpool attending a meeting, a statement confirmed by a call to the man's partner. No doubt, Tomos had been on the phone to his brother the minute Harri had left, but there was nothing he could do about that. Dylan, the brighter of the two brothers, in Harri's opinion, would already have got his story straight about Gwennie's altercation in the bar.

Dylan was working from home this morning for the pharmaceutical company who employed him. It was a Swedish organisation, with Dylan working as a sales rep liaising with the GP practices in Wales. Harri briefly wondered if he represented metformin, the drug he took for his diabetes and whose brand continually changed depending on which rep had visited his pharmacy.

Dylan's photo was on the company website. Harri was struck again by how much he looked like his brother, except for a small scar about his lip. Working as a sales rep in a multinational organisation was an interesting choice of profession for a farmer's son. As far as Harri was aware, he hadn't attended university but, according to the website, had joined the company as a trainee and worked his way up to be a major account manager.

Harri and Siân entered the gardens fronting a large modern bungalow, boxy, but with wooden windows and a Welsh slate roof. Harri approved of the construction quality and wondered how much it would cost in this affluent town. Money surely wasn't a factor in the killing of Gwennie Jones, but might Jaci, all those years ago, have had a secret that might have put into jeopardy Dylan's progress upwards in society? In the driveway sat a large SUV, its windows tinted more or less to the legal level. As they waited, Dylan came to the door holding a wailing baby as he invited them into the house.

'Sorry about this. Marie has had to go to the pharmacy to get some more Calpol. Bethan has a tooth coming through and it's mayhem.'

Harri with a pang remembered those days of reddened cheeks and tear-stained faces. It had been up to him to make late-night dashes to the twenty-four-hour Tesco in Carmarthen, Paula's fatigue the first sign of the illness that consumed her. Ben and Ellie were now teenagers, well able to look after themselves. Paula. Well Paula was gone to wherever you go and Harri was trying to make the best of things.

Siân shot him a look. A crying baby was a good distraction technique, and they had arranged the meeting for 11.30 a.m., which both Dylan and his partner were aware of. In Siân's opinion, Harri suspected, the baby was a ruse. Never mind. If Dylan was a killer, all the gummy babies in the world wouldn't prevent an arrest. They followed him into a living room where a thermometer and notebook showed they were monitoring the baby's temperature, so perhaps Siân had done him a disservice.

'We're here,' said Harri, 'to talk about the argument your brother Tomos had with Gwennie Jones on Thursday evening.'

Dylan nodded, not bothering to hide the fact he'd spoken to Tomos. 'I believe it's there on CCTV. You'll know then that I was a mere bystander, and I have to say the term argument is a little strong for what went on. We were having a drink, Gwennie flew in and started jabbing her finger at Tomos's chest, and he showed admirable restraint.'

'Did she say why she was so upset?' asked Harri.

Dylan shrugged. 'Something he'd written online about the TV programme they're making into the Jaci Jones disappearance. Gwennie was involved in some way; don't ask me what. She thought it was her big chance, you know, the next Scarlett Johansson.'

Interesting choice of actor, thought Harri, remembering Tomos's blonde comment.

'That's a little harsh, given Gwennie is dead,' said Siân.

Dylan shrugged, but said nothing, the approach of hardened criminals. His manner made Harri more watchful.

'Did you see the comments themselves?' he asked.

Dylan shook his head. 'I'm not on social media at all. I don't see the point of it. I have an email address and a mobile.'

'Do you use WhatsApp?' asked Siân. 'That's a form of social media.'

Dylan curled his lip. 'Only because Marie messages me on it. I keep getting added to groups and I leave straight away. I'm not interested.'

After a glance from Harri, Siân read from her tablet. 'Your brother wrote, "Another shit TV programme about missing Jaci and Gwennie Jones using it as her chance of stardom. Disgusting. I remember Jaci and she'd have thought Gwennie were a loser."' There was a brief silence. 'What did you think he meant by that?'

Dylan jigged the baby. Little Beth was clearly going to be the prop when things got difficult. 'I dunno. What did he say?'

'We didn't have the actual words when we went to interview Tomos.' Harri didn't say that it had taken a couple of hours to track down the post appearing in a closed group that they'd waited six hours for approval to join. 'So, what did they mean?'

Up and down the baby went again. 'Tomos and I knew Jaci a little bit because she used to babysit for us. When she went missing, we were both upset. I guess it's still a bit raw.'

'Jaci babysat for you?'

'Jaci and Eleri both did, and recently Gwennie started babysitting for Beth, although Marie doesn't really like leaving the baby alone.'

'How did you find Gwennie?' asked Harri.

'Pretty bright, to be honest, and she reminded me a bit of Jaci. You know, aspirations beyond this small town. I can relate to that.'

'How did she come to babysit for you?'

'I often see Eleri around. She makes cracking cakes and sells them locally. We were reminiscing about her babysitting days, and she mentioned Gwennie might be up for some work. I liked the idea because I know the family.'

'Were your parents friends with Marion?' Harri wondered how long it would be before his paths crossed with Gwennie's grandmother.

Dylan frowned. 'You've been to the farm, haven't you? Well, the Jones family lived for a time in a cottage at the top of the lane. Marion had split up from the girls' father and was looking for somewhere reasonable to live. Da let them use the cottage, although it was a bit far out of Ceigwyn for Marion. She moved into town after a year or so.'

'Jaci can't have been much older than you both.'

'About eight years. This was when we were about ten. Ma would have left us on our own in the house, but there'd been that fire up the valley where the children died.'

Harri remembered the case. A family where the parents had got up at five to go to the fruit market in Cardiff. The children had been left sleeping in bed and a fire had broken out. A tragedy made worse by the controversial conviction of the parents for neglect.

'Did either of you keep in touch with Jaci after she moved to London?' asked Siân, her eyes on the baby.

'Not really. Jaci would come home sometimes and I'd see her in the pub and say hello. That's what it's like around here – everyone knows each other – but that was it.'

'You never went to Wimbledon to see her?' asked Harri.

Dylan shook his head looking unconcerned. 'Never.'

'You do go to London with work, though.'

'I do now but not back then.'

'What do you think happened to Jaci?'

Dylan shrugged. 'Probably one of her London boyfriends. She should have stayed in Wales.'

Harri fought back a sigh. He'd be rich if he had a pound for every person he'd heard say that so-and-so should have stayed in Wales. As if serious crime never happened here.

'You never heard talk of Jaci having someone around here?'

There was the sound of a key in the door and Dylan lowered his voice: 'Look, the little I knew of Jaci, she was as quiet as a mouse. All these stories of hotel trips away and a hidden love life didn't ring true. I reckon you've been barking up the wrong tree all these years.'

Dylan's partner entered the room. She had long dark hair and a petite build with a bindi in the middle of her forehead. Was she the reason Tomos had smirked when he'd said Dylan liked blondes? A bit of covert racism, perhaps. Harri and Siân left to the sound of both of them soothing the baby.

# 27

Julie Edge was everything that Mallory was not. She had dyed auburn hair cut into a blunt bob that should have made her look harsh, but gave her a look of no-nonsense authority. She wore a pair of huge thick-rimmed glasses that were all the rage at the moment, which added to her air of terrifying competence. Mallory in her hurriedly bought Primark dress felt the pinch of shame that her life involved a rented house and an uncertain relationship. There must be a path not taken, and she suspected her journey to her current situation had begun long before her accident.

They were in an upmarket coffee shop on Battersea High Street that Mallory had walked to, hauling her rucksack and carrier bag to the meeting. Julie briefly glanced at the supermarket bag but said nothing.

'What would you like to drink?'

Mallory was still reeling from the breakfast and ordered a mint tea. She felt a long way from Wales with its older population and slower pace of life. London, she realised with a shock, was no longer her home, and she wanted this meeting finished with so she could get back to the heart of the investigation. With their drinks in front of them, which neither of them seemed inclined to touch, Julie looked at her watch.

'I've only got half an hour. Something's come up which I need to deal with. I was very anxious to talk to you as I've never been properly spoken to since the initial interview I gave. Whenever Jaci's name appears on the TV I feel conflicted. They're talking about someone I knew, but I've only ever been on the fringes of the investigation into her murder. It's not like she was family, but I still care.'

'Did Marion ever try to speak to you?'

Julie's confidence slipped a little. 'No. I often wonder if they blamed me or at least her workplace for what went wrong.'

'Why would they think that? We thoroughly looked into her work relationships.'

Julie shrugged. 'I don't know, but I sometimes think we let Jaci down. That's the trouble with the working environment: you're superficially close to people, but you often don't know what's really going on in their lives. That was the case with Jaci. She was my PA, but I had nothing significant to tell you about her personal life. I think Marion might have resented that.'

'I think Jaci's disappearance was difficult for a lot of people,' said Mallory. 'Not least because there's no body and not even a hint of what might have happened.'

Julie grimaced. 'I was hoping that perhaps the police knew something that they were keeping back from the public.'

'There was nothing at the time of significance that we hadn't shared with the public. However, a few things have come to light in the last few days that I want to discuss with you. First off, I'm a little confused about the colour of Jaci's hair at the time she went missing. The photo we used showed Jaci with brown hair, but I've since seen a photo with dark blonde hair.' Mallory deliberately kept the photo album in the box. She wanted to see what Julie knew.

'She was blonde by the time she went missing. She'd started dyeing it around Christmas time the previous year, maybe a little earlier. It suited her – it was only a few shades lighter than her usual colour. Does it matter?'

'I think it does. When Jaci initially went missing, we put out multiple appeals for information. People were looking out for a dark-haired woman when, in fact, she was blonde. When time is of the essence, someone might have dismissed a sighting because the woman they saw was blonde.'

'Bloody hell.' Julie looked stricken.

'It's not your fault,' said Mallory. 'It's ours. We should have double-checked the accuracy of the photo we were given, but there is something we can do now by revisiting some of the information we received at the time. Look again at any reports of a blonde woman in distress, for example.'

'Will you do that?'

Mallory shook her head. 'Jaci's disappearance is still a live investigation that I'm not involved in, although they do know I'm here and passed your contact details to me. I'll be handing over what I've discovered to them. That also includes a Dictaphone that we suspect was taken from her workplace.'

Julie glanced up. 'Really? Was there anything on it?'

'The tapes had been wiped.' Mallory couldn't reveal the contents without Cal's permission, she decided.

'I'm not surprised. Workplace etiquette was to delete tapes and respool them to the start. It helped ensure confidentiality in the days before GDPR. I'd dictate information into the machine, pass the tape over to Jaci, which she'd type up using a different machine and headphones, and then wipe the tape.'

'But you could wipe the tape with the Dictaphone too, couldn't you?'

'Of course. Do you think it significant?'

'I don't know. Was Jaci a fan of reading?'

Julie shook her head. 'Not that I know of. We never discussed books.'

'The classics, for example.'

Julie grimaced. 'I really don't remember, but I don't think so.'

Mallory could feel the stress pouring from Jaci's old boss. 'Did she ever mention anyone called Gemma or use that name in relation to herself. An alias she might have used?'

Julie massaged her temples as she thought. 'No, not Gemma. The name means nothing to me, but you could always ask to check our personnel files if you think there might be a work connection. We've always had a lot of temps coming and going.'

Mallory shook her head. 'Again, it's something for the cold case team.'

'But you're here talking to me,' said Julie. 'Do you think that Gwennie Jones might have been killed by the same person?'

'I think it's a possibility, which is where I come in, but I feel I'm trying to catch a butterfly in trying to find a connection to Wales. Did Jaci ever mention a hotel called The Cedar Tree? I believe it's on the borders in Monmouthshire, although again, there are hotels similarly named in Staffordshire and Northumbria.'

Julie shook her head. 'I'm sorry, it means nothing to me.'

'What about her mother, Marion, and sister, Eleri? Did she talk about them much?'

'Not her sister, but I think I knew she had one. Marion stayed with Jaci for a short period of time, which wasn't easy in a small flat, but they got on well enough from what Jaci told me.'

'And you knew about her trips away mid-week?'

Julie finally picked up her coffee. 'I knew she was taking time off, of course, because I approved the leave. At the time, I saw nothing untoward about them as she was very matter-of-fact about her holidays. She saw them more as a source of fun than anything deceitful or underhand. I quite admired her. I had two young children at the time, a series of nannies, none of whom stayed, and a huge mortgage. I think I envied Jaci's freedom.'

'Even that's significant,' said Mallory. 'If she viewed her trips as fun rather than underhand, it suggests she wasn't involved with a married man, for example.'

'Hmm.' Julie regarded the table.

'Am I barking up the wrong tree?'

Julie shrugged. 'Something was going on. Jaci was, as you know, a dark horse. She had the look of someone keeping a secret, although God knows what that was.'

Mallory felt a surge of self-righteous justification. Jaci's private life *had* been complicated and hidden. She'd taken all the flak from Jaci's family after Terry's appearance on TV, but her words had been essentially correct. First Cal and now Julie were confirming it.

'I know this is going to sound like a strange question, but do you think Jaci had multiple lovers or just the one,' she asked.

Julie thought for a moment. 'You know, she never had that unmistakable glow that comes from a new relationship. If she'd had a series of lovers, she'd surely have come bouncing in as the relationship began. I saw none of that, so I'd say she'd known the man since she began working for me.'

'But she was looking forward to the trips away?'

'I'd say so, yes.'

'Did she ever mention anyone called David or someone known as "B"? I'm particularly thinking of someone who might have passed away, a former boyfriend, for example.'

Julie shook her head. 'Not that I recall. You asked me about "B" at the time, but it didn't mean anything to me. Funnily enough, she did once say that someone she knew when she was growing up died young. She looked near to tears when she told me, and I got the impression it might have been a former boyfriend. I felt like it was a long time ago.'

Mallory frowned. 'I don't think you mentioned it when we interviewed you.'

'I probably forgot. I've spent the last seventeen years thinking about our conversations.'

'She definitely said they were dead.'

'Definitely.'

'Died young? Did you get the impression it was someone from back in Wales.'

Julie shrugged. 'Probably, as much as I gave it any thought.'

–

Cal wasn't available when Mallory visited New Scotland Yard. She'd been called into a meeting, probably to do with the Jaci Jones case, given her niece was lying dead in Carmarthen mortuary. Mallory handed the box over to a member of Cal's team, the kind of strapping lad once seen all over the force when there had been a minimum height requirement. He took it gingerly from Mallory, as if it contained a ticking bomb, and Mallory was glad to get rid of it. It was possible that forensics might be able to recover some of the wiped tape, which might crack the case open, but it was a long shot. It was Cal's problem, not hers. It might take weeks for any analysis to come through, and she was looking forward to the trip back to Wales.

On the newspaper stand at Paddington, Gwennie's murder dominated the headlines. One specifically mentioned the 2008 case: '*Jaci Jones's Niece Dead*'. Poor Gwennie, reduced to an appendage in her aunt's life. Despite their shared history, Mallory felt a flash of pity towards Eleri Jones, mourning the loss of her daughter after her sister. Surely there was a limit to tragedies.

The journey to Swansea was uneventful as Mallory read through her notes. She texted Harri suggesting an update. He replied immediately but sounded busy:

> I'll call tonight. Let's catch up properly tomorrow. I think you might want to come down the station. Forget what I said about staying away.

It was typical Harri to taunt her like this, but he must be drowning in work. She was more intrigued than miffed and desperate to get home to a hot bath. She picked up her car from near the station and drove straight home. As she parked outside the small terrace, her eyes wandered up the street to where Gwennie had been killed. In many ways, her trip to London had been a failure in terms of Gwennie's death. She'd found no link between the two investigations except for a hunch by Beck Cowan, which amounted to little, and the sparse contents of a long-forgotten cupboard. But… but… she was sure there was something.

Opening her front door, Mallory was struck by the silence and sense of Toby's lingering presence. He'd collected all his things to take back to London, but his essence was still in the building. How hard it must be for Eleri Jones, who'd still be surrounded by Gwennie's possessions. Mallory dumped her dirty washing into the machine, set it going and got out the hoover to freshen up the downstairs. As she was plumping up the sofa cushions, she spotted a keyring that had fallen down the edge of the seat. She pulled it out and saw it was a little figure of a pirate with a single Yale key attached. Toby must have left his London key here, although it was odd he hadn't called about it. Perhaps Joe had already had a new one cut.

It was dark at four o'clock, but the nights were beginning to get lighter, if only by a sliver. At a loss as to what to do next, she ran a bath and lay back in the bubbles. Naturally, her mobile rang when she was at her most relaxed, but she saw Harri's number come up on the display.

'How you doing?'

'I'm in the bath,' she said. 'I've had a long day, but I'm desperate to know what you've been up to.'

'All right for some.' Harri sounded tired. 'I've got a fair amount to update you on, but I wondered if you'd ever heard of the Bethel brothers. Did their name come up in the original investigation?'

'Bethel? Was one of them called David?'

'Unfortunately not. These are Dylan and Tomos. They look like twins and bizarrely dress alike but are in fact regular brothers. A tight unit. Gwennie is on CCTV arguing with Tomos on the day of her murder, which makes him a suspect. Tomos swears Gwennie only had a go at him because he'd made a rude comment about the TV programme.'

'And Dylan?'

Harri sighed. 'Dylan is outwardly more respectable. Living in Ceigwyn with his wife and child and a decent job as a pharmaceutical sales rep. However, he's more guarded than Tomos.'

'Did they know Gwennie?'

'Yes, she babysat for Dylan, apparently, and interestingly enough, Jaci looked after them when they were kids. They're not acting suspiciously and both were relaxed when I asked about Jaci. Tomos made a throwaway comment about Dylan liking his women blonde, rather than brunette, as Jaci was.'

'Oh.' Mallory told him about the photos in the hatbox.

'That's interesting in terms of the cold case, isn't it, although we'll need a lot more than that if we're to link Dylan Bethel with Jaci. Anything else that can't wait until tomorrow?'

'I've got some leads in relation to Jaci that I've handed over to Cal. A hotel called The Cedar Tree, the name Gemma and a Dictaphone where the tape had been wiped. It's a long story, but we missed a cupboard during the original search.'

Harri was silent.

'I know, I know. A fuck up. Anyway, the tape's been wiped, as I said, but what is there is a couple of quotes from *Wuthering Heights*.'

‘Anything else?’ Harri sounded harassed.

That I miss you, thought Mallory suddenly. ‘I met with TV producer Beck Cowan today.’

She could see she had his attention now. ‘What did he say?’

Mallory laughed. ‘That he was trying to get hold of you. I’d speak to him if I were you. He’s also looking into the Welsh angle in relation to Jaci Jones.’

‘I’ll leave it to Siân to interview him,’ said Harri sourly. ‘Keep at it, Mallory. Love you.’

‘Love you back,’ said Mallory. She got out of the cooling bath and put on a pair of leggings and an Aran jumper to keep warm.

As she was contemplating the contents of her fridge, the doorbell rang. She crossed into the hallway and switched on the light before opening the door. In the dark, drizzle falling on her hood, stood a woman, a few inches taller than Mallory, her gaze up towards where Gwennie had been killed.

Mallory took a step back. ‘Hello Marion.’

# 28

The impression Mallory had got from talking to both Cal and Beck was that Marion was diminished in some way, but the woman who turned to speak to her was as physically imposing as she'd always been. Tall and lean, Marion Jones was wearing a beige mac with the collar turned up against the cold. She'd always liked hats, Mallory remembered now, and tonight she wore a woollen beret pulled down over her forehead. She appeared to be taking in Mallory too, her eyes skimming over her casual attire.

'You've not changed one bit,' she said without rancour, but Mallory, with their shared history, tensed.

'I think you'll find I have, I'm afraid. How did you know I was here?'

'This is West Wales. No one goes under the radar here, however much they try. I want to speak to you.'

The presumptive tone which brought back so many painful memories made Mallory's hackles rise. 'I don't think that's a good idea, Marion.'

She kept the door ajar. There was so much she wanted to talk to this woman about, but it had to be on her own terms. She saw that Marion slumped where once she would have tensed for the fight.

'Can I come in please, Mallory? I haven't come here to rake over old coals. Eleri doesn't know I'm here, and

I had to slip out before she spotted I'd gone. She's been keeping a watchful eye on me since my diagnosis.'

'Diagnosis?'

'I have early-stage dementia. At the moment I've problems with memory loss and difficulty finding the right words. I have medication that helps, but we all know how this is going to end, don't we?'

Mallory hesitated and then nodded. So Cal had been right. Marion wasn't the person she'd once been. In the course of her job, Mallory had been called to people with dementia. Sometimes they'd locked themselves out of their homes or driven down the road and been unable to remember where they were going to. Once, however, she'd gone to a nursing home where a resident had attacked another as the sun set. Sundown syndrome it was called, a patient's agitation increasing as daylight faded. With a shock, Mallory realised that the dynamic between her and Marion had shifted, and she'd need to proceed with caution. Some of the fire must still be there, but some of her testimony might now be suspect.

She ushered Marion in, who followed her into the living room and took in the newly lit fire. 'I used to visit this house when Mrs Hope lived here. Old Mother Hope, we called her. She lived until she was a hundred and one.'

'It's a holiday cottage now, which the owner is trying to sell.'

Marion shrugged, uninterested. She sat down on the pistachio-coloured sofa and blew out her cheeks. 'I know you and I have a lot of history, but I need to talk to you. I'm still OK. My short-term memory isn't great, but I've not lost my desire to find out what happened to Jaci, and now Gwennie.'

Mallory took a seat opposite. 'I'm sorry about your granddaughter. It must be a terrible thing to go through again.'

Marion slid her gaze away from Mallory and nodded. 'Gwennie was like Jaci in some ways. Naive and after a life she couldn't have.'

Naive? It was an interesting adjective. Mallory hadn't heard it applied to Jaci, and especially not by her mother. It suggested a personality flaw rather than a compliment. Instinct told her to remain silent and let Marion lead the conversation.

'Are you working on the investigation into Gwennie's death?'

Mallory hesitated. Marion had tracked her down this far, so she must have some knowledge of her life here. 'I don't know if you'd heard, but I left the Met after an injury sustained while working. I'm now a civilian investigator, occasionally contracted to help with serious crimes. I'm not officially involved in the investigation into Gwennie's death, but I am pursuing a line of enquiry for the team.'

It was a partial truth which Marion was inclined to accept. 'I'd heard you'd left policing. In the years after Jaci's disappearance, I used to try to keep track of what everyone was up to. A form of stalking, I suspect, but I didn't have anything else to do. I heard you married Joe, that handsome DC.'

'We did, and had a son, although we're no longer together. As a mother, I think I began to understand the terror you must have felt at Jaci just vanishing.'

Mallory, to her surprise, realised that this was true. Her fear of Marion and her sharp words had lasted into Toby's childhood as she'd struggled to reconcile work, marriage and motherhood. Only as she'd encountered her own difficulties with Toby had she realised how bloody hard motherhood was.

Marion nodded. She appeared deflated, the fire that she'd once had extinguished. Both Cal and Beck had expressed concerns about Marion's mental well-being before Gwennie's death. There was a detachment now visible that Mallory hadn't seen before.

'The reason I'm here is that I want to know if you take on private work.'

Mallory's heart thumped. 'Private… what? Do you want to hire me?'

Marion shrugged, her gaze back on Mallory. 'I've done a lot of thinking over the years and in some ways, I think I probably blamed you for all that stuff about Jaci's love life. I'd hoped you'd feel some affinity with Jaci, but it came across as a trashing of her reputation, and I unfairly put all the blame on you. The thing is, you were always good. I know we never got on, but you had an excellent reputation, and it's that competence which is the reason I'm here. You're on my doorstep and I need help.'

Mallory shook her head. 'I can't help you in relation to your granddaughter's murder. You need to trust the investigation team. They're very good, I promise you. I can't update you on progress because that's something they need to do, but finding Gwennie's killer is a matter of urgency.'

Marion pulled the collar of her coat up tighter, shivering despite the fire. 'I've no reason to think they won't be successful and I'm sure there are new forensic tools and other technologies that weren't around when Jaci vanished.'

'I also know DI Harri Evans well. He's leading the investigation and you can trust him to drive everything forward.' She nearly said 'he's no Terry Foster' but it felt like an act of disloyalty.

Marion picked at her lip. 'I'm worried about history repeating itself. I've spoken to Eleri and she's pushed DI Evans away already, even though he was nice when she had the break-in.'

'Break-in? What break-in?' Harri hadn't mentioned this on the phone.

'Someone got into her house. I was en route from Bristol, so the house was empty.'

'Was anything taken?'

'Eleri doesn't think so.'

Mallory tried to think. It surely wasn't a random attack, and it suggested Eleri might be under threat. 'Is Eleri OK? The FLO could stay at her house if she's feeling threatened.'

Marion shook her head. 'She sent him away. They were never much use to us in Jaci's disappearance, and in any case, by the time one was assigned to us, Jaci had already been missing two weeks. Again, Eleri might be taking her cue from how I behaved back in 2008.'

'I understand how hard it is with memories of Jaci's case, but in relation to Gwennie, try to remember that policing has moved on in nearly two decades. We've learnt from our mistakes.'

'Do you think Gwennie died because of what happened to Jaci?'

It was the question Mallory had been waiting for Marion to ask. 'I honestly don't know. What do you think?'

'I… I just don't know either. Although I've never got my life back since Jaci went, I thought that Eleri and Gwennie were making a go of it here. It's not been easy because we're known as the family that lost Jaci, and not just here in Wales but also in my neighbourhood. Random strangers even occasionally stop me in the street. It's been horrendous, made all the worse as there have never been any answers in relation to Jaci. Now we'll be associated with a double tragedy.'

'I can't even begin to imagine it,' said Mallory. 'I've lived with the case for years, but it's not the same as your loss.'

Marion nodded. 'There's something I've wanted to ask you. Do you think as a family we might be under suspicion?'

Mallory froze. 'Not as far as I'm aware. Why do you think that might be the case?'

'Well first there was Jaci and now Gwennie. The police will obviously be looking at family.'

'From what I know, Eleri was serving at her stall in the quay when Gwennie was killed. Do you have a witness for where you were?'

Marion said, 'I had a doctor's appointment at five p.m. which I attended. I couldn't have got here in time.'

Mallory did some rapid thinking, trying to remember Marion's alibi for Jaci's disappearance. She'd spent the summer staying with Jaci but had gone to live in Somerset, near Weston-super-Mare. It was an odd location, neither London nor West Wales, but it was where Marion had been living with her ex, and she'd made friends there. If she was living in nearby Bristol now then it sounded like she'd settled in the area.

'You had a rock-solid alibi for Jaci's disappearance. Weren't you singing at a gig?'

That was it, Mallory remembered. Marion had been a decent singer in a folk band, and she'd augmented her income with part-time work as a childminder. She'd been almost famous in the 1970s, and Mallory remembered searching for her on the internet and listening to one of Marion's songs. She'd been gigging at an arts venue the night that Jaci might have gone missing and had toured for the weekend with the van around Somerset. Her band members had alibied her and none of them had any links to Jaci.

Marion nodded. 'Green Velvet were having a bit of a revival after one of our tunes was used in an advert. Nothing major, but it meant we came back together to play some venues.'

'Are you still together?'

Marion made a face. 'After Jaci vanished I kinda got obsessed. You know that as well. I had no time for anything, let alone the band.'

Mallory let out a deep sigh. 'We never thought Jaci had come to harm as a result of your actions. From memory, Eleri alibied well too. Is there anything you want to tell me?'

Marion rubbed her face. 'I was so sure that Jaci had been abducted by a random stranger. I didn't recognise my daughter from the descriptions DI Terry Foster gave of her. She was well liked at work, and I saw nothing untoward when I lived with her over the summer.'

'Tell me about the summer,' said Mallory. 'Why did you go and live there with Jaci? Is there anything else we should have known?'

Marion scratched her shoulder as she thought. 'You know, I just wanted to spend a summer with my daughter, and I craved the city. We really did have a great time, although Jaci was secretive. She acted like the cat who'd got the cream, but I didn't think it was to do with a boyfriend.'

'Why not? It's surely the most obvious conclusion.'

'Because she never said a thing. Her flat was so sterile and, I dunno, loveless. It can't have been a man.'

'Did she go away mid-week while you were staying with her?'

Jaci shrugged. 'No. I wondered if she'd had a fling and it was all over, but it had made her feel good about herself. Only, now I'm wondering…'

'What are you wondering Marion?'

'If the killer was closer to home because of what's happened to Gwennie.'

Mallory nodded. 'Tell me, who's David?'

# 29

*December 2008*

Mallory was still reeling from the fallout after Terry's appearance on *Crimewatch*. She'd heard that the BBC in general, and the programme in particular, was hoping to attract a younger audience, so God knows why a dinosaur like DI Terry Foster had been given a starring role. Mallory had dealt with a wrathful Marion, who first screamed down the phone at her and then had made an official complaint against Terry. Joe had watched the broadcast alongside Mallory at her flat and thought Terry had come across as the wide boy he was, with a slightly patronising attitude towards Jaci. Marion was calling it for what it was: casual sexism, and Mallory agreed with her.

But, and here was the issue, something was off. There wasn't enough personal stuff in the flat, a lack of detritus you collected as a single woman. Mallory should know. She was seven years younger than Jaci and her apartment was full of the bits and pieces you pick up when you live in London – discarded travel cards, passport photos, receipts, earphones, flyers, free magazines. There was nothing like that in Jaci's flat. She could have lived a minimalist life, which was fine, but her days off remained unaccounted for. All they had were some missing things, most importantly her mobile, and a couple of cash payments for around a hundred pounds into her bank account.

Mallory folded her arms and regarded the screen she was looking at. Now that she'd discovered the make of the perfume alongside the brand of hair straighteners, an appeal had been put out for people to look out for such discarded items. The mobile phone was also an enigma after it was switched off the evening she disappeared. She was trawling through the emails from people who'd sighted any of these three items, and there were a lot of them.

The doors of the office burst open and two colleagues strode in, laughing. Dan and Mark were in their late thirties, happy at the way their careers were progressing and inclined to patronise her.

'*Duw, duw*,' shouted Mark. 'What an *awful* thing to happen.' It was his attempt at a Welsh accent, and Mallory remembered they'd been sent to Wales to interview Eleri, Jaci's sister. Given that Eleri had a decent alibi for the week of Jaci's disappearance, she wasn't a suspect, and Terry had been happy to leave the interview to Dyfed Powys police. However, after the *Crimewatch* appeal, a witness had come forward to say Jaci was a tart and she should leave her man alone. The call had been anonymous, but the police officer had stated that the woman had a Welsh accent, so it had been a trip to Wales for Dan and Mark.

Mallory got up and walked over to them. 'Did you speak to Eleri?' she asked.

Dan shook his head. 'She wouldn't talk to us. Slammed the door in our face. So we wandered around and popped into The Feathers for a chat. The customers were full of gossip about all the Jones family. Marion had seen off two husbands and Eleri was expecting, father unknown.'

'What about Jaci?' asked Mallory. 'What did they say about Jaci?'

'A dark horse, according to the regulars. Left and never came back. A bit up herself apparently. She liked nice clothes, expensive make-up. Ceigwyn was too parochial for her so she couldn't wait to get away.'

'Oh,' said Mallory. 'So there's nothing for us in Wales? No male friends there or suggestions of hotels she might have visited?'

Dan put his feet up on the desk. 'Nothing to worry your pretty little head about. Trust me. Wales is another dead end.'

# 30

In the absence of any other viable suspects responsible for Gwennie Jones's murder, while his team chased down the presence of a possible new boyfriend, Harri considered the Bethel brothers. Gwennie knew Dylan and babysat his daughter, and then she had had an argument with Tomos. Before the evening was out, she was dead, which made Tomos at least a potential suspect, although he couldn't think for the life of him what Gwennie might have that Tomos would want to kill for. They were both remarkably cool, a not uncommon attitude among those who had already got away with a serious crime. Harri suspected one of them had attacked Jane Callender, had never been brought to justice and had chanced their hand once again when Gwennie had stormed into the pub. Jane had no history of falling out with people, and yet days after a disagreement with Tomos, she'd been hit around the head. The problem was they'd need more than the video images to build a case against them. What he needed was a motive.

He needed to pursue the TV angle, which meant catching up with Mallory and seeing how far she'd got before Siân interviewed Beck Cowan. Harri scratched his armpit, aware of the roll of fat underneath his arm. He needed to go on a diet and start swimming or something. He felt when he was with Mallory that they must look like an odd couple. Mallory with her extreme leanness against his Welsh stockiness running to fat. Mallory had sounded tired on the phone this evening. Perhaps he should have offered to drive down there and speak to her, but there was so much to do in the office.

His phone rang and he saw it was his sister, Fran.

'Is everything all right?' he asked. 'I'm going to be working late tonight.'

'Both kids are OK, if that's what you're worried about. Listen, I've been watching the news. Is it really Jaci Jones's niece who's died?'

'I'm afraid so. I was out early in the morning and didn't see you. You remember the Jaci Jones case, then.'

'Harri, I *met* Jaci.'

Harri frowned. 'You met her?' Harri did some rapid maths. Jaci would be around Fran's age now, her late forties. 'Were you friends?'

Fran groaned. 'I can't talk about it over the phone. Can you get home so I can tell you to your face? You're not going to like it.'

–

Harri drove back to his house in Carmarthen in a state of confusion. He was more used to having these 'you're not going to like this' conversations with Mallory rather than his sister. Mallory was the seek-forgiveness-not-permission type, while Fran most definitely was not. He wondered how his sister's path might have crossed with Jaci. Fran was a solicitor, but she dealt in property law, and Jaci had lived in a rented apartment a long way from Fran's place of work. They could hardly have known each other professionally.

As he drew up to his house, Ben opened the door, his hood pulled up to face the cold outside.

'I'm going to the pub,' he told his dad, while putting a stick of chewing gum in his mouth. 'I didn't think you'd be home this early. We saw you at the news conference on TV. You were looking a bit fat.'

'Oh, thanks very much.' The honesty of youth. 'I'll be going back to work after I've sorted something out with Fran. Where are you going?'

Ben pulled on his gloves. Jesus, the lad was dressing like he was off on an arctic expedition. 'We're meeting at the Duke of Clarence. Not sure where we'll be going after that.'

Harri nodded. Another night at the pub, but Ben wasn't like Harri had been as a teenager. For Ben, a pint, two maximum, was enough and he switched to soft drinks. It was the same with Ben's friends, not like Harri's youth where he'd booze for hours.

Fran was waiting for him, but he saw she wasn't anxious. Whatever their chat was going to be about, it wasn't a confession, he could see. She was four years older than him and had given up her own home to come and live with him after Paula died to help him bring up the children. She was their constant in their lives, and she wore the responsibility lightly. Harri had never been able to ask her if she'd have liked kids of her own. It was a conversation too far, and he didn't want to upset the delicate equilibrium of their situation. She'd even welcomed Mallory into their home without fuss. Whatever happened in the future, he needed Fran close by.

'Do you want some tea?' she asked him, switching on the kettle.

'God no. I think I'm turning into a teapot with the amount of stuff I've drunk today.'

'How's Mallory?'

Harri grunted, not wanting to think about Mallory right now. 'I've given her a job in relation to the investigation that we're keeping quiet about for the moment. Otherwise, she's fine. Why do you ask?'

'I was just asking, Harri.' Fran never took offence at his grumpiness, the older sister's prerogative, he guessed.

Harri looked at his watch. 'I've not got long, as I need to get back to the office. You said you wanted to tell me something about Jaci. You've never mentioned meeting her before.'

'I didn't meet her, exactly. Look, it won't take long; I just wanted to let you know. I gave this information to the original investigating team, but I got the impression that it was just added to the masses of data they were receiving at the time. Certainly, no one ever got back to me about it.'

Harri was suddenly thirsty, but determined not to drink any more tea. He filled a glass of water from the kitchen tap and sat opposite his sister, who had brewed herself a strong coffee from a machine in the corner, which only she knew how to use.

'So, tell me. How did you know Jaci?'

'I didn't know her; I met her the once. At a hotel.'

Harri carefully placed his glass on the table. 'Go on.'

'I was at a conference on something to do with property law. It was a Wednesday-to-Friday event in Monmouthshire. Everything started at nine a.m. prompt, and I was going to go down the night before, which the company was prepared to pay for. However, I'd had a stressful time of it, so I booked two days leave so that

I could travel there Monday and avail myself of the spa facilities.'

'Can you remember the name of the hotel?'

'I couldn't, but I've looked it up and I'm pretty sure it was The Cedar Tree hotel. It's the only place in the area that matches up to the façade, and I think the pool looks the same.'

'The Cedar Tree? OK, carry on.'

'I was a single woman staying the night at a hotel, so I did what I usually do, which was have a facial and massage, and then I booked myself a six o'clock dinner. It's late enough that I don't feel like a schoolgirl but early enough that I avoid coupledom, large parties, etc.'

'Was there anyone else there from your company?' Harri had a fair idea where this was going, and his sister's account would need corroborating.

Fran, ever the lawyer, shook her head. 'I'm afraid not. Anyway, while I was at the table, I saw that there was another woman dining alone. She was beautifully dressed, I remember that. A long floaty dress and strappy heels. They'd sat us near each other as they probably thought we'd want the company when in fact the last thing I wanted was to chat with a stranger. She must have felt the same as we avoided eye contact until we were about to go.'

'Can you remember the date?'

'I've got down my old diaries from the attic, and I think it was February 2008. I certainly went to a conference then and the time fits.'

'So seven months before Jaci disappeared. And the woman sitting near you was Jaci?'

'I'm pretty sure it was. She had the same hairstyle, the Rachel from *Friends* look, achieved with hair straighteners. You know about my work as a super recogniser.'

Harri nodded. It was one of the reasons he was taking Fran's account so seriously. People often made mistakes with identification, especially after significant periods of time. Fran, however, had taken part in a programme after the 2011 civil disturbances when police were looking for super recognisers, able to pick out faces in a crowd following riots. She now occasionally worked for the police, mainly in South Wales, as a consultant when it was important to identify people in a crowd. 'If you say it was Jaci, I believe you. Tell me about what happened with her.'

'She spoke to me first as she was getting up, something innocuous about the lovely meal. I started because of her accent. Welsh, but hardly noticeable.'

'What did you say to her?'

'I said the food was excellent and asked if she was here on holiday. She answered without hesitation and said she needed to get away and this place had great online reviews. She was friendly, relaxed, but clearly was only making chit-chat and wanted to get back to her room for whatever she had planned for the evening.'

'Did she say her name?'

'Nope, and at the time, I wasn't aware I was a super recogniser. I just thought I had a good eye for people. That all came three years later, but I was confident enough to ring the hotline for the police team and pass on that I'd met Jaci in a hotel earlier. The person at the other end of the line was polite enough, but I never heard anything else.'

'Did you get the impression she was waiting for someone, or perhaps had a man back in her room?'

'Absolutely not. I'd say that, like me, she was having a mid-week-night pamper away.'

'And you say you gave this information to the investigating team. Do you remember who?'

Fran shook her head. 'Unfortunately not. It's the sort of thing I'd have written down at the time, probably in a notebook, but I haven't kept those. It was a man, though. Youngish, I think. He took the information and thanked me for calling it in. I've no idea if it was ever checked out.'

Harri thought of how many calls the missing persons team would have fielded back in the day. Fran's would have been graded low priority because there was no evidence of a male companion and no confirmation it was actually Jaci Jones. Hopefully someone from the team would have followed it up. He needed to speak to Mallory to ask her.

'Is there anything else that struck you? Something you've perhaps remembered in the meantime?'

Fran made a face. 'I don't think so.'

'Did you see her again?'

'Only briefly. I was getting dressed the next morning and I saw her putting her suitcases in the car. She was obviously getting away early before breakfast was served. I guessed she had something else on that day.'

'Can you remember the make of the car? Colour, even?'

Fran frowned. 'It was large-ish, an estate I think, but I can't remember. I'm sorry.'

'You said suitcases plural,' said Harri. 'How many did she have?'

'Well, that was the only unusual thing. I travel light, as you know. A small case on wheels and a large handbag, which is all I take for the weekend. This woman had two large suitcases. The sort of thing you'd take on a plane for a week away.'

'Two. And you're sure there was no one with her?'

'No one. She put the cases in the car and drove away without a backward glance.'

'Two suitcases?' Harri stood and threw the rest of his water down the sink. 'Whatever did she need those for?'

# 31

Mallory did something she never thought she would ever do. She opened a bottle of wine and shared it with Marion, who had looked confused at the name David when Mallory had mentioned it. It was an example, perhaps, of how her cognitive functions came and went. Harri had tried to call her, but she ignored the ringing. She'd been specifically told to keep out of the way of any Jones family, so she had no idea how he'd take the fact that Marion had turned up on her doorstep. Mallory didn't know if this rapprochement was a temporary truce or permanent, but it was her only chance in seventeen years to talk to a member of the Jones family and she wasn't going to let the opportunity slip through her fingers. She'd asked Marion about David because it was the only lead she had, but Marion had immediately clammed up. She needed to go in more gently.

'Tell me about Jaci,' said Mallory. 'Right from the beginning. Tell me what she was actually like. Did she want to get married, for example? Or was she more interested in her job? It's a long way from Ceigwyn to Wimbledon. I want you to tell me Jaci's journey.'

Marion closed her eyes, as if the act would help her to remember. 'She was a quiet one. As a baby she hardly made a sound. When it's your first, you barely know any different, but when Eleri came along with a pair of lusty lungs, I realised how quiet Jaci was.'

'A lot of people described Jaci as quiet or reserved. How did this translate into friendships?'

'It makes her sound shy, and she wasn't. She loved to chat, but she was quite secretive. She liked to live in her own head.' Marion stopped, clearly remembering Terry Foster's comments.

'Did she ever use an alias? The name Gemma, perhaps?'

'Gemma?' Marion's voice rose. 'Why would she call herself Gemma?'

'It's a name I've come across recently.' Mallory kept her voice even. 'Let's go back to the younger Jaci. Carry on describing her.'

Marion shot her an angry glance. 'She had three good friends here when she was a teenager. One left and I think moved to Scotland. The other two, Cerys and Amy, are still here, but they're married with kids. I see them out in town sometimes and it's hard.'

'A reminder of how things might have been with Jaci?'

Marion shook her head. 'She'd never have stayed here. The place was too small for her. Jaci liked dressing up, even from a young age. You know, wearing make-up, putting on her heels, wearing a smart frock. I mean, who dresses like that round here? We're a jeans and boots town, so she'd get some comments, but Jaci wasn't bothered. She wanted a job where she could dress up like that every day, so it was no surprise when she left school that she joined Squire Insurance in Swansea.'

'She was there for a few years, wasn't she? I believe she applied for a transfer when a job came up.'

'They were trying to get her to move for a year or so. It was hard to retain staff in London, and Jaci had a reputation for being competent. London is a long way from Wales, though, so they'd arrange for her to go to meetings there and get to know the staff. She met Julie Edge, her boss, that way and when Julie's PA left, she thought, why not?'

'And male friends?' This was the key question, and her reaction would be a measure of how far Marion had come since 2008.

Marion sighed. 'She got the Swansea job at eighteen and moved into some lodgings with two other girls. As far as I know, she didn't have a boyfriend. She was a pretty girl, so she must have been dating, but she never told me about the men.'

Mallory remembered the team coming to a similar conclusion. In Swansea, there had been a man called Simon who had dated Jaci for two months, but it had fizzled out without any rancour. Jaci had actually attended his wedding a few years later. There had also been the rumour of a casual boyfriend called Alun, but the two men by that name working in the insurance company absolutely denied ever having had a relationship with Jaci.

'So then we come on to Jaci's London friendship group. She'd arrived in Wimbledon six years earlier and found herself a decent flat in a former council block. Her neighbour Eddie Novak kept an eye out for her.'

Marion shivered.

'What is it?' asked Mallory. 'Didn't you like him?'

'It's a bit weird, isn't it? A sixty-year-old man keeping an eye on a thirty-year-old woman. Besides, Jaci didn't need looking after.' Marion bit her lip as if realising what she had said. Jaci had most definitely needed looking after and Eddie Novak had taken on a neighbourly role. He'd had no alibi for the night of Jaci's disappearance, but had walked on crutches since a car accident three years earlier. The tiny man would never have been able to overpower Jaci and dispose of the body.

'We looked into Mr Novak, but he had only a few friends from his local church. There was no predatory male we could identify and no proof that Jaci had ever been concerned about his intentions.'

Marion reluctantly nodded. 'Fair enough. Anyway, I know she had a couple of boyfriends in her office too.'

'She did, and they were questioned and ruled out of the investigation. Which leads me on to David. Tell me about him,' said Mallory, remembering Cal's account of meeting Marion and her comment that Jaci should have stayed in Wales and married David.

'David?' Marion's brows knitted together. 'I don't know a David.'

'What about from around here? Wasn't there a David in her life?'

'I've told you, there was no one. No David, no anyone.' There was a flash of the old Marion. Mallory was pretty sure Cal hadn't got her facts wrong, and yet Marion looked more confused than deceitful. Perhaps this was how Marion was diminished. 'You don't mean David Bethel, do you?'

Bethel. Harri had mentioned two brothers in his phone call, but neither had been called David. 'David Bethel? Did he live in Ceigwyn?'

'Poor David. No, he lived on a farm out in Felinfach. He was one of three, a lot older than the others, and mad about motorbikes. My girls used to babysit the younger brothers and Jaci always had a thing about David.'

'Did he feel the same?' asked Mallory, trying to sound casual. She was terrified any false step might cause Marion to clam up.

'Probably, but as I said, he was motorbike mad. If he'd had to choose between his bike and Jaci, he'd have gone for the bike, I promise.'

'Is he still living in Ceigwyn?'

Marion let out a long sigh and rubbed her head. 'He died. I can't remember how. Jaci had gone by then. I had to ring her to tell her what happened.'

'Maybe it was on his bike,' said Mallory. After seeing how people drove around there, it was more than a lucky guess.

Marion's face cleared. 'That's it. A smash on the Ceigwyn Road. Jaci came back for the funeral. Quite cut up, she was.'

'Can you remember what year? Was she living in Swansea or London?'

'Definitely London. It was a year or so before she disappeared.'

'Around, say, 2007?' Mallory could see the question was confusing Marion. It didn't matter. She could find out easily enough when a David Bethel died. The question was how relevant it was to the case.

Mallory could see Marion frowning at her mantlepiece, clearly distracted by something. 'Is everything OK?' she asked.

Marion pointed towards the keyring Mallory had found half-buried in her sofa. 'Why do you have my key?'

With her heart thumping, Mallory crossed and picked up the fob with the pirate figure. 'This is yours?'

Marion nodded. 'I left it last time I visited, and Eleri said I could pick it up when I next came to Wales. I haven't looked for it yet – Eleri said she'd be in the house when I got back.'

'Do you know where it was kept in the house?'

Marion shrugged. 'On a keyring by the front door. It's an all-purpose spare.'

Feeling sick, Mallory looked at the key. If it did belong to the Jones household – and she'd need to check – it was not only evidence, but directly linked this house to Gwennie, given that her bag was missing. But she'd never seen the key before. It was possible it had been left by one of the previous guests at the cottage, as Mallory had moved in to find the house already furnished, but she had given the place a good hoover before leaving for Ireland, and she'd have surely seen it then. Which meant Gwennie or Eleri had been in this house when Toby had been here. Toby?

## 32

Mallory ushered Marion out of the house shortly afterwards as she grasped the key in the palm of her hand, as if willing it to disappear. She grabbed her mobile and tried Toby's number, but it went straight to voicemail. 'It's Mum, can you call me?' she said into the phone, trying to remember Toby's demeanour when he'd left her. He'd been agitated, but she'd put that down to him viewing the crime scene, which he'd willingly admitted to. It didn't make sense that Gwennie or Eleri had been in this house; there must have been some other reason for the key to be here. She wondered if it had been planted while she'd been in London overnight, some sick joke by the killer. It was possible, and she should really speak to Harri about it. Torn, she decided she would first check it belonged to the Jones property, given Marion's cognitive problems, even though she'd sounded so sure. At that moment, her mobile rang and Harri's name came up on the screen. Mallory did some fast thinking – deflection would be good at this point.

'Hi,' she said, trying to sound her usual self. 'You'll never guess who's just left my house. Marion Jones.'

'Marion? Jesus, how was she?'

'Changed a little, I'd say. She asked me to help find Gwennie's killer but became easily distracted, and we quickly moved onto Jaci. How's it going with you?'

'All right. We have two lines of enquiries. The first concerned the Bethel brothers, which we're digging into. There's also the possibility that Gwennie had another boyfriend, an out-of-towner, maybe, according to Liam Ball, who she'd been seeing.'

Christ. This was the point she should tell Harri about the keyring she was still clutching for dear life, but she wanted to speak to Toby first.

'Are you any nearer to finding what Gwennie's attacker took from her bag? That might lead you to a new boyfriend.'

Harri sighed. 'No nearer. She had her phone on her, but her purse and asthma inhaler are missing.'

'What about keys? You said there was a break-in. Did the thief have a set of keys?'

Harri's tone sounded puzzled. 'Gwennie's keys are missing, but the burglar forced a rear window. Why do you ask?'

Mallory sat on the sofa, her legs shaking as she tried to concentrate on Harri. Until she knew what was going on, she needed to deflect him away from her question. 'I'm just approaching it from all angles. So I've discovered who David was, and there's a connection to your enquiries. David Bethel, older brother of the two Gwennie was seen with in the pub on the evening of her death.'

'David Bethel?' She heard Harri's sharp intake of breath. 'Bloody hell, Mallory. What's going on? You sure he's dead?'

'I think Marion can probably be believed on that one, but we need to check dates. What his connection with Jaci's and Gwennie's death might be, I've no idea, but it's a lead of sorts.'

'I'll get on it tonight. We'll be able to get a date quick enough, and as far as I'm concerned, it pushes the Bethels up my suspect list. Tell me about the trip to London.'

Mallory began to relax as she recounted her interviews over the previous two days. 'Fran's got an interesting story about meeting Jaci, she thinks in 2008. It would back up your assumption that it was the Monmouthshire hotel that Jaci visited. The trouble is, I'm not sure of the relevance of this information in relation to the death of Gwennie Jones. I think it might just be something for the cold case team. Do you think it's something you should pursue, or do you want to come in and work on the team picking up other leads, like the potential new boyfriend?'

Christ no, thought Mallory.

'Could I at least visit the hotel tomorrow and if I get nothing that links to the Gwennie Jones murder, simply pass it on to Cal Bentley? She has the contents of the box.'

'All right, but you have tomorrow only, and then I need you at HQ. Tell me about the hotel again?'

'We never found any evidence of Jaci having a long-term boyfriend, but there was the feeling in the workplace that she was involved with someone. This is because she talked about going away for a few days mid-week, plus new clothes and perfume were purchased.'

'Jaci was well dressed, wasn't she? Fran said she was very smart for someone dining alone, and Fran takes care of herself.'

'Yes, exactly. Jaci spent a considerable amount of her salary on clothes, make-up, hairdressers and nail bars, but she was thirty-one and living in a rented flat in London. It's what you spend your money on, but it gave colleagues the impression there was someone.'

'Married?' asked Harri.

'Possibly, given that he never came forward when Jaci went missing, although Jaci seemed to have no shame about the relationship. He, however, was probably petrified that his wife would find out.'

'And he'd have been a suspect in the inquiry.'

'Of course. And I think he was our missing "B", but we spent considerable resources trying to track him down and were never able to discover his identity.'

'So which hotels did she visit?'

'This was the thing. We couldn't tell. There was absolutely nothing on her credit or debit card, which suggests that the room was paid for by someone else or in cash. Now hotels don't like taking cash because they want a deposit if you buy a drink from the bar or if you're a no-show. So our guess was that the room was being paid for by someone else, possibly on a company credit card.'

'So what do you make of Fran's view that Jaci was there by herself?'

Mallory bit her lip, thinking. 'It doesn't make sense. She had two suitcases, which suggests another person. However, I have to tell you, we never found evidence that Jaci had a car. She passed her driving test at the age of twenty-two and bought a small Clio when she was in Swansea. She kept it for a year when she moved to Wimbledon, but found she rarely used it and so she sold it. Did Fran remember what car she was driving?'

'She can't remember. She's good at recognising faces, that's all. She even had to hunt down the hotel through the internet.'

'It's possible Jaci hired a car, which she occasionally did when she returned to West Wales, although she preferred to travel by train. I'm sorry, but I wish we'd looked at this in depth back in 2008.'

‘I know,’ Harri sighed. ‘She said she called a member of the team at the time and they were perfectly polite, but she never heard back from them.’

‘It’ll have been logged, prioritised and investigated. I can do the follow-up tomorrow.’

Harri put his hand over the phone, answering someone. ‘I have to go. Look, come into the station tomorrow and we’ll have a proper catch-up. Marion’s not going to be an issue any longer, although Eleri might yet have something to say about you being in their midst.’

‘But do I have permission to speak to Eleri now that my presence here is known?’ If Mallory could wangle a trip to see Eleri, she could try the key in the lock. Then, she promised herself, she’d talk to Harri about her find, even if he was furious with her.

‘I suppose so. In the meantime, I’ll look into David Bethel and confirm whether he was on the scene in 2008. Tread carefully, won’t you, Mallory? There are two other Bethels who could be our “B”, and I’d hate to think of you going into battle with one of them.’

‘Sure.’ Mallory gazed at the keyring, aware of a line just crossed. God knows what Harri would say when he found out that she’d hidden a potential piece of evidence from him.

# 33

Snow was forecast for the following morning around the Pembrokeshire coast and the slate grey clouds matched Mallory's mood. Toby hadn't returned her call and his phone remained switched off. She toyed with the idea of calling Joe, but he might have been on shift and would probably have confronted Toby himself without Mallory's input. She'd just have to verify that it was Gwennie's key at some point during the day and then speak to Toby and Harri, in that order. Feeling that she had a rough plan of how to handle the situation, she dressed in a smart jacket and trousers and headed west, the day brightening as she left the coast. Her car, usually languishing on the street, had got more use in the last few days than the previous month. It stood out, however, against the other SUVs and high-end vehicles in the large car park to the side of The Cedar Tree hotel. It was a Georgian house that had once probably belonged to a wealthy farming family but had been turned into a luxury hotel. There was a glass extension that had a spa look to it, but the frontage remained graceful, with Virginia creeper climbing up the pale red bricks.

Mallory wondered idly if they needed a night manager. It had been her first job after medically retiring from the police. Night work had suited her, but she had missed the camaraderie of an investigation team. Come to think of it, she still missed it. In the distance, towards the rear of the house, stood a cedar tree which retained its papery brown leaves, Monmouthshire having milder weather than the blustery town where Mallory lived.

She slipped her pass out of her pocket and walked to reception. A woman in a blue suit with a red neckerchief gave her a bright smile, reminding her of cabin crew back in the days when she actually travelled on planes.

'I'm Mallory Dawson from Dyfed Powys police. I wonder if it would be possible to speak to the manager.'

The woman raised her eyebrows and took a step back. 'Would you hold on?'

She disappeared into the back office where Mallory could hear some mumbling. A face appeared at the door and withdrew. There were more mutterings and the receptionist reappeared. 'Follow me, please.'

She took Mallory across the large foyer where a couple were reading the papers. In the distance she could hear breakfast being cleared up and the hum of a hoover. The hotel didn't feel full, but there were plenty of cars outside. It suggested a place where you could hide away, a place to feel cocooned, but anonymous. The manager's office was situated behind the main staircase. Their arrival had been telephoned ahead in advance and a woman stood on the threshold of her office, dressed in the same uniform as the receptionist.

'Do you want to come in?' She was in command of herself and sat smoothly behind a large desk. 'I'm Bridget, the manager here. Would you mind if I saw your ID?'

Mallory handed over her pass. 'I'm working with the team investigating the recent killing of Gwennie Jones. You might have seen the death in the papers.'

'I'm sorry, it rings a bell, but I don't get much time to look at the news. Where did this take place?'

'In a town called Ceigwyn in Ceredigion. I don't expect you to have heard of it, but the victim was the niece of Jaci Jones, a woman who went missing back in 2008.'

'The woman who disappeared from her flat?'

'That's right.'

'Goodness, the poor family. I remember reading about it at the time. How can I help you?'

'While we've been looking at a possible link between the two crimes, someone has come forward who remembers seeing Jaci at this hotel around February 2008. We've also recently found a pencil with the hotel's name embossed on it. Do you still produce those?'

Bridget smiled. 'Pens now, and we're thinking of phasing them out as people write everything into their phones these days, even the guests. Do you have it on you?'

Mallory had photographed the contents of the box before handing it over to Cal. Bridget looked at the pencil and nodded. 'Definitely one of ours, but I'm not sure how I can help. The records will have been deleted by now.'

'They will?' asked Mallory, her hopes sinking.

'Of course. I mean, we had computers back then, but nothing like now. I used to download client details onto USB sticks, but I remember having a mass clear-out of that when GDPR came in. Now we have to get everyone's permission to sign up for our newsletter, for example.'

'I guess the whole industry has changed.'

'Beyond recognition. We still get some bookings direct – a couple of regulars still write to us to say they're coming – but most of our trade comes through sites such as

Booking.com. We have to continually change technology to keep up with progress.'

'How long do you keep records for?'

'It depends. For HMRC, we keep records for seven years; for credit cards, we hold details for seven days in case of discovered damage. After that, everything is deleted.'

'And security footage?'

'Ninety days and then it's wiped. I'm sorry but we have nothing from seventeen years ago.'

'So there's no way of discovering who stayed with her back in 2008?'

'Not unless you want to go analogue.' The manager smiled for the first time.

'I'm sorry?'

'You could ask me; I've been manager here for nearly twenty years, but it was a long time ago.'

'Oh!' Mallory pulled out her phone. 'Here's a picture of Jaci Jones taken the summer before she went missing. She had dark hair usually but had lightened it for the summer, and we now believe her hair was lighter still.'

Bridget took the photo and regarded it. 'I don't remember her, I'm afraid. Did she come here with someone?'

Mallory shrugged. 'We don't know. It's possible, but our witness thought she was here on her own.'

'We get plenty of solo travellers and, in fact, we make an effort to give them a special stay. I'm single myself and I hate it when everything is geared up for couples.'

'But you don't remember this solo traveller?'

The manager shook her head. 'I'm afraid not.'

'What about the name Gemma? There's a possibility it was one of her aliases, or even the name of her lover.'

Bridget frowned. 'The name means nothing to me. I mean, I assume there have been Gemmas staying at the hotel but, as I say, our records are only recent and I can't do a search without a warrant.' She looked across at Mallory, her forehead puckered with anxiety. 'I hope you understand.'

'Sure,' said Mallory. 'I do.'

-

It had been a long shot, reflected Mallory as she gazed back up at the hotel, and she wondered how much of the trip had been to simply distract her mind from the pirate keyring. She thought, however, that this hotel might still have something to tell her. If the guest had been Jaci, and as a super recogniser Fran was a convincing witness, then this hotel was an odd choice of location. Bridget had been convincing enough, although her name was interesting. Could Bridget be 'B'?

Mallory's next step was to speak to someone she was pretty sure would not be pleased to see her, but she finally needed to tackle the key found in her living room. Next stop, Eleri Jones.

# 34

Harri had a doctor's appointment that morning to discuss the results of his latest tests. After losing his wife Paula to cancer, Harri had a simple attitude to any form of medical investigation. He distracted himself while the tests took place and then forgot all about them until twenty-four hours before the results were due. Then he acted like a man condemned until the news was delivered. Today was reckoning time for his six-monthly diabetes review. At least it wasn't with a doctor. Nurses, in Harri's opinion, were far less scary and easier to ignore. The news, however, was depressing. Despite cutting back on the carbohydrates a little and on biscuits a lot, his HbA1c level had increased. He'd need new medication to manage his condition. She also told him he'd put on two kilos of weight.

'I see you're a policeman. Do you still have to take a regular medical?' she asked, reading through Harri's notes.

'I do now,' said Harri grimly. 'I informed my boss when I was first diagnosed with diabetes and was deemed medically fit after an extended assessment. I now take a shortened form of the test every year. At the last one, they were more concerned about my increasing BMI, which was nearly thirty.'

The nurse turned to a chart on the wall. 'It's thirty-one now, which puts you into the obese range. We should be able to get it down with Ozempic. Have you heard of it?'

'The fat jab? I don't want to look like one of the Kardashians.'

The nurse laughed. 'It's called that, but it was originally manufactured to treat diabetes. It suppresses your appetite, which should cause some of the pounds to fall off, although there are some side effects, such as nausea. Do you want to give it a go? We'd start you off on a low dose and see how you got on.'

Harri thought about that roll of fat under his arm and nodded. God knows what Mallory must think of him naked. 'Why not?'

–

In the car, he took a call from Eleri Jones. Her preference now was to ring him direct rather than bother with Siân or a family liaison officer. As long as communication remained open with the family, Harri was inclined to go along with it.

'How are you?' he asked. 'Is Marion with you?'

'She is,' said Eleri, lowering her voice, 'but she's more hindrance than help. Generally, she's OK, but her mind wanders sometimes. Did you know she went to see someone called Mallory Dawson, who was a detective on Jaci's investigation? I believe she's working for you now.'

'I know Mallory,' said Harri. An understatement, but essentially true. 'Our plan was to make sure she didn't come into contact with the family, given the past history, but I believe Marion made the first move.'

'She'd never have gone there in the past. It's an indication of how bad things have got with her mind.

When I asked her what they'd talked about she couldn't remember.'

'How can I help?'

Eleri took a deep breath. 'I know I've sent you away multiple times, but I'm beginning to feel quite anxious. This is going to sound weird, but I have this terrible feeling that ever since the break-in someone has been watching me. At first I thought it might just be a natural reaction to having an intruder in your home, but now I'm not so sure.'

'I don't think it's ridiculous. Do you feel this while you're at home?'

'I don't think so. I'm a bit paranoid, obviously, as someone clearly knew I was out when they entered my house. But my fabulous neighbour has put up a light in the passage opposite so anyone standing there is going to be in full view. No, it's not in my house that I sense someone.'

'Where then? At work?'

Eleri ran a business delivering cakes and other sweet treats to coffee shops in and around Ceigwyn. The thought of her produce made Harri's stomach groan.

'Not while I'm driving. I've been keeping an eye on the cars and vans following me and I've not seen anything. Just when I'm walking around town and at my stall down by the quay. I feel like I'm being observed.'

'More than just curiosity? You're well known in Ceigwyn.'

'More than that,' said Eleri. 'I feel under threat. I know it's only a day since my break-in, but…'

'Don't worry; you're right to be cautious. I'll send a car past your house on a regular basis and someone over to the market this Saturday. They can have a look around while you're trading.'

'Do you think I could be in danger?'

Harri thought of the burglary. 'It's best we keep an eye on you, Eleri, given that both your sister and daughter have been killed. Is there anyone who might have a grudge against your family?'

'What? A twenty-year-old feud? The answer's no.'

'I think we need to explore whether or not something has remained dormant for that period of time and, with that in mind, you might be getting a call from Mallory Dawson. If you're up to it, I'd appreciate it if you could answer any questions. We're inching forward and she's good at finding patterns in things. She was around in 2008 and that might be key to us finding Gwennie's killer quickly.'

Eleri had clearly been giving her mother's visit to Mallory some thought. 'All right. I'll speak to her. I owe Gwennie that.'

–

At the station, Siân was hovering near her desk, her eyes on the door to the CID room. Harri had called ahead to say he was on his way in after the medical appointment, and his DC was clearly waiting for him. She had something on her mind, her pale face blotched with red.

'Can I have a word boss?' She had in her hand a sheaf of papers. 'There's some new intel I need to show you.'

Harri could feel his colleagues assiduously staring at their screens, absorbed in their typing, deliberately ignoring the interaction. What the hell was going on?

'Sure, come on in.' Harri gestured towards his office. Siân had attended the post-mortem of Gwennie Jones and he'd asked for an update when he got in. Something must have come up for Siân to be this agitated.

'Take a seat,' Harri said, shaking off his coat. 'Got the PM results?'

'What? Oh, yes.' Siân fanned the papers in front of her glowing face. 'Gwennie died from a traumatic head wound which caused swelling on the brain. It was initially thought this might be survivable, but the brainstem was damaged, which disrupted critical functions.'

'So nothing in addition to what you were able to tell me immediately after the autopsy?'

'No, but the weapon we're looking for is a blunt instrument like a cricket bat. Flat and wide.'

'Could it actually be a cricket bat? I mean, that's not something that's easy to conceal in January.'

'*Like* a cricket bat. It's that sort of shape we're looking at.'

'All right. So what have you got in those papers you're holding? There's something you're wanting to tell me.'

Siân swallowed, looking unhappy. 'There's a lot of CCTV around Ceigwyn town that we've been analysing, especially from those Ring doorbells. I guess there must have been a sales push there recently because there's more than I'd expect. We've had one officer reviewing all the footage and he's come up with something.'

Siân laid a picture in front of him which showed a thin girl, recognisable as Gwennie from the orange jacket she was wearing. She was walking while looking at her phone, oblivious to the outside world.

'It's definitely her. Where was this taken?'

'On the hill down towards Evans's Pharmacy. It's the route she would have taken from her house. About thirty seconds later, she's followed by a boy about her own age. Here's a picture of him.'

Harri frowned. He looked like every teenager out there with his pale baggy jeans and grey hoodie with a padded gilet over the top. 'You think he's following her?'

'It's got to be a possibility, hasn't it? We've checked other Ring doorbells in the street, and the next one, which leads to the pharmacy. Here they are again, and again.'

Siân laid more photos in front of him.

Harri studied the images. 'It's also the direct route into town, isn't it? Perhaps he was just going to the *Mari Lwyd*.'

'The issue is that after Evans's Pharmacy, there's no sighting of either of them. Gwennie we know was waiting outside first the cinema and then the shop, but the boy, if he was going to the *Mari Lwyd*, should have been identifiable by the doorbell cameras as he continued into town. He's not there, nor do we have any recording of him going back up the street. We're assuming he used one of the rear paths behind the terraces.'

'Then he's definitely a person of interest,' said Harri. 'Do we have a picture of his face?'

Siân nodded. She passed her final image to Harri. Harri felt his heart thump hard as he looked at the boy. 'Shit,' he said. 'It's Toby.'

'I'm sorry, boss,' said Siân, looking like she meant it.

# 35

When Mallory received the call, she felt physically sick. Not only was Toby on camera following Gwennie before she'd died, Mallory herself had in her possession potential proof of a connection between the pair that she'd not mentioned to Harri or anyone else in the investigation team. She pulled over the car and vomited into a hedgerow, to the disgust of the elderly driver who had been tailgating her for the last few miles. As she held her head in her hands, she thought about what she should do. She was halfway between the border and West Wales and every fibre of her being wanted to turn her car towards the capital and accompany Toby on the journey down to Carmarthen. However, Harri had been adamant. She was to come back to HQ and wait. Toby would be brought to the station by Joe, who would be allowed into the interview with his son. When they had a statement from Toby, she would be informed of the reason for his interview. The threat was clear. This was the only way she would be able to stay on the investigation and even then, depending on what Toby said, it would be touch and go.

Joe called her as she was swilling out her mouth with water. 'What the hell's going on Mallory?' She could hear the terror in his voice; like her, he had never imagined their shy, introverted son would be questioned about a murder.

'I don't know. I've just received a call from Harri to say they want to interview Toby in relation to the death of Gwennie Jones. They won't give me any more information.'

'But why?' shouted Joe. 'Why would they want to interview Toby?'

Mallory thumped her steering wheel. 'Because they must have some evidence linking him with Gwennie. You know how it works.'

'Toby never mentioned her to you? He's certainly never said anything to me.'

'Only that he went to see the body when he heard there had been a murder. I took it as normal teenage curiosity. I mean he wouldn't be the first person to gawp at a crime scene. He also told me, perfectly naturally, that he'd gone to see the *Mari Lwyd* the evening of Gwennie's death and there was no sense that he was stressed about the evening. What's he been like since he got back to you?'

'I've hardly seen him, but not in a bad way. He went to college this morning and seemed fine. It's got to be a mistake.' Mallory was silent. 'What is it?' asked Joe.

'I found a key in my house that I don't recognise. You don't have a single Yale to your front door that Toby carries on a pirate keyring, do you?'

'In London? My place is like Fort Knox. Toby needs two mortice-style keys to get through the front door and he usually has them hooked to his belt.'

Mallory sighed. 'I thought as much. Marion Jones came to visit me yesterday and said the key belonged to her. When I dug deeper, she said it hung on a hook at the side of the door at Eleri Jones's house.'

'Bloody hell. Is that what the team have on him?'

'Um, no, because I haven't told them yet. Marion has early-stage dementia and the key could belong to anyone. I was going to see Eleri Jones this afternoon.'

Mallory waited for the explosion that never came. Joe was probably reflecting that he'd have done the same himself, although Mallory doubted she'd get the same understanding from Harri. 'How are you getting Toby home from college so you can travel to Wales?'

'I've said something urgent has come up and I need him home quickly. I told him his mum was OK, so he's not fretting on his way back here. He's replied to say he's on his way and doesn't seem bothered. I'll meet you at the station, but I can assure you no one is interviewing him without me there.'

–

On the drive back to Wales, Mallory did some hard thinking. This was crunch time and she'd face it square on whatever the consequences. For the last few months, she'd become increasingly aware that life as a civilian investigator wasn't for her. It was something that had been niggling away at her while she was in Ireland with Harri, and it had been brought into sharp relief by Toby's current situation. It just wasn't working, being in a relationship with her occasional boss. She didn't like being sidelined in the current investigation, which was an occupational hazard for someone in her role, and she'd realised that if it came to a choice between her job and being a mother, she would choose the latter. The other issue was that it wasn't just her and Joe that had history with the Jones family. Now, Toby would be included. The one time he hopefully would ever be a witness in a criminal investigation, and it would be connected to Jaci Jones. The case would never leave her alone until the killer was brought to justice, and even then, it would be a subject never to be spoken of except in hushed terms.

At the station, Siân was waiting for her, looking harassed. 'I'm sorry about this, Mallory. I know it must be hard for you, but we need to do this by the book.'

'I don't understand why he's here. I know Toby was around the night Gwennie died as he said he saw the blue lights when Gwennie was killed and went to take a look, but surely that's natural curiosity.'

Siân took a deep breath. 'Let's start from the beginning. I need to take a statement from you about what Toby said to you when you got back from your holiday. This was the day after Gwennie was killed. Let's sit down somewhere?'

Mallory nodded and followed Siân into an interview room. There was to be no warm coffee shop chat this time, but an official setting. Siân opened a tablet and began to type onto the screen while Mallory was conscious of the key burning in her pocket. She would have to mention it in an official statement, and part of her was relieved that the confession would be to Siân and not Harri.

'OK,' said Siân, looking up. 'You got back from Ireland on Friday morning, didn't you? Was Toby at home when you reached your house?'

'He was. He told me there had been a murder and that when he heard it on the news, he went out to look at the crime scene.'

Siân nodded, her eyes back on the screen. 'What was his manner when he was telling you this?'

'He was calm.'

'How did he describe the body?'

Mallory closed her eyes. 'He said there was blood everywhere.'

Siân frowned and looked up. 'He said that?'

'That's what he said. Why?'

Siân shook her head. 'It doesn't matter. How was his tone when he described the scene to you?'

'He was a little perturbed but not especially upset. He used the experience to ask me whether I thought he should join the police.'

'Really?' Siân snorted. 'Did you put him off?'

The comment dissipated some of the tension in the room and both women laughed. 'I was worried that he was only considering the option because he was the son of police officers. It's the first time he's ever raised the possibility. I personally don't think it's the right career for him, but we didn't talk about it in depth.'

'OK,' said Siân. 'What happened next?'

'We then went out for some lunch and we saw you and Harri; you'd just come from the crime scene. You saw how he was.'

'And for the rest of the day?'

'In the afternoon, I drove into Aberystwyth to get some ready meals for dinner. After eating, Toby went to his room and I relaxed in front of the TV. I spoke to Joe, his father, mainly because I was thinking about the Jaci Jones case and hoping I'd be asked to be involved in the investigation. I mentioned Toby had spoken about joining the police.'

'And you took him to the train station the following day, correct?'

'Yes. He caught an earlier one than planned but that was because I wanted to get to the meeting that didn't happen.' Mallory hesitated. 'Do you have CCTV of him with Gwennie? Is that why he's been summoned?'

Siân opened the flap of an envelope and pulled out some photos. It was the first image she'd seen of Gwennie, apart from the single photo that the newspapers were using. In that, Mallory could see no resemblance to Jaci at all, although these images were too indistinct to make much impression.

'You're sure this is her?' asked Mallory.

'She was wearing a distinctive orange jacket that matches the one here, and the timings fit. We're pretty sure this is Gwennie Jones. Could you confirm this is your son Toby?'

Mallory didn't need to look twice. Even without the picture where he was facing the camera, she could see by the way he hunched his bony shoulders that it was her son.

'It's Toby. Can I ask where these were taken?'

'On Mwnt Road, which leads to Evans's Pharmacy where Gwennie was found. He's clearly walking behind Gwennie. However, we've then analysed Ring doorbell footage from the road that leads down into the town and neither Gwennie nor Toby can be seen on any camera. Gwennie, as we know, was waiting outside the pharmacy, which accounts for her movements, but not Toby's.'

'Are there any side roads or passages?'

Siân shook her head. 'Yes, but we need an explanation as to why he might take these routes. What we do have is an image of Toby returning half an hour later.'

'Half an hour? But wasn't Gwennie attacked on the main road? Someone didn't spend half an hour killing her.'

'Do you know what Toby might have been doing for the half hour?'

Mallory shook her head. 'I have no idea, but there's something I need to show you.' Mallory put her hand in her pocket and pulled out the keyring, placing it carefully in front of Siân. 'When I was hoovering my house yesterday evening, I found this key. I didn't think too much of it, assuming Toby had left it behind. However, when Marion Jones visited my house yesterday, she suggested it might belong to the Jones household.'

Siân stared at the key, her eyes widening in shock. 'You think this is Gwennie's missing key?'

Mallory rubbed her face. 'I don't know. Marion has dementia and I was on my way to Eleri's house to check with her now.'

Siân's face set. 'How many people have handled this since you discovered it?'

Mallory swallowed. 'Just me.'

'And does the boss know?'

Mallory shook her head. 'He has no idea. This is my screw-up and I take full responsibility for it.'

–

When Siân had gone, Mallory put her head on the table. Her leg was throbbing, as it always did when she was under stress. The door opened and Harri came into the room wearing a raincoat. He'd been into town and had bought her sandwiches and a can of Coke, her go-to when she needed a sugar rush. He crossed over to her and placed the provisions on the table, but took a step back, his gaze steady.

'Toby is nearly here. We'll get this sorted, but he does need to answer some questions.'

'Toby wouldn't hurt anyone. You don't think he's a potential killer, do you?'

Harri looked away, his face flushed, and Mallory realised he was trying to hide his anger. 'Toby needs to be questioned and eliminated from the inquiry. The fact you're working for us is an added complication, but that fades into insignificance given the fact you've deliberately withheld a piece of evidence from us.'

'I—'

'Don't give me the "I was going to check it belonged to Eleri" bullshit because if you'd discovered it anywhere else, you'd have been straight on the phone to me. You were protecting your son, and I need to consider how that leaves you as a member of my team.'

Mallory nodded, consumed by misery. 'I'm so sorry. I was going to ring you as soon as I'd checked with Eleri that it did fit in her lock. Christ, I've been such a fool.'

Harri frowned. 'Did you believe him when he said he went to look at Gwennie's body?'

'Of course. Why wouldn't I? I'd have probably gone for a look myself.'

'And he said there was blood everywhere?'

Mallory frowned, trying to remember Toby's exact words. 'Something along those lines. Why?'

'There was no blood, Mallory. I saw the scene myself. Even though Gwennie's body had been removed, there was no staining on the pavement. She was hit with an object, most likely a cricket bat or something similarly shaped, and it caused massive internal bleeding. It was probably one violent swing and Gwennie was out cold.'

'So why did he say there was loads of blood?'

Harri shrugged. 'Kids are a pain in the arse and I'll never understand them. Fran's better at the parenting stuff than I am. Maybe I'll ask her when I get home tonight.'

Mallory groaned. 'And the weird thing is that when Toby told me about the blood, my mind went to my own stabbing. All that blood on the pavement – it could have described my own attack.'

'Perhaps Toby's read an account of what happened to you. It was a horrific event; he might have found something online. The thing is, Liam, who'd been seeing Gwennie, thought that she'd found someone else, possibly someone from out of town. I need to see if that was Toby.'

'Toby? Christ, he was only on his own for five days. It can't be him. What about the Bethel brothers?'

Harri shook his head. 'I can't discuss them with you. Not while Toby is being questioned. Any work you did in looking into any other suspects might be seen as an attempt to exonerate your son. I'm thinking like a defence lawyer.'

'Can you at least tell me when David Bethel died?'

Harri hesitated. 'He was killed in a motorcycle accident in December 2006. Three days before Christmas. Jaci probably did attend the funeral if she was home for the holidays. Whoever we're looking for, it's not David Bethel.'

'But there could be a link with his brothers. I—'

The door opened and Siân stood at the threshold. 'They're here now.'

Mallory put her head back into her hands. 'Christ.'

# 36

Harri had never met Mallory's ex before, and in other circumstances, he would have been interested to see the man she'd spent her twenties and early thirties with. Now he felt for him as a father; he couldn't imagine how he'd feel if either of his kids were in this situation. Harri had agreed that Siân and Freddie would conduct the interview, with him watching proceedings from the observation room. They were both settling down opposite Toby and his father. Joe, he saw, was a muscular man with a broad chest, clearly the result of working out. He looked like the officers he saw in the armed response unit – calm, but focused. Toby looked his usual self, distant but with an open expression.

Siân was leading on the questions. 'Thank you for coming in today, Toby. We want to talk to you about your movements on the night of the eleventh of January, last Sunday. Can you tell us where you were that evening?'

Toby looked at his father. 'I was staying at my mum's house. It was the night of the *Mari Lwyd* festival.'

Interesting, thought Harri, that he's not mentioned the murder.

Siân placed two photos in front of Toby. 'I'm going to show you some photos that were taken on the night in question. Do you recognise the female in the images?'

Toby looked down at them. 'It's the girl who was murdered. Gwennie Jones.'

'Yes, it is,' said Siân. 'Did you know Gwennie?'

Toby paused and looked at his father again.

'Tell them the truth, son.'

Toby swallowed. 'I met her once. I was in the Chinese takeaway, and we were both waiting for food. She said she'd had a row with her mum and was going to eat her food on the street corner as she didn't want to go home.'

'OK,' said Siân.

'I said she could come back to mine – well, Mum's – as she was away in Ireland. So she came and ate her takeaway.'

'Where was that?' asked Freddie. 'Which room did you eat your meal in?'

Toby scratched his head. 'In the living room. We watched some TV while we ate.'

'When was this?' asked Siân, taking back the photos.

'Wednesday night.'

'Wednesday the seventh of January?'

'Yes.'

Harri was impressed by Toby's responses. He was calm and radiated honesty, but Siân would need to dig down to why he'd decided to say nothing about this meal with Gwennie.

'How long was Gwennie in your house for?' asked Siân.

Toby bit his lip as he considered the question. 'Less than an hour. Maybe forty-five minutes.'

'And what did you talk about?'

'We didn't really talk; we just ate and watched TV.'

Harri could well believe this, judging by his own children's behaviour. Conversation was a dying art.

'Did she say anything about herself, where she lived, for example?'

Toby shrugged. 'She said she lived up the road. That's all.'

'Did she mention a boyfriend?'

'I never asked.'

Siân crossed her arms. 'And did you make any arrangements to meet again? On the Thursday night, for example.'

'Definitely not. It was just a casual thing, inviting her to eat her food with me. I didn't expect to see her again.'

Siân pushed across the photos she'd shown Harri. 'I'd like you to take a look at these images. Can you tell me who's in the picture?'

Toby glanced down. 'That's me.'

'Did you go out the night of the eleventh of January?'

Toby licked his lips. 'Only for about half an hour. I wanted to see the horse's head going around town.'

'And did you see it?' asked Siân.

Toby was silent. Joe nudged his son. 'Answer the question, Tobe.'

Miserable, Toby shook his head. 'It was freezing. I… I feel the cold really badly because I'm so thin, and I couldn't bear it. I got to the spot where the giant inflatable Santa is, halfway down the hill. I could hear people shouting and suddenly I didn't want to go down there, so I turned around and went back to the house.'

'Where exactly did you turn around?' asked Freddie, showing Toby a map. 'Can you point it out on here.'

Toby found the spot immediately. Harri was too far away to see where he was pointing.

'For the record, Toby has pointed to a spot by the old cinema. Did you see Gwennie waiting there?' asked Freddie.

'I saw her, but she didn't look at me. She was rifling through her bag as if she was looking for something, and she had her head down. I wouldn't have been able to have confirmed it was Gwennie.'

'Rifling in her bag. Do you think she might have been looking for her key?'

Toby frowned. 'I don't know.'

Siân passed the key that Mallory had found, now encased in an evidence bag, over to Toby. 'Your mother, Mallory, found this on the sofa recently. We believe it may have belonged to Gwennie. Could she have left it while she was with you?'

'I don't know. She never came looking for it and I never noticed it was there.'

'OK,' said Siân. 'Let's go back to Thursday night. You saw Gwennie standing on the corner. Did you walk past her?' asked Siân.

Toby shook his head. 'I don't think so. I was cold and missing London, so I just turned around and walked back up to Mum's house.' He shot Joe an anxious look.

He's lying, thought Harri. Joe, it seemed, had also spotted this. 'You need to tell the truth Toby.'

There was a short silence while Toby assessed his options. 'I… I… OK, I was a bit embarrassed that Gwennie hadn't noticed me. I mean, she was clearly waiting for someone, and I sort of hung around for her to look up, but she kept searching her bag. I was a bit upset that I was being ignored, so I thought I'd go and see the horse, but avoid the crowds. I decided to go into town the river way.'

Siân frowned and picked up the map. 'The river? There's no river in Ceigwyn.'

Toby's finger traced the outline of the route he had taken. 'It runs down the hill behind the houses. There's a thin path next to it. I thought if I used that, I could avoid the crowds, so I went that way, but the music got louder and louder, which was stressing me out, so I turned back and trudged up the hill.'

There was a short silence as Siân and Freddie digested the information. Siân was studying the map. Harri remembered the end of the terrace before the old cinema. There was a thin passage that had been searched, but it had been full of stunted bracken and thorny bramble. Only a determined walker like Toby could have squeezed themselves down there.

Harri wrote a note on a piece of paper and handed it to Belle, the DC standing next to him. 'Can you get the CCTV from the old pump house towards the bottom of the hill? It might be able to corroborate Toby's story.' He turned his attention back to the interview.

'Did you come back the way you went down?' Siân was asking.

Toby nodded. 'Yes.'

'Was Gwennie still standing there?'

'Yep, and this time she noticed me and smiled, but I think she was waiting for the person behind me.'

'Behind you?' asked Siân. 'Someone else was coming up the river path?'

'Yeah. I could hear them. It was really hard going because of the weeds, and I was worried that they might be following me, but then I came out onto the road and turned back up the hill.'

'You didn't turn around to take a look at the person?' asked Freddie.

Toby shrugged. 'I wanted to get home.'

Siân folded up the map. 'You told your mother that you went to see the body when you saw the blue lights. Why didn't you tell her about the earlier meeting?'

'I was still digesting what had happened and I didn't think it was important. I mean, I only met her the once.'

Harri saw Joe roll his eyes and cast a glance towards the observation window.

'And did you get to see the body?'

Toby shook his head. 'I went to my room and was on my iPad. I never saw anything.'

'So why did you tell your mother you went?' asked Freddie.

Toby folded his arms. 'It was just something to say.'

# 37

It was Harri who told Mallory of the outcome of the interview, coming to find her as she nursed a cold cup of coffee.

'We're releasing him without charge. We need to check CCTV to confirm his story, but we have nothing to hold him on. You can go and talk to him if you want.'

'Harri, I—'

'Not now, Mallory. Go to your son.' Harri left, still fuming, she suspected, about the front door key.

Mallory's relief at the outcome of Toby's interview was tempered by the worry of what the experience might do to his fragile mental health. She found Joe and Toby in another room, Joe wearing a stunned expression at finding himself in a Welsh police station. Toby, however, showed resilience to the turn of events.

'I think police work is cool. I'll talk to the careers adviser.'

Joe looked over to Mallory and shook his head. 'No,' he mouthed.

Siân came in with a plate of sandwiches and put them down in front of them. 'You've a long trip back to London. Have something to eat before you go.'

There was something in her manner that suggested she knew about Toby's eating issues. Harri must have told her when they were preparing for the interview, but Mallory still appreciated the gesture. She grabbed a sandwich and wolfed it down, and she watched Joe do the same.

'Have something, Toby, please.' He looked at her in surprise. She normally didn't force the issue, but subtlety had deserted her. He picked up a sandwich and nibbled around the edges. After a few minutes, the atmosphere grew awkward.

Joe looked at his watch. 'I really need to be getting back. Shall we go, Toby?'

He nodded, and they all rose. As they were leaving the building, Toby slightly ahead of them, Mallory wanted to say something to Joe, to thank him for being there, but the words wouldn't come. 'I wish I could come back to London with you.'

Joe shook his head. 'There's honestly no need. You're better here, working on the case, if they'll let you. Plus, Toby likes coming to visit. It's as near an equilibrium as we're ever going to get. Keep going, Mallory; you're doing it for both of us.'

'It's more than just us two who have been affected by the case, but I do know what you mean. Take care of him.'

Joe nodded and Mallory watched the pair leave with a pang. Harri had sped off to a meeting, and there was no reason to hang around, but she wanted to thank Siân for the way in which she'd handled the whole Toby episode. The DS owed her nothing but had shown compassion towards Mallory rather than her usual detachment.

Siân was at her computer and looked up. 'I was about to ring you. Eleri Jones wants to see me and asked me to bring you along. She's in a bit of a state, wound up and gaggling a bit. Apparently, she's been expecting you to show up after your meeting with Marion and wants you there to hear what she has to say. It sounds like she's found something.'

'Found something? Did she give any clue what it might be?'

'Nope, except she's discovered something in Gwennie's possessions and wants to talk to us about it. She wouldn't tell me what, but I need to go up there anyway and try the key in the lock.'

Mallory bit her lip. 'I'm not sure Harri will want me there.'

Siân shrugged. 'Until I'm told otherwise, you're part of the team.'

Mallory reached out and squeezed Siân's arm. 'Thanks, Siân, for everything, including how you handled Toby. I mean it.'

Mallory followed Siân's car on the journey to Ceigwyn, so there was no chance to chat. Driving through the Welsh countryside, she had trouble marshalling her thoughts. There were so many strands that needed further investigation – David Bethel and his brothers, Jaci's visit to The Cedar Tree hotel, the implications of Jaci's changed appearance – but she couldn't settle on any to untangle as she headed back to Ceigwyn, her distracted brain full of concern for Toby. It had been a strange twenty-four hours, but it seemed this day had more in store for her.

Mallory could see Eleri peering through the front sitting room window when they drew up. She'd put a cone outside in the busy street, which Siân took as Mallory drove past her to her own house to park outside it. By the time she'd got back to Eleri's, the kettle was on and Marion and Siân were in the sitting room examining the pirate keyring.

'It's definitely mine,' said Eleri, ushering Mallory into the room. 'I hadn't realised Gwennie had lost it. She never mentioned it, and now I'm wondering if she was standing on that corner because she had no way of getting into our house.' She sighed heavily. 'Something else to beat myself up about.'

'She was meeting someone,' said Marion. 'She was going to give them those postcards you found.'

'Postcards?' asked Mallory, perching on the edge of the sofa. Marion looked more perky than she had the previous evening, which suggested she was having a good day. Despite her illness, Mallory needed to make sure she didn't underestimate Marion. Back in the day, Eleri had done nothing without her mother's permission, and even now it looked like Marion wanted to dictate even the course of the investigation.

Eleri rubbed her eyes. 'Mam, let me do the talking.' She looked across at Mallory, her mascara smudged onto her cheek. 'You know, I've seen you around town a couple of times and I thought I knew you from somewhere. You've distinctive features, but it took a while to place you. When Gwennie died, I thought a lot about Jaci's investigation, and that's when I remembered who you were.'

'And you told Marion?'

Eleri glanced at her mother. 'I told Marion, although I'd have thought twice about it back in the day. She's changed over the years.'

Marion lifted her cup to her lips, happy to be the centre of attention.

Siân pulled out her iPad, taking charge. 'Before we get onto the postcards you found, can I ask if you've had any other incidents relating to your break-in? You told DI

Evans that you thought someone was watching you. Is that still your feeling?'

Eleri nodded. 'Nonsense,' said Marion.

'Mam!' Eleri rubbed her eyes again. 'I'm worried. Gwennie might have been murdered for something she had that the killer never found. That's why I've been looking around the house for what it might be.'

'You say you've found something in Gwennie's possessions,' said Siân. 'We sent forensics to have a look at Gwennie's room the day before yesterday. Is this something that you've discovered since?'

'Room?' asked Eleri, some of her old acerbity back. 'They searched my whole house. It brought back some of the old hurt. Gwennie was like all teenagers, very private, so she wouldn't have stashed anything around the house unless it was in her room. But they went through my kitchen cupboards and bedside drawers.'

'And nothing of significance was found,' said Siân. 'It's something we have to do as we're looking for any information relevant to Gwennie's death. It's unlikely to be a random killing, and we need to create a timeline of Gwennie's last few days.'

'I hear you've got the Bethel boys in your sights,' said Marion, glancing at Mallory. 'Mallory asked me about David Bethel, but I hear you've been talking to Dylan and Tomos.'

It was no surprise, thought Mallory, that the questioning of Tomos and Dylan had got around the town.

'We're talking to a lot of people,' said Siân, avoiding Mallory's eyes. 'We'll update you as soon as we have something definite to tell you. You mentioned on the phone that you'd discovered something.'

Eleri reached into a tote bag on the sofa next to her and pulled out a thin box file covered in a floral pattern. She lifted the lid and inside was a blue scarf with a pattern of a gold chain, a thin watch, a torn photo and a couple of postcards.

'What are they?' asked Mallory.

'Some bits and pieces that Jaci sent me over the years. The scarf and watch were birthday or Christmas presents. I don't really remember which, but when she went missing, I just couldn't wear them any longer. I put them in my dressing table drawer and forgot about them. Also, here are the postcards Jaci sent me over the years, along with a photo. They were in a kitchen drawer for years, and Gwennie and I used to get them out occasionally and look through them. It's something she liked to do when she was a little girl.'

Siân took the box. 'Where did you find it?'

'It wasn't hidden at all. It was on one of Gwennie's tables in her room. The forensic team probably saw it and thought nothing of it. It's just a bit of cheap-ish jewellery, some postcards and a photo of Jaci.'

Mallory looked across at Siân, whose pale skin was flushed with red. The team should definitely have clocked the postcards and photo, if nothing else.

'Can I see the photo?' asked Mallory, holding out her hand. Eleri handed it over, clearly reluctant to let it go. It was an eight-by-six-inch image that had been torn in half, with only Jaci showing. She was in a white gown, the sunlight on her hair making it difficult to tell whether she was brunette or blonde in the photo.

'Did she send it to you with the other person torn out?' asked Mallory.

Eleri shrugged. 'Yes, but Jaci was full of oddities, and very private.' She stopped. 'You know all this. I liked the photo of her, so didn't think too much of it. Gwennie liked it too.'

'So you've no idea who the other person was?' asked Mallory.

'A man,' said Marion. She saw all eyes were on her. 'I don't know who.'

'You mentioned you kept the watch and scarf in your bedroom and the postcards in a kitchen drawer. Who put the items in this box?' asked Siân.

Eleri looked over to Marion. 'It must have been Gwennie. I've never seen this box before, so she's got it from somewhere and collected everything together that I had from Jaci. She didn't just ask me if she could have them. Of course, they have sentimental value for me, but Gwennie was Jaci's niece. I wouldn't have minded her having them.'

'Perhaps it was for the benefit of the TV company,' said Mallory. 'They like personal items. Given that you'd declined to appear in the programme, perhaps Gwennie didn't feel able to tell you that she wanted to show them on camera.'

Eleri folded her arms. 'Do you think she was planning to give them to that guy? What was his name?'

'Beck Cowan,' said Mallory. 'I get the impression that Mr Cowan is a professional. There's no way he'd have taken something that belonged to you, but perhaps Gwennie might have been persuaded to show them on camera.'

'Bastard,' muttered Eleri. She looked across at Marion, who was sitting with her eyes closed.

'Can I look at the postcards too?' asked Mallory.

In 2008, the investigation team had asked the family if they had information on places that Jaci might have visited. They'd mentioned Portugal, where Jaci had holidayed a couple of times, including that summer with Marion. The first three were from the Algarve, brightly printed photos with palm trees and golden sands. The messages were anodyne and talked about enjoying the sun.

'She went alone, didn't she, except for that final time with you, Marion?' said Mallory. They'd checked plane tickets and Jaci had travelled to these places solo.

'She liked to do her own thing and top up her tan. If she'd lived, she'd have paid the price for all that sun worship.' Eleri took the cards off Mallory, who was staring at the other two cards in her hand. The first had been sent from a hotel in Monmouthshire called The Golden Lion. Rather than a photo to advertise the place, the hotel had commissioned an artist's etching, the black-and-white image suiting the traditional style of architecture. The second was a photo of the Georgian Cedar Tree Hotel. Fran had been right about Jaci's trip to the place.

Mallory turned the card from The Cedar Tree and read the message. 'Back in my special place, love Jaci.' Mallory experienced a surge of anger which she fought to hide.

'Did you show these cards to anyone in Jaci's investigation team? I haven't seen them before.'

There was a silence that no one felt inclined to break. Eleri looked across to Marion, who shrugged. 'After the TV broadcast, we lost faith in the investigation. These were found about six months after Jaci disappeared and we went to the two hotels to ask if they remembered Jaci.'

'*You* went?'

'Well, why not?' Marion retorted. 'At least we were trying to protect Jaci's reputation. Someone in your team was leaking everything to the press. If we'd given you the cards, there would have been pictures in the newspapers and more stories insinuating that Jaci was a tart. At least we were able to ask discreetly.'

'You went to The Cedar Tree and The Golden Lion and asked if they had seen Jaci? What did they say?'

Eleri shrugged. 'Neither remembered her at all.'

'Did you tell them you were relatives of a missing person?' asked Siân.

Eleri shook her head. 'There was no one we could trust. Our story was that my sister had left a ring that was a family heirloom at the hotel and we were checking to see if anything had been handed in. Our sister was abroad, so we weren't a hundred per cent sure which hotel she'd stayed at. In both cases, there was no record of a Jaci Jones having stayed there, so we showed a picture of her. Neither manager nor reception of either place recognised her.'

'So she either stayed in the hotel under an alias, or she was accompanying someone else.' Mallory read the message written on the card from The Golden Lion. 'Wish you were here woooo. What does she mean by this?'

Eleri took the card and read the message. 'I didn't really know. There was a house near where we lived as children that was supposed to be haunted. Every time we passed it, we'd shout "Woo", so I guessed she must have been staying in a haunted room. I never thought much about the message, to be honest. I was more concerned about who she'd gone to the hotel with.'

The hotel also had an old-fashioned feel to it, although it was much less luxurious than The Cedar Tree.

'Was Jaci much of a reader?'

Eleri frowned. 'She liked romances. You know, anything with a pastel cover. Is that what you mean?'

'I was thinking more like the classics. Emily Brontë, for example.'

Siân was focusing on her tablet, too professional to give away the fact that she had no idea why Mallory was asking the question.

Eleri snorted. 'Not Jaci. Why is it important what books she liked?'

Marion stirred. 'She asked me that too.' Her gaze rested on Mallory. 'Why are you asking?'

'Just some information we've discovered that suggests Jaci was reading *Wuthering Heights*.'

Mallory saw Marion was looking alarmed. Eleri too had spotted it. 'What do you know, Mam? Tell us.'

Marion shook her head and closed her eyes again.

Mallory returned to her scrutiny of the postcards. The postmarks were still visible: the one from The Golden Lion was dated May 2008 and The Cedar Tree was from June 2008. Fran had been sure that she'd seen Jaci in February of that year, so Jaci had been more than once, which made sense of her message '*Back in my favourite place.*'

'Can you remember who you spoke to when you went to The Cedar Tree? Was the manager male or female?'

'It was a woman,' said Marion. 'Both managers were women, in fact. I can't remember their names, though. They're probably long gone by now.'

'I'm not so sure about that.' Mallory looked across at Siân. 'When you showed the photo of Jaci to the managers, was it the same one that was appearing in the press?'

Eleri shook her head. 'That photo was all wrong. Jaci was blonde when she disappeared, and had been all year. We had another from her Portugal holiday that we used.'

'But the photo we had was given to us by Marion,' said Mallory. 'It formed the basis of enquiries.'

Eleri looked at the floor and shrugged. 'I was here in Wales. You need to ask Marion why she gave you an out-of-date photo.'

Everyone looked at Marion, who was still sitting on the sofa with her eyes closed. 'Is she asleep?' Mallory mouthed at Eleri, who shook her head. She made a whirling gesture with her finger at the side of her face. 'Gaga,' she mouthed back.

I'm not so sure about that, thought Mallory. In fact, Marion had been very clever. The question was, what did she know about Jaci's activities that she'd been so keen to keep hidden?

# 38

Harri had to leave the station just to stop himself fuming. The problem with secrets like the one Mallory had been keeping, albeit for only twenty-four hours, was that the reverberations rippled far beyond the origin. Toby now knew his mother would cover him no matter what and Harri was now complicit because he hadn't reported the breach to his boss, Steph Morris. He would, eventually, but a phone call to her office had revealed she was taking a day's leave, which meant that, including the weekend, he had until Monday to keep Mallory on the team. Decisions needed making, and he and Mallory needed a proper chat.

St Dwynwen's church was as Harri remembered it. It probably hadn't changed in centuries. Still the black iron gate leading on to a small churchyard, still the shaggy grass covering the bottom of the tablet graves. Harri had offered to meet Jane Callender at her home, but she'd preferred to come to the church. Despite everything, she was still the warden here, and opened and closed the door to visitors every evening. She was standing in the small porch as she waited for him. This isolated church held no terrors for her, but she'd moved from the cottage where the attack had taken place, and now lived in Cardigan.

She handed Harri a small object that made his hand glow with warmth. He looked down. 'What is it?'

'Hand warmers. You pop them in the microwave and they keep the heat for an hour or so. I thought you'd appreciate it in this weather.'

Harri remembered his mother's phrase 'warm hands, warm heart'. He grasped the gel pad and squeezed it.

'I won't keep you long,' said Harri. 'I want to go over the statement about your attack. I know it's going to be painful but it's important.'

Jane looked out onto the frosted churchyard. 'Has he done it again?'

'Maybe. I don't know. I need to make sure we didn't miss anything about the attack on you. You said at the time you thought it was Tomos Bethel who'd stolen the items from the church cupboard. Did you have any suspicions in relation to anyone else?'

Jane dug her hands further into her pocket. 'Who else could it have been? We don't have regular worship here any longer. There's just a handful of us with a key to the door. We employed Tomos Bethel to do some carpentry in the church and days later the plate and candlesticks were missing. What did he say when you questioned him about it?'

Harri thought back to the interview and his dismissal of the 'brass tat' that had gone missing. 'He said they were hardly worth stealing.'

'That's not much of a defence, is it?'

Harri felt a wash of shame. 'No, it's not.'

'Did you tell him I'd made the accusation against him?'

She'd asked the same question in hospital but must have forgotten his reply. 'Of course not. I said we were questioning anyone who had recent access to the church.'

'Still, he came after me.'

'We found no proof of that. He was alibied by a family member, and he only had access to one vehicle, his work van. None of the cameras we have dotted around here showed he's been near your home.'

Jane snorted. 'There are back roads to my old house where you'd never pass a camera. Didn't you think of that?'

'Of course, and he might have had access to a car, for example, or persuaded an accomplice to take him to your house. The problem is that we had no evidence against him, so we were unable to prove he'd been near your house.'

Jane looked up at him. 'Has that changed?'

Harri shook his head. 'No, but I suspect there will be no quick fixes. Is there anything you've remembered about your attack that you want to share with me? It's been seven years. You might have remembered something that you didn't want to bother us with.'

'I don't remember much. I was working part time in the adult education college and I'd just finished classes. It was daylight, so I wasn't taking much notice of my surroundings. I drove up outside my house and that's the last thing I remember. My next conscious moment was in Glangwili hospital.'

'OK.' Harri rubbed his face. It had been a long shot, but he needed to make sure he'd extracted everything from what he suspected was Tomos Bethel's previous crime. 'Have things got better now you've moved?'

Jane shrugged. 'I was getting priced out of my old village. Sports cars, SUVs. My poor old banger was standing out like a sore thumb.'

Harri gestured towards his car. 'I know the feeling.' An image of Dylan Bethel's Range Rover came to mind.

'Tell me, did you see one of these SUVs near your house around the time of your accident? I mean, something that you weren't used to?'

Jane frowned. 'I don't think so. I know one of my neighbours said that a car had been blocking their drive, idling with its engine running. I never connected it to my attack. This was a few days earlier.'

But they'd questioned Tomos two weeks earlier about the theft. Had he enlisted the help of Dylan? 'Are your neighbours still there?'

'They moved. They just said it was a large silver car that drove off when they sounded their horn. They told me I should report it to the police, but I was just out of hospital and desperate to move on with my life. I… I was also afraid of repercussions from my attacker. I hope you understand.'

'Would the occupants have had a good view of your driveway?' asked Harri.

Jane nodded. 'Oh yes.'

–

As Harri was starting his car, his phone rang. It was Mallory. 'We need to talk.'

Harri sighed. 'I know. I'm sorry. Shall we speak over the weekend? I can come and see you; there's a lot to discuss.'

'I've an even better idea. How about we go away together for the night, maybe Sunday?'

'You think we'll be able to chat better away from the crime scene?'

Mallory coughed. 'Um, not exactly. Am I still on the team?'

'You've got a few days' grace, as I won't speak to Steph until Monday afternoon as she's away at a conference. Where are you suggesting we go?'

'Siân will update you soon, I'm sure, but Fran's memory was spot on. There's more to extract from The Cedar Tree hotel. What do you think?'

Harri thought about their trip to Ireland, the last time he'd felt relaxed. It now felt an age ago. 'Count me in.'

# 39

Harri's mood surprised Mallory. She'd expected him to be reserved, cold even, but if anything, he seemed buoyed up by their trip and had smartened himself up for their visit to The Cedar Tree. Mallory had offered to take him in her car but he'd preferred to drive. By mutual agreement they had decided not to discuss the case, and Mallory's role in it, on the journey down. Instead, he told her a little bit about his childhood and touched on his marriage to Paula. Mallory had spent little time thinking about his wife, and hadn't liked to bring up the subject. She'd died of cancer, and Harri had coped with the significant help of Fran. If anything, it was Fran who had most daunted her, but she'd proved friendly enough.

It was Fran, of course, along with the pencil and postcard, that had led them to The Cedar Tree hotel, and Mallory was certain she had unfinished business there. She was going to get to the bottom of Jaci's presence at the hotel and discover the reason behind the two large suitcases. First, however, they were going to look in on The Golden Lion hotel, which was en route to their destination.

Mallory was intrigued that Jaci had chosen two hotels within ten miles of each other. It suggested an arrangement that meant Monmouthshire was mutually agreeable to both parties, and if one hotel was fully booked, then the other would do as backup. Given that The Cedar Tree hotel had been described by Jaci as 'her favourite place', Mallory guessed that The Golden Lion was their plan B.

It was an old coaching inn on the outskirts of Chepstow, a tall building with latticed windows and winter pansies planted in window boxes. It had a more homely feel than The Cedar Tree – companies such as the one Fran worked for were unlikely to hold corporate events there – but nevertheless, it was well appointed, and according to the website, rooms started at a hundred and fifty pounds a night. It was too early for lunch when they arrived, so they bought some soft drinks and took them into the large lounge area where a cleaner was giving the place a dust. While Harri checked his emails, Mallory went back to the bar to enquire about rooms. The server was young and not much interested in selling a stay in the hotel.

'There are fifteen rooms: five at the front, eight at the back and two in an annexe off the car park.'

'Which are the best ones?' asked Mallory, picking up a leaflet.

'The annexe, I guess. You can actually book both rooms, as they're interconnecting, so they're popular with families.'

'What about for a couple?'

The server glanced across at Harri. 'The largest room is at the front right. It's supposed to be haunted, so some guests especially ask for that one.'

Mallory thought about the message on the card. 'Can I take a look at the room, unless it's occupied?'

The server glanced at the book. 'There was no one staying last night.' He lifted the key off the latch. 'Follow me.'

Mallory winked at Harri as she passed him, but he was concentrating on his phone. She followed the server up a narrow stairway that opened into a wide corridor. Once you got beyond the bar, it was a decent space, one that made you feel as if you were far away from the rest of the world. The hum of cars passing was the only sign that they were on a busy main road. At the end of the corridor was a double-aspect room containing a four-poster bed covered in thick drapes.

'It's lovely,' said Mallory. 'And you say people come here for the ghost. What is it?'

'An old woman; not that exciting. If it was a crying child or white lady it might be more romantic, but an old lady wearing a lace cap who sits in the corner knitting? It doesn't do it for me.' Perhaps remembering that he was supposed to be selling the room, the man smiled. 'Sometimes, guests will swear they saw something, but I've never seen the ghost myself.'

Mallory looked around the room. There was no particular atmosphere; just the stillness of a space that was currently unoccupied. 'I can't feel anything either.' She took the postcard out of her pocket. 'We came to take a look because a friend of ours sent us a postcard a while back with an etching of the hotel. Have you seen this before?'

The server took the postcard and looked at it. 'It's new to me. Who sends postcards nowadays?'

Mallory shrugged. 'No one, probably. Have you worked here long?'

'Six months. It was shut for a while when it changed hands, and we were worried in the village that it might not reopen. But someone from the Isle of Wight bought it and gave it a new lick of paint.'

Mallory nodded. The room wasn't going to give up its secrets, and she needed to move on.

Back with Harri, Mallory told him of what she'd seen. He'd been doing his own sleuthing while she was away. 'I've just spoken to the cleaner. This place changed hands last year and the previous owner had it for five years before that. My guess is that it's a difficult place to turn a profit. God knows who had it in 2008. I'd turn the information over to Cal and get her team to look into it.'

'It's what I'm planning to do once we get back from The Cedar Tree. At least we know that manager was working there at the time.'

They got back into the car and drove towards the second hotel, Mallory's mind still on the room. 'I'm sure The Golden Lion was a backup hotel, but it's an odd choice, in my opinion. It's not very romantic, more, I dunno, functional. Even the haunted room has a sense of anonymity about it. There must be other high-end hotels around here. And also, why send a postcard from a place like that?'

'It's an odd choice, I agree. It's a shame those postcards weren't shared with you at the time. There might have been people who remembered Jaci, especially if she was a regular.'

'The thing is, Bridget told me she was a manager in 2008. I can understand her not remembering Jaci after all this time if she'd stayed there the once, but surely she'd have remembered her if she was a regular. And given that she comes across as a competent manager, how come she didn't remember Marion and Eleri going to the hotel and asking after Jaci? The disappearance was all over the news.'

'Maybe she did remember and didn't want to tell you.'

'That's what I'm thinking too.'

They fell silent as The Cedar Tree came into view, the building visible through a gap in the trees. Harri whistled as he drove up the sweeping driveway, pointing at a stone fountain where an immaculately dressed couple were holding up their dog, allowing it to drink from the clear water.

'This is a step up from The Golden Lion.'

Mallory smiled as she checked her hair in the visor mirror. Jaci had loved designer clothes and make-up. She'd have fitted in well here, unlike Mallory and Harri, who dressed for comfort rather than show. However, they'd packed small cases, and made sure that they brought smart clothes for their evening dinner, which was included in the price. As they wheeled in their cases, the same woman was on reception, although she didn't recognise Mallory from her previous visit, her gaze fixing on Harri instead. He took the key to the first-floor rooms, even though the booking was in her name, and steered her into the lift. When they reached their room, Mallory gaped at the cream furnishings and thick carpet.

Harri was eyeing up the bed. 'Is it too early to—'

'Yes,' said Mallory, putting her case on the stand. 'We've got some detecting to do first.'

Harri grinned and pulled her towards the bed. 'It'll wait.'

-

With her head on his shoulder, Mallory frowned at a bruise on his stomach. 'What's that?' she asked. 'Have you hurt yourself?'

Harri squinted down. 'Oh. I've started taking the fat jab, if you must know. It's supposed to suppress my appetite, but I don't think it's started working yet. I'm famished.'

'Are you trying to lose weight?' Mallory winced. One thing she loved about Harri was his solidity. With her son like a wraith and her uncertain relationship with food, Harri and his family represented normality on the occasions she'd sat around their dinner table. 'You know you're fine as you are.'

'It's just a few pounds, Mallory. Don't stress.' He reached across for the room service menu. 'Christ, have you seen the prices here?'

Mallory didn't need to look. 'We can probably get some sandwiches from the bar. It's a few hours until dinner.'

They got dressed, went downstairs to the foyer and ordered some food. Their dinner wasn't until eight, and Mallory found she was hungry. There was a bustle about the place. Most of the staff were youngsters, probably working their way through college. Once they'd finished eating, Mallory nudged Harri. 'Shall we have a look around?'

They explored the ground floor. There was a dining room, where white linen covered tables were being laid for dinner. In the corner was a piano, which would no doubt annoy Harri, who hated music in restaurants. A closed door had a sign which announced it as the library, but when Mallory pushed it open, she saw it was occupied by a group of men, one of whom was standing at a whiteboard. Mallory glanced at the writing – '*Tasks for the Year Ahead*' – and withdrew.

At the end of the corridor was the spa, where a girl was on the telephone. 'We're fully booked for treatments,' she said, putting her hand over the receiver.

'Just having a look around,' said Harri evenly, probably aware he didn't look like its usual clientele.

They hurried away, trying not to laugh. 'I should have brought my swimming costume,' said Mallory. 'I could have interviewed the lifeguard. I feel like I'm on a wild goose chase.'

'Probably,' Harri yawned. 'I could get used to this luxury.'

-

Before dinner, as they were having a drink at the bar, Mallory saw Bridget walk over and have a conversation with the bartender. As they were chatting, her gaze swept the room and settled on Mallory, who was struggling to drink her glass of prosecco. Bridget smiled and crossed the room to greet them.

'It's good to see you back here. Did your work enquiry tempt you to book a return visit?'

'It did.' Mallory gave the woman her brightest smile. 'This is my boyfriend, Harri.'

It was the first time she'd referred to him as that, usually calling him her partner. However, given Bridget knew her to be a police officer, she didn't want Harri's presence to sound official. Harri, playing his part, gave the manager a genial smile.

'Amazing place you've got here. Mallory was telling me you've been manager for nearly twenty years.'

Bridget nodded, her eyes straying to another couple who had entered the room. 'That's right. I'm part of the fittings. Will you excuse me?'

'She couldn't wait to get away, could she?' said Harri, after a moment, finishing his glass of wine.

'Could you try to act less like a detective? A bit of small talk wouldn't have gone amiss before you started probing.' Mallory wondered if Harri had done it on purpose. He might have fixed a smile on his face, but his first words to Bridget had made him sound like a policeman.

'Don't fool yourself. I've been recognised as a copper before now, and we were never going to hoodwink her. We might as well keep Bridget on her toes while we're here.' Harri looked at his watch. 'Let's have dinner.'

The food was excellent, but Bridget didn't make another appearance. Mallory glanced around at the other guests and saw only a single diner sitting alone. Perhaps any other solo guests had adopted Fran's tack and dined earlier.

They were both tired after the three courses and were about to make their way back to the bedroom when Mallory saw the library, this time empty.

'Humour me a second.'

Unlike many such places, the hotel hadn't just bought a job lot of books in bulk. It looked like care had gone into the choice of titles – Dickens and Austen as expected, but also a local author section, which included books by Arthur Machen. It was this that Harri gravitated to. 'I wonder if they have a copy of *Wuthering Heights*.'

'I wouldn't be surprised. We could look, I suppose.'

She was studying a shelf of guides to the area which included a history of the house. She pulled the book off the shelf and idly glanced through it.

'Mallory, look.'

Harri had in his hand a thick blue book and was flicking through the pages. Mallory moved across to him. 'What is it?'

'The guest book from 2019. You know, the type where you write comments from your stay. There are others too.'

The books would have been easy to miss. They were all identical, the same blue binding and creamy white pages. On the spines was simply a number, the first stamped with a '1'. Mallory pulled it out and saw it began in 2002. There must have been earlier volumes, probably stored on the shelves above, but it was these that she was interested in.

'Let's work backwards from when we know she was here. The postcard is stamped the twelfth of June 2008, postmarked Chepstow.'

They pulled the book over to the central table and opened it so they could pore over the contents. It wasn't a guest ledger but a visitors' log containing comments such as '*wonderful setting*' and '*we'll be back*.' Not everyone left their full name, but there was enough information to begin to rule people out. Women were more likely to write comments than men, putting their names before their husbands. Two days after the postcard was sent, Mallory spotted the message '*Our favourite place. Jaci and B.*'

# 40

They scoured the rest of the books and there was one other message, from November 2007, where Jaci had written '*Wonderful discovery. We can't wait to return. Jaci and B.*' The message suggested that this was the first time that the couple had stayed in the building. They had returned once in February 2008, when Jaci had been spotted by Fran, and again in May 2008, when she'd sent the postcard. The hotel's luxury had probably appealed to Jaci, who liked nice things, and she had wanted to congratulate the hotel on her first visit.

'Why do you think Jaci doesn't put B's full name? Do you think he's asked her not to?' Mallory looked up at the clock. It was nearly eleven, and they'd been in the small room for nearly an hour. They'd need the relevant visitor books as evidence, which meant a confrontation with the manager.

Harri yawned. 'Probably. The question is, can we definitely make a link between Jaci's disappearance and Gwennie's death? If the answer is no, you need to inform Cal about the discovery.'

'We can't risk these going missing. We're going to have to take the books after speaking to Bridget.'

They jumped as a shadow appeared in the doorway. 'Did I hear my name?'

Mallory frowned. It was unlikely to be a coincidence that Bridget happened to be passing as Mallory and Harri discussed the books. She wondered how long the manager had been standing there listening to their conversation. Perhaps she'd been wrong to dismiss Bridget as the elusive 'B'.

The manager entered the room and looked down at the bound books. 'Doing a bit of detecting after dinner? We hold murder mystery weekends, if you're into that kind of thing.'

Mallory looked to Harri who seemed amused at Bridget's exasperated tone. She let him explain what they were doing as he would need to make the call on how much to reveal to Bridget.

'I didn't realise the library was out of bounds to guests?' he said evenly, as he stacked the books in a pile.

Bridget made an attempt to relax. 'I think if you're part of an official inquiry, you could at least be honest about your reasons for staying here.'

'I'm the officer in charge of investigating the recent murder of Gwennie Jones which includes any potential link to the killing of her aunt Jaci. Yesterday, we found a postcard from Jaci that definitely proved she was here in the summer of 2008 and, on my day off, we decided to come and stay at the hotel to see what type of establishment you have here.'

Mallory watched Bridget bite her lip. 'As I said to your colleague, I don't remember the woman. We have hundreds of guests every year. I'd like those books put back where they belong.'

Harri shook his head. 'We're taking these and I'd like *you* to tell me if you have anything else that you decided not to reveal to Mallory when she came here.'

Bridget glanced at the books as if she'd forgotten about their existence. Mallory suspected she was overworked and underpaid in this exclusive setting, or perhaps, more worryingly, hadn't taken Mallory's questions at the time seriously.

Harri glanced across at her. 'So, do I have your permission to take them? The alternative is that we return with some of the investigation team and a search warrant and close the hotel for a day or so.'

Mallory had forgotten how hard Harri could present himself. She was used to the softer side of him, but he hadn't reached his position in the CID by allowing witnesses and suspects to walk over him. Bridget, she noticed, was still making an effort to remain calm.

'Why don't you sit down?' asked Harri, pulling out a chair.

Bridget nodded and sat down, crossing her legs and clasping her hands over her knee. She looked ready for an interview. Mallory let Harri lead. They had crossed from two lovers having a welcome night away to colleagues, and it wasn't an easy transition. Mallory batted away the thought that things couldn't continue as they were and concentrated on Bridget. At their previous meeting, Mallory had left with the sense that the manager was concealing something. Now the stonewalling was more palpable.

Harri laid out the two books in front of Bridget. 'Jaci Jones stayed in this hotel in November 2007 and May 2008. She left two messages in the hotel guest books, as you can see. We also have a reliable sighting in February of 2008, although it appears she didn't sign the guest book on that occasion. So that's three times at least that Jaci stayed here.'

Bridget glanced down at the book. 'It's signed by a person called Jaci Jones, I'll grant you, but it could be someone else.'

Mallory still had Jaci's postcard in her bag, but Harri made no mention of it, most likely keeping it for a formal interview if Bridget continued to deny any knowledge of the missing woman.

'I can tell you, we're pretty certain it's Jaci, and so, I think, are you. What I find interesting is you're pretending that you don't remember her when you clearly do. Are you responsible for her disappearance?'

Bridget's head snapped up. 'Me? I didn't even know her. Why would I want to kidnap her? I barely leave this place, and my priority is always the guests' safety. I tell you, I don't remember the woman or her stay here.'

'You know, I don't believe that. You've been a manager here for nearly twenty years. I've watched you working this evening. You know everything that goes on and who comes here. The question is, were you in on the deceit?'

'What deceit?'

Mallory kept her eyes on Bridget. They were now on uncertain ground, as neither she nor Harri had worked out what was going on yet. Harri kept his nerve.

'Jaci was an ordinary girl on an average salary who stayed at this exclusive hotel every few months for about a year before her disappearance. She didn't pay for the room, as far as we can tell, which means she either stayed here for free, or someone else paid for it. Which was it, Bridget?'

Bridget shook her head. 'It's a long time ago. I've told you, I don't remember.'

'I think you do. Whatever it is you're hiding, you're masking a killer. Unless you were involved yourself.'

'I… I was not.' Bridget paused her eyes on the blue books, as if willing them away. 'I just allowed it to happen.'

Mallory hardly dared breathe. Bridget had admitted that there was something going on that she was party to, but not the orchestrator of. Mallory's suspicions of Bridget's initial account had been correct.

'You allowed what to happen?' asked Harri.

Bridget uncrossed her legs and slumped in her seat. In her relaxed posture she looked years younger. Mallory had seen burnout before with colleagues who'd left the force and discovered a new *joie de vivre*. Perhaps Bridget's confession would do the same for her.

'You have to understand that hotels like these need an amount of upkeep, and it's all about filling rooms,' said Bridget. 'We don't just cater for the ordinary guest wanting a nice break in the countryside: we have to advertise spa weekends, themed stays and corporate hospitality events. It's how we make our money.'

'Go on,' said Harri. 'Was Jaci involved in any of these speciality events?'

Bridget swallowed. 'It wasn't that. There was this film company.'

Film company? Mallory felt a rush of nausea and closed her eyes.

# 41

*December 2008*

Mallory was hungover for the second time in a week. Joe had invited her out for a drink the previous evening and they'd got stuck into the G and T's in an upmarket wine bar, probably chosen to impress her. After a few glasses, they'd gone back to his place before Mallory had left just before midnight. She needed her sleep and a change of clothes before she faced the next day in this infernal investigation. Joe was now working across from her in the busy office. Freshly shaved and showered, he looked like the alcohol hadn't touched him, which was typical of men. Either that or maybe she should stop trying to match him glass for glass.

Attempts to find hotels that Jaci might have stayed at had proven fruitless. DI Terry Foster was convinced they needed to look reasonably close to Wimbledon. His reasoning was that you wouldn't travel to Scotland, for example, for a mid-week night away for some hanky-panky – his words, not hers. So they'd focused on contacting places within a two-hour radius of London, which ran into the tens of thousands of establishments. There had been some interesting leads, but nothing concrete to focus their attention on. It would take time to sift through all the information, and privately, Mallory thought they'd never get through the hotels, nor the information called in by the general public on the dedicated hotline.

Their main problem was that Marion and Eleri Jones were no longer cooperating with the inquiry, which had cut off a vital means of confirming or ruling out any rumours. Mallory, who had a pleasant but distant relationship with her own mother, was willing to bet neither knew the name of any boyfriends, but Jaci might have hinted at places she'd visited recently. If that was the case, Marion in particular was now saying nothing.

Terry came over to Mallory's desk and pulled across a chair, sitting so heavily that a giant creak came from the supporting shaft. 'Can I run something by you?'

Mallory frowned. He was the guv'nor, so why was he looking so uncomfortable as he fiddled with the button on his jacket? 'Sure,' she said.

She could see Joe's eyes on them as they chatted, probably wondering why Terry had singled her out. Perhaps, after the disastrous *Crimewatch* broadcast, he was looking to his female colleagues to prove he wasn't the unreconstructed male Marion was making him out to be. Whatever was on Terry's mind, it hadn't been mentioned at the team meeting.

Terry coughed. 'I've been going through the leads given to us after the *Crimewatch* appeal. It's going to take weeks, if not longer, to catch up with everyone, but two separate people have called in with an interesting angle. Both said that Jaci looked like an actress, if you can call it that, who appeared in a porn film they'd watched recently on DVD.'

Mallory screwed up her face. Marion's words the last time they spoke were still ringing in her ears. 'You're trying to ruin my daughter's reputation with your lies and insinuations.' Never mind that it had been Terry who'd appeared on *Crimewatch* with his old-fashioned copper's attitude.

'Do you think it's true? We've not had any other intelligence about Jaci being in the porn industry. Could they be mixing her up with someone else?'

'Possibly. I doubt they were looking at her face.'

Mallory kept her expression neutral. 'Can either of the individuals actually identify the movie, or even better, provide us with a copy?'

'They say not, and both declined to reveal their names. Anonymous tips are the worst for diverting investigations. I'm thinking of letting it drop. I'll mention it in the team meeting tomorrow, but wanted a bit of female input.'

Christ, thought Mallory. Get me out of here. 'All we've got are statements from work colleagues that Jaci liked to go for nights away, which has been confirmed by Marion. It's a big jump from that to her appearing in a porn film. Anyway, don't they have studios for that kind of thing?'

Terry sighed. 'You're right. I'll pass the tip on to Vice and see if they can come up with anything. Even if all they do is find someone with a resemblance to Jaci, it means we can discount this particular lead. Carry on looking at those hotels, OK?'

'Sure boss.'

Later that night, she recounted the conversation to Joe, who snorted. 'Even if they're genuine tips, and they don't sound it to me, they're probably mistaken. What do you think?'

'That I hope to God Marion never hears of this rumour.'

# 42

The investigation was getting wilder by the minute. Harri had agreed to come away with Mallory to The Cedar Tree hotel despite his dismay at the way she'd behaved because he cared about their relationship and saw how much the Jaci Jones inquiry meant to her. It was a common misconception that detectives never took any time off. Like doctors and lawyers, his hours were irregular, but he was entitled to his weekends like everyone else. Fran had agreed to look after the kids, as much as they needed looking after, and he'd been glad to leave the inquiry behind for a day or so.

He'd half-hoped they'd get around to discussing their relationship, but events had overtaken them, as was often the case when two detectives were in a relationship together. The discovery of the visitor books had been too good an opportunity to miss and clearly struck a chord with Mallory. Her face when Bridget had mentioned a film company suggested that he wasn't going to be taking a plane out to Hollywood anytime soon. He glanced across at Mallory, as if to say 'I'll take the lead on this', but she wasn't having any of it.

'Tell me about this film company,' she said to Bridget. 'Are we talking about pornographic films?'

Bridget looked behind her, got up and shut the door. 'Not hardcore. I wouldn't allow any of that. More art-house erotica; you know, four-poster bed, leading lady in a lacy nightgown, the man in hunting breeches. There was a market for it back then. It was shot with a soft-focus lens.'

'You wouldn't have found it in your local Blockbuster though, would you?' said Harri.

He tried to remember what it had been like in 2008. The internet had been around, but there had been very few free sites which would tempt you with the odd video before you had to get your credit card out. Not a road a serving detective wanted to go down, and besides, Paula's death had killed his libido stone dead for a few years. Then again, even as a teen, he didn't think lacy nightgowns and men in breeches would have done it for him, but he was perfectly willing to believe there was a market for it. In his opinion, there was a customer for most things, however outlandish.

'How did you get involved?' asked Mallory. 'Surely all it needed was a camcorder in a bedroom. Why did they let the hotel manager know what they were up to?'

Bridget scowled, Mallory's downmarket dismissal obviously rankling her. 'It was more sophisticated than that. There was a script, film lighting, a cameraman and a director. I'd have noticed that many people going into a room.' Bridget glanced at Harri. 'You were right when you said that I know everything that goes on in the hotel. I've had to kick out a few unsavoury guests in my time. I make sure my staff tell me what's going on.'

'So how were you approached?' asked Mallory.

'The director of the films came as a guest sometime in 2007. I suspect he'd been checking out locations, and we're by far the most exclusive hotel in the area. He approached me in my office and laid it out as a business opportunity.

I'd allow filming in one of our suites and in return they'd pay a fee plus full board for a night for all the guests.'

'And you said yes?' asked Mallory, her voice incredulous.

'Look. I've seen some corporate events turn into much worse than a woman in a nightie. In fact, I've seen it all. I didn't see any harm in it, and they booked three rooms mid-week when trade was slow.'

'Who was in the rooms?'

'Jaci was in one with the male actor. Then the director was in one of our twin rooms, which he shared with the cameraman.'

'And in which room was the filming done?' asked Harri, trying to envisage the scenario.

'In the third room. They booked the honeymoon suite for the night.' Bridget looked at the floor.

Harri was incredulous. 'Didn't anyone… hear?'

Mallory, despite the tension in the room, shot him an amused look. Bridget looked contemptuous. 'This is a hotel. Sex in the honeymoon suite isn't going to bother anyone. And I told you this was art-house erotica. No group sex, no swinging from the chandeliers. They were discreet about taking in the camera equipment and lights too. You'd have thought they were businessmen setting up for a presentation.'

'How many times did they come here?' asked Mallory.

'Four or five times. I had to stop it because once a guest caught on about the filming. I'm not sure they realised what the content was, but they kicked up a fuss about wanting a quiet mid-week retreat and I thought the complaint might get escalated to the owners.'

'There were no shots of the exterior of the building or its grounds?' asked Mallory. 'I'm thinking Mr Darcy coming out of the lake.'

Bridget folded her arms. 'Absolutely not. I thought the filming could discreetly take place in private, but I was clearly wrong about that, so I called a halt to the visits. This was months before Jaci disappeared.'

'Did you recognise her from the images when she went missing?'

Bridget shook her head. 'No. Only when her mother came to visit and showed me a picture. I never put two and two together.'

'You didn't think of getting in touch with detectives on the case once Marion had been to see you?'

Bridget shook her head. 'I didn't see the relevance. As I said, this was months before her disappearance.'

'OK,' said Mallory. 'Let's get down to specifics. Who was the male actor with Jaci? If they were sharing a room, they were presumably a couple off-screen too.'

Bridget sucked in her teeth. 'I'm not so sure about that. It was always the same man, but I never saw Jaci spend much time with him, and he never joined her for dinner. I couldn't describe him to you.'

'So you don't think they were a couple?'

'I… I don't know. I mean they were sharing a room with a double bed, so maybe they were, but he definitely kept to the background.'

'And the director?' asked Harri, holding his breath. 'The person who arranged and paid for everything.'

'Beck Cowan.'

He looked across at Mallory, who was looking numb, as well she might have been. She'd interviewed the director days earlier and thought she was the one duping him, when in fact he'd been the one withholding vital information. The bastard. They needed to get in touch with him quickly because Harri suspected he also had vital information in relation to the murder of Gwennie Jones.

'Are you still in touch with Mr Cowan?' asked Mallory, shooting Harri a furious look.

Bridget shook her head. 'Of course not. I've not seen or heard from him in over a decade. He's probably doing something better than art-house erotica. He was a very serious young man.'

Mallory pulled out a postcard from her bag and laid it in front of Bridget. 'In June 2008, Jaci stayed at a nearby hotel. Were you full that time or had something happened?'

Bridget frowned. 'I honestly don't remember. Can I look at the visitor book?'

They found the volume for her and she flicked through. 'June is a busy month for weddings but they're usually on a Friday or Saturday.' Bridget paused over an entry. '"Thank you for everything, Red Brick Creative",' she read out. 'They're a London-based advertising company who book out most of our rooms. The CEO likes the honeymoon suite. I'll have had no rooms spare that week.'

'What about this – was it taken here, do you think?'

Bridget picked up the picture of Jaci squinting into the sunlight. 'I can't tell. Maybe.'

'Any idea of who the other person in the picture might have been? It looks like someone was torn out.'

Bridget shook her head. 'I'm sorry, no.'

Something about her triumphant expression riled Harri. He leant forward. 'The team looking into the disappearance of Jaci Jones have been looking for leads in relation to the hotels she might have stayed in for over seventeen years. Why did you think it was OK to keep this information quiet after Marion Jones came to see you? It was all over the papers by then, so you must have made the connection.'

Bridget's face went puce and she looked near to tears. 'Because this is all I've got. I've no other home but here. A decent pension, but what will I do when I retire? I want to stay here as long as I can and ignore my youthful mistakes. I'd never allow anything like that now. It just seemed all so… romantic. I heard the woman, Jaci I mean, reciting her lines. They were from *Wuthering Heights*, my favourite book.' Bridget looked like she was about to recite them but changed her mind. 'I'm sorry.'

Harri saw to his surprise that Mallory's features softened at the speech. 'That's fine,' she said, looking at her hands. 'This case has made fools of us all.'

# 43

Mallory looked around the hotel room and made a face. All right, they weren't in the honeymoon suite, but their bed was a half-poster with thick damask drapes and linen bedsheets. 'Art-house erotica' was the phrase Bridget had been keen to emphasise, but Mallory wondered who she was kidding. If Jaci and her mystery partners were being paid to have sex on camera, they were taking part in pornography. The nearest Mallory had ever got to artistic porn was watching *Last Tango in Paris* with Joe on a DVD of uncertain origin. She'd thought it boring and definitely geared towards the male gaze. Urgh. She really hoped that Jaci's participation in the whole enterprise had been consensual because the alternative was that she'd been coerced by Beck into coming to the hotel. Mallory sat on the bed and took off her shoes.

'You know, I preferred those quaint little rooms in Ireland to this luxury. I just don't feel at home here, and I'm sure Jaci wouldn't have either. How did she get involved in that stuff?'

Harri took off his jacket and tie and flung them over the dressing table chair. 'Almost certainly through Beck, or perhaps the actor. Interesting that he liked to keep to their room while Jaci had dinner.'

Mallory shrugged, less interested at this moment in the male actor than in Jaci's well-being. 'Tell me again, did Jaci seem OK when Fran saw her? I'd really like to know she wasn't being forced into something. I didn't ask Bridget because I'm not sure I'd have believed her answer, but Jaci's old boss Julie said she seemed matter of fact about her nights away.'

'Fran's a good judge of people, and as far as she was concerned, Jaci was another solo guest in the hotel. I don't think we're looking at coercion here, Mallory, but what we do have is a person of interest who knew both Jaci and Gwennie.'

'Beck Cowan.'

'Exactly, and he's just overtaken the Bethel brothers as my chief suspect. He's almost certainly the "B" in her email correspondence.'

'Oh God.' A horrible thought just occurred to Mallory. 'You don't think he was trying to get Gwennie involved in a similar kind of movie?'

Harri grimaced. 'I thought Mr Cowan had become a respectable film maker. I think I saw mention of a BAFTA nomination. I doubt they're stripping off while quoting Emily Brontë in his recent films.' Harri began to undo the buttons on his collar and stopped, looking at his lit-up phone on the table. 'Siân's just sent me an email, so she's still up. I'm getting her on Zoom to chat about what we've just discovered.'

Siân was in fact still at work, reminding Mallory of the days when she'd put in similar hours. She appeared on Harri's phone screen, her face grey with fatigue and mascara smudged, drinking from a can of Lucozade. Oh to be in your twenties again, thought Mallory. Harri updated her on their conversation with Bridget and she whistled.

'That's got to be a strong lead, hasn't it? I've just been running his name through the database as you were talking, and he doesn't have a record. We need to see if we can place Beck in Wales, and more specifically Ceigwyn, on the night Gwennie was attacked. We'll start by tracking down the vehicle he drives. Do you have any ideas why he might have attacked Gwennie?'

Harri glanced across at Mallory. 'We've talked about the possibility that Gwennie might have been asked to take part in something similar to Jaci. I think it's quite unlikely, as Beck is very respectable these days, but we need to keep it in the mix at the moment.'

Mallory rubbed her tired head. 'Another possibility is that Gwennie had discovered the identity of the person Jaci is posing next to in the photo that Eleri found. The image is torn in half. Imagine if Gwennie had found the other half or had proof through the discovery of another image.'

'And you think that person intended to meet Gwennie on the night of her death and take it back. Why kill her?' asked Siân.

'Gwennie didn't have them with her. Perhaps she'd been doing a bit of thinking herself. Gwennie wanted to be an actor, so perhaps she was using the photo as a bit of leverage without understanding its significance. Money might have changed hands. She didn't necessarily get the money from Beck, so perhaps we're looking at a bit of amateur blackmail. However, Toby says she was rifling in her bag when he passed her, and don't forget she'd left her key at my house. It suggests a disorganised personality. Whatever happened, that was still in the house when she died.'

'Which would explain the attempted break-in,' said Siân.

Mallory could see Harri wasn't convinced. 'That's a lot of "perhaps". I think we need to get Beck in for questioning once we've tracked down his movements on the day Gwennie died. If he has a good alibi, we need to work out what else is going on, but he's not off the hook for Jaci Jones.'

'Do you want me to get started on this?' asked Siân, her voice strained with exhaustion.

Harri pulled the phone closer to him. 'Absolutely not. Go home and get some sleep. We'll need fresh eyes in the morning. Get anyone who can come in on a Sunday there and we'll get started.'

'All right, boss. Before I go, can I ask Mallory how she thinks this might be related to Jaci's disappearance. How might Beck have orchestrated that?'

Mallory took the phone off Harri. 'I need to speak to Cal again but I'm pretty sure Beck's name was never mentioned during the initial inquiry. However, we had plenty of tips, including two that specifically mentioned Jaci having appeared in a porn video, so we need to trawl through everything again.'

'I suppose,' said Siân, 'given their professional relationship, he's someone that Jaci would have opened the door to without a doubt. He's seen her at her most vulnerable and behaved, we assume, professionally.'

'So why kill her?' asked Harri, turning to Mallory.

'I don't know,' she said. 'That's the problem. We still don't know why she disappeared that night.'

Siân took a final swig from her can and deposited it into the trashcan by her desk. 'And why – if he is the killer – make a documentary about her disappearance? By doing so, he's creating a connection that we'd never have made ourselves.'

There was so much work still to do, thought Mallory. 'I don't know that either. He looks innocuous, but then some killers do look like the guy next door. It might be difficult to find a motive for him harming Jaci, but digging into his past will give us some insight, and I do have an ace up my sleeve.'

'What's that?' asked Harri.

'He wants to interview me for the TV show.'

'No way,' said Harri. 'I'm getting him in to question him about the death of Gwennie Jones. Jaci's death takes a backseat for this.'

'But you don't have anything on him in relation to Gwennie's death except that he'd contacted her. There's a much stronger link for interviewing him over Jaci's disappearance.'

Harri grunted, his face creased in annoyance. 'Let me think about it.'

–

They were both too wired for sleep after the end of the call. Mallory changed into her flannelette pyjamas and slid into bed.

'Sorry it's not a lacy nightgown,' she said. 'Although after tonight's conversation I don't think I'll ever look at one in the same way.'

Harri folded his arms. 'You know, I have a friend who used to work in the Vice Squad when it was still called that. He's in the South Wales Police but we've tapped into his knowledge over the years. I might give him a call, if you don't mind. I know he keeps late hours – he's been off sick with stress from the job, but I believe he's back at work. I won't Facetime him, now you're in your jim-jams.'

'No problem, but put him on speaker, would you? I want to hear what he has to say.'

There was a lot of chat that Mallory had to listen to first. Arnie sounded dry and professional, as far as you could imagine from the sexism of Terry Foster, but like her old boss, he had a tendency to wander from the task in hand. Harri had warned him he was on speaker, but it made no difference.

'...so I've been told it's light duties only, but the super isn't interested. I only got back from work an hour ago. If it carries on, I'll be signed off again.'

'You need to take it easy, Arnie. Look, I've a scenario from an old case that might have relevance to the current murder inquiry into the killing of Gwennie Jones.'

'Oh no, if you're ringing me, that doesn't sound good.'

'I'm going to be putting this through official channels tomorrow, but I wanted your take on it tonight. It's been quite an evening for revelations.'

'Go on. I'm all ears.'

'There's a possibility that a suspect in my current investigation might have been involved in the disappearance of Gwennie's aunt, Jaci Jones.'

'I know the case,' said Arnie.

'You weren't contacted at the time?' asked Mallory.

If Arnie was wondering what Harri was doing in a hotel room with another detective, he didn't comment on it. 'Not at all. That case has never passed through my team.'

'The suspect now has a reputable production company that's making a documentary into Jaci's disappearance, but we've discovered that he started life as a producer of soft porn – sorry, artistic erotica – shot in hotel rooms. You know, women in nighties, men just come in from the hunt.'

'Got a name for me?' asked Arnie.

'Beck Cowan. It's his real name, apparently. Siân has run it through the computer already and he doesn't have a record.'

'Why should he? If it involves consenting adults and the huntsman doesn't bring his horse, you're all clear. Jesus, Harri, you know what we have to deal with here. We're not going to be bothered about some small-scale entrepreneur. Do you know how much the pornography industry brings into the UK's revenue?'

'Surprise me.'

'In 2021, over five billion pounds, which is set to double by the 2030s. Now, in addition to the usual stuff, we've got OnlyFans, where people sell pictures of their feet, and pornographic content is creeping onto social media sites as quickly as we can get it removed. We focus on monitoring the extreme stuff, which I won't ruin your evenings by detailing, and where the industry is being used to launder money. Otherwise, he's not going to be on my radar.'

'This Beck Cowan might be involved in Jaci's disappearance. Her as an actor and him as director. How might that have spiralled into murder?'

Arnie took a long puff on something, probably a vape. 'That's an interesting one. When something's illegal, people will go to extreme lengths to protect their business and their reputations, often both. With legal stuff you'd be looking for more conventional motives. Was Beck having an affair with Jaci, for example, and did her leading man take offence? Or perhaps, Beck had a day job that wouldn't look kindly on him as the new Hugh Hefner, and she was threatening to expose him. You know what motivates people when it comes to crime, Harri. I don't think you need Vice to help you with that.'

'Just because he hasn't got a record doesn't mean he's not known to you.'

'The name doesn't ring a bell. What's his film company called?'

'Black Stripe Productions.'

'Black Stripe? Sounds a bit morbid, but it means nothing to me. I can have a good look in the morning.'

'What are the chances of getting hold of a film? I'm not being prurient. We need to build a case, and at the moment, we have the word of one witness that the filming even took place.'

Arnie chuckled. 'You think we keep a library of these things? If it's not evidence, we're not interested, but leave it with me. There are odd collectors out there. One of the team might be able to help.'

Harri cut the call and looked at Mallory. 'Things are moving, finally, and I don't like it at all.'

# 44

The following morning, Harri wouldn't let Mallory go to London to interview Beck without Siân. Her place on the team, according to him, was still under review and he needed someone there who was solely focused on the murder of Gwennie Jones. The deaths of Jaci and Gwennie were most likely entwined, especially if Beck was the killer, but the priority was finding out who had attacked Gwennie and why. Mallory could understand Harri's rationale. She was on the team because of Gwennie's murder and discovering that person's identity would go some way towards reassuring the residents of Ceigwyn, especially Eleri, that they were no longer in danger. At present, they didn't have enough evidence to interview Beck as a suspect in either case, only as a witness, but Mallory guessed that the interview would drive the investigation forward, given what Bridget had told them about the hotel filming.

They drove back to Carmarthen in silence, each absorbed in their thoughts. They went straight into a team meeting where Harri updated the team on what they'd discovered. There were now multiple strands to investigate, and Freddie was to be dispatched to Chepstow to formally interview Bridget.

‘Do you think Marion and Eleri guessed what Jaci had been doing?’ asked Siân. ‘It would account for a lot of their behaviour.’

‘Marion stayed with Jaci over the summer from July onwards. There’s no evidence that any filming took place then, but that’s not to say it didn’t come out another way. Those suitcases that Jaci had in her car were probably her costumes. Perhaps Marion spotted them.’

‘It’s quite a leap from the discovery of a lacy nightgown to concluding she had a starring role in a film,’ said Harri. ‘Perhaps Marion thought it was evidence of dirty weekends away.’

‘It was the fact that Jaci took time off during the week that stumped us,’ said Mallory. ‘We took it as evidence of a lover who worked shifts rather than cheap hotel rooms.’

‘Why do you think Jaci did it?’ asked a detective sitting at the back. ‘Money?’

Mallory shrugged. ‘Everyone said Jaci was quiet and reserved, but that didn’t fit with her abduction, nor the hotel stays we couldn’t locate. It’s how I came up with the phrase of a complex and hidden love life, even if it was too clumsily stated. If you want my opinion, I think Jaci did it for the excitement. There was more to her than a girl from a small town in Wales.’

‘Why spend all that money on the nightwear, though?’

‘Unless we see the film, which seems unlikely, we’ll have to assume it was harmless erotica. Perhaps Beck gave her the money for the costume.’

‘Tax deductible?’ asked Harri with a laugh.

‘Why not? I suspect Beck pays his taxes like everyone else.’

Harri groaned. ‘Sometimes I hate this world I’ve brought my children into. Today she’d have an OnlyFans page – there's a teacher in Aberystwyth who has one, apparently. Her school isn't that happy, but she's still got her job.'

Mallory wasn't so sure that it was equivalent to these new sites. Attitudes towards pornography had changed, admittedly, but it would have been a big thing for a girl from the west of Wales to get involved in. There was something they were missing.

'Are we ruling out the Bethel brothers, given the argument with Gwennie?' asked Freddie. 'There's something fishy going on with both of those men, and we know Gwennie was meeting someone, most likely a local who knew the river path.'

'Agreed,' said Harri, 'but it looks like it's not relevant to the present investigation.'

After the meeting, Mallory followed Harri into his office. 'What's next for me?'

'I've got a meeting with Steph and that's where your fate will be decided. I want you to get on the train with Siân immediately. Beck'll meet you because he doesn't know about your activities with us. I can't say I'm happy about it. He's potentially a double killer.'

'We might get a confession.'

Harri snorted. 'People like Beck don't just confess. You're going to have to convince him that you're on the trail of that picture, which will put yourself in danger. I don't like it.'

Mallory shrugged and said nothing. The issue was more than just this case. There was a tension between her as a civilian investigator, her place on his team and their relationship. She had decided to apply for a job she'd seen advertised online and she'd have to let Harri know sooner rather than later.

For the second time in as many weeks, Mallory made the return trip to London, this time with Siân. Mallory had also arranged for Cal Bentley to meet them at the station before the meeting so she could update the cold case team lead. Beck had been pleasantly pleased to hear from her, and they'd made arrangements to meet at his office, although she wondered what their reception would be when he discovered the presence of Siân. The four-hour trip gave her the chance to catch up with her colleague, who she discovered had a new boyfriend and was studying for her sergeant exams.

'Would the team lose you if you got promoted?' asked Mallory, wondering if Harri's CID was about to be decimated.

Siân shrugged. 'Once I pass the exams, it's a case of waiting for a job opening. The station is continually in turmoil in terms of recruitment, so it's anyone's guess. You know, for a while, I was worried this case was going to be a millstone. I mean, it's hard going into a job interview when your current investigation is stagnating.'

'Stagnating?' asked Mallory. 'This is early days.'

Siân blushed and looked down. 'I mean, I hope it's not going to be a Jaci Jones scenario.'

Weary, Mallory nodded and texted Cal that the train was ten minutes late. When they reached Paddington, the cold case lead was waiting for them outside Burger King. Mallory saw Siân's eyes light up as she shook Cal's hand. Here was a woman whose career path she could aspire to, a woman about her own age leading up a team.

Cal updated them as they walked out of the station. 'I've searched the files we have on the computer multiple times and, as far as we're aware, no one ever gave the name of Beck Cowan as a suspect in the Jaci Jones investigation.'

'I was sure too, but we never did take forward those men who called saying that they'd seen Jaci in an erotic video.'

Cal shrugged as they took their place in the taxi rank. 'Beck has got offices in Bloomsbury, but we'll get off at Leicester Square and walk the rest of the way. I don't want to be seen with you, given that the focus of your questions is the Gwennie Jones case. He might not be as surprised to see you've brought along a colleague as you think.'

'Do you think he might have been doing some digging about me?' asked Mallory. 'I hope we're not walking into a trap.'

'OK.' Cal handed her a small pendant in the taxi. 'I want you to keep this in your pocket. It's the type of thing the elderly wear around their neck; they press the button for help when they fall. We usually rely on technology you download onto your mobile, but this is all I've been able to sort out, given the urgency of the meeting.'

'If I press it, will it go through to a call centre?'

'It'll come to me and I'll be in the building in seconds. It's a three-storey terrace and Black Stripe Productions is on the second floor.'

'Funny – someone I spoke to recently called the name morbid. I wonder what he meant.'

'Black Stripe? Maybe he was thinking about black armbands, the edge around funeral envelopes, that kind of thing.'

'Maybe.' Mallory was jolted forward as the cab came to a halt. 'This is us.'

Mallory and Siân walked the streets to Bloomsbury in silence, both glad to know Cal was following in their wake. This part of London was still recognisable to her, even if the occupants of the buildings had changed hands in the intervening years. The noise of Leicester Square and Covent Garden receded into the background as the street got quieter and traffic thinned. Black Stripe Productions was halfway down a row of terraces, some of which were still in residential use. When she got to the front door, she pressed the bell for the TV company. There was no answer. Instead, she tried the one above; the person on duty answered her call.

'It's Mallory Dawson for Beck Cowan on the second floor.'

Rather than reply, a click indicated the lock had been sprung, and Mallory pushed open the door.

A plaque on the door of the downstairs suite of offices announced it as '*Golden Safari*'. If there was anyone working behind the doors, they were making no sound. They climbed the carpeted stairs to the first floor and stopped outside the panelled door, expecting Beck to open it in response to the sound of their footsteps. He'd been happy enough to arrange the meeting and appeared keen for them to talk. Mallory pushed open the door and stepped over the threshold. There was a small foyer which led into an open-plan office with three desks pushed together. On one wall were photos of Beck at various functions – white tie, casual, accepting an award.

'Hello. It's Mallory Dawson. Are you there?'

Mallory crossed the office, where one of the three laptops was still on, while Siân took some photos on her phone. 'It's a bit eerie here, isn't it?' she whispered to Mallory. 'Where is he?'

‘I don’t know.’ Mallory could feel a knot in the centre of her chest, the tension making her breathless. ‘I need to check he’s not hiding somewhere.’

To the right was a small kitchen with a couple of glasses in the sink waiting to be washed. The only other door led onto a small room dominated by a long table with video conferencing equipment set up at one end. She put her hand on the equipment, which was cold.

‘I’m not sure he’s made it here today,’ she said to Siân. ‘Maybe he got wind of you coming.’

‘How would he know I was coming? There must be something else going on, given the door’s unlocked.’

Mallory crossed to the window and looked out. By the gates of the small park, closed to the public, stood Cal opening a bottle of fizzy drink.

Mallory took out her phone and messaged her. ‘No one here. We’re having a look around.’

She wondered where Beck had gone. He must lock the door to this office in the evening, which suggested he’d only left temporarily. His laptop had a screensaver on and was locked when she jiggled the mouse. She took a seat facing the door and waited with Siân, who stood watching the entrance to the building. After ten minutes she rang his mobile, which went to voicemail. After another forty minutes with her nerves taut with anxiety, she called Cal.

‘He’s not here.’

# 45

Minutes later, Mallory received a phone call from Harri. 'How's it going?'

'Beck isn't here. There's a really odd vibe about this place. I think the next step is to visit his house. It's possible he's not there, but there's no point in returning to Wales without trying to track him down.'

'Look, I'm taking one of the pool cars and driving to Twickenham, if you want to meet me there. Arnie got in touch to say there's a collector of unusual erotica that might be able to help us with tracking down Jaci's films. When Arnie says "help" he means it's in this chap's possession. I'm going to make the trip myself as I'm now officially linking the deaths of Jaci and Gwennie Jones.'

Mallory held her breath. 'What's happened?'

'We've traced Beck's current vehicle, which conclusively places Beck in Wales and specifically Ceigwyn on the night Gwennie was killed and again on the evening of the break-in at Eleri's house.'

'Bloody hell. Is that enough for an arrest warrant?'

'Yes, according to Steph, and it's being arranged, but will take a few hours. There's more. Freddie has been following the trail of the Rav 4 Beck was driving in 2008. The ANPR system was of no use, of course, given records are only kept for a twelve-month period. The car was sold in December 2008, which is significant, given it was just a few weeks after Jaci disappeared. The buyer was a woman in Isleworth who held on to it for three years. It was then sold a further three times to various people around London. In 2021, it was involved in a minor prang, but the insurance company had deemed the repairs more expensive than the cost of the vehicle and was scrapped.'

'You think you might be able to track it down?'

'It's worth a try. Meanwhile, we'll see what this man in Twickenham has to show us.'

'He's got a video of Jaci?' Mallory winced. 'God, it's what we want and what we don't.'

'You don't have to come,' said Harri quickly. 'I can go. We'll go on to Beck's place afterwards as we'll have permission to carry out a search by then.'

'No way,' said Mallory. 'I need to see this.'

-

Arnie's contact lived in Twickenham, an anodyne-looking suburb with attractive houses once you got away from the centre. Greg Mann lived in one of these tall terraces. He answered the door without any embarrassment, a tall thin man who seemed to fit in his narrow home. He'd clearly been waiting for their arrival. There was the sound of a kettle whistling on the Aga and biscuits being laid out on a plate. He ushered them into his study. It was impossible to ignore the walls of the room, which were covered in boxes of film canisters, VHS and Betamax tapes, and some DVDs. Greg saw Mallory take in the shelves with amusement.

'The first thing you need to know about me is that I'm an academic, so a lot of the stuff I have here is exactly for that purpose. Academic.'

Yeah right, thought Mallory.

'Just in case you're thinking, "yeah right",' continued Greg catching Mallory's expression, 'I've worked with various police forces for over ten years. It's Arnie who sent you my way, isn't it?'

'It is,' said Harri. 'I think he explained the situation. We're trying to track down a specific set of films – we've no idea how many, but I'm guessing no more than five. They were period dramas, if you can call them that, with a script made by a professional filmmaker who's gone on to greater things.'

'It's interesting,' said Greg, offering them a biscuit, 'because my specialism *is* the art-house stuff. I'm not interested in the more salacious rubbish, and certainly nothing illegal. I leave that to your colleagues.'

'How did you get into this world?' asked Mallory. 'I mean, you don't study this stuff at university… do you?'

'You do and I did. My undergraduate degree was in sociology and film studies, and the two specialisms collided. I got interested in the making of pornography between the 1920s and 1950s, after which it became much more commercialised. After that period, I'm only interested in those with a historical theme that hark back to earlier times.'

'Like the Jaci Jones films.'

'Exactly. Arnie piqued my interest when he called. I remembered seeing some films at the time but wasn't sure I had any in my collection. They're neither historically significant nor particularly well made.'

'That's interesting in itself,' said Mallory, her eyes still drawn to the rows of films. 'The director has gone mainstream and is well regarded in the industry.'

'The director is only as good as the team around him. The camera operator is decent enough, but the actors are strictly amateur and not in a good way. These are people trying to recite lines from a script in a natural manner and failing miserably.'

Mallory remembered the Dictaphone that Jaci must have been using to learn her lines. Poor Jaci. She waved her hand around the shelves. 'Is your archive catalogued?'

'Of course. Some of the formats are now unplayable and some of the discs I have run on obsolete software, but I'm gradually moving everything onto a digital format to preserve what I can. Even if the film is unplayable, it's still catalogued, so I'm aware of its contents.'

'And you found a film?'

'I found two, but before you add me to your list of suspects, please bear in mind that I'm a gay man. It's the man in breeches who caught my eye, not Jaci.'

Mallory held her breath. 'And are they still playable?'

Greg nodded. 'They're in DVD format, so that isn't an issue.'

'Can we see the films?' asked Mallory, ignoring Harri's frown. 'I need to confirm it is Jaci Jones, look at the identity of the male actor and check if their involvement was consensual, as far as I can tell. That's all, I promise.'

'No need to promise me anything. It's harmless enough. I've already transferred them both to digital so you can see them on this laptop.'

Greg turned the screen of the laptop on the coffee table towards them. Mallory was aware of Harri's discomfort but blanked out his concerns to concentrate on the screen. The screen went from black to the title image, emblazoned with the name '*Black Stripe Productions*'.

'Interesting it's the same name.' She was conscious that the quality of the image was nothing like that of the films she watched with Toby. They'd sat and watched the latest James Bond film before her trip to Ireland, and even on her basic TV the shots had been of cinema quality.

'It's not very clear, is it?' she said.

Greg looked over the top of his glasses at her. 'This is a top-spec MacBook, and what you're seeing was state of the art at the time, but it's a standard-definition compressed image.'

The scene opened with an image of a bed next to leaded light windows, a room Mallory instantly recognised as The Golden Lion's haunted suite. Over the image, a title had been superimposed, '*Lady Gemma's Secret*'.

'Gemma,' whispered Mallory.

The camera panned on a supposedly sleeping Jaci, her fair, wavy hair spread out on the pillow. It looked natural enough, although no one slept with their hair fanned out in such an artistic way. The camera's gaze was soft focused, but Jaci was instantly recognisable with her petite features and attractive face. She opened her eyes at the sound of a door opening and sat up, clutching her nightgown at her breast.

'Who is it?' The acting was excruciating and Mallory tried hard not to cringe.

The camera panned away from Jaci towards a man standing in the doorway. He was tall and attractive in a brooding way. His face was stern, trying hard to be Heathcliff to Jaci's Cathy. Over his broad chest, he wore a white collarless shirt tucked into breeches, the two straps of his braces hanging to his knees. Mallory heard a sharp intake of breath.

'What is it?' asked Mallory. 'Do you recognise him?'

Harri shook his head as if he couldn't believe what he was seeing. 'Bloody hell, that's Tomos Bethel.'

# 46

Harri wanted to switch off the film once Tomos had taken off his shirt and climbed into bed with Jaci, but Mallory insisted on seeing it through to the end. Greg watched the discussion play out between Harri and Mallory with an amused expression, which put Harri in a foul mood. They didn't have to watch the bloody thing all the way through to the bitter conclusion, if that was the right expression. They had proof that the video existed, they'd seen the essence of its contents and Harri had identified Tomos Bethel. That was enough for him. Mallory, however, for reasons that he thought he could understand, was interested in issues of consent and the dynamic between the two actors, so Harri forced himself to calm down and watch the action.

It was vanilla sex, made more for the art-house market, and even in 2008 it would have been tame viewing. Jaci looked neither drugged nor an unwilling participant. Harri had long had to reconcile himself to the knowledge that some women saw pornography as a valid career choice. The money involved hadn't been substantial. Mallory had mentioned small amounts unaccounted for in Jaci's bank accounts and presumably Tomos had also received a similar payment. His motivation for taking part in the filming must have been one of curiosity and perhaps bravado rather than financial.

When the film had finished, the three of them sat in silence for a moment. Greg was unmoved and studied a poster he had on the wall of a film called *The Good Old Days*. He must have watched thousands of movies over the years; Harri wasn't sure he wanted to know what motivated the man. He wasn't buying the 'academic interest' angle, nor his disassociation as a gay man. You could find these films of prurient interest whatever your sexual orientation or career, and to him, Jaci was being exploited by two men – Beck as director and someone from her childhood, Tomos Bethel. As the credits rolled, Harri noticed that 'Beck and the production team' were the only indication of who was involved in the production. Neither Tomos nor Jaci were mentioned.

'Is that usual, to not have the actors mentioned by name?'

Greg shrugged. 'It depends. No one's looking at the credits, are they? Some actors want anonymity, others try to build a career on their name. What do you think your two were doing?'

'They definitely wanted anonymity,' said Mallory. 'Although appearing on camera was a strange way to do that. Do you know what the distribution of a film like this was? I mean, presumably they were sold in sex shops.'

'Could be as little as a couple of hundred copies. Don't be deceived by the arty feel. No cinema would have touched the movie; it was a straight to DVD market and niche at that. For what it's worth, it's well shot.'

Well, that's all right, thought Harri. Congratulations, Beck. 'Tell me, how do you go from soft porn director to BAFTA nominee?'

Greg laughed. 'The line between mainstream and the sex industry isn't clear. Take a look at Andy Warhol's

*Blue Movie* sometime. Your guy probably started with a portfolio career and carved out a niche in a more respectable side of the industry.' Greg had turned the laptop back towards him. 'Would you like to look at the second picture? It's more of the same, in essence.'

'Not now,' said Harri.

'Yes, I would,' said Mallory, shooting him a glance. She'd probably guessed she might not get another look at the movie once the files were handed over to forensics. Harri sighed and nodded, ignoring Greg's amused expression.

'Let's get it over with.'

With the laptop facing them again, Harri and Mallory watched as '*Lady Gemma's Revelation*' appeared on the screen. It was all so bloody cliched. This time, Jaci was brushing her hair at a dressing table. She was in a different room, more upmarket than the previous one, so Harri was guessing they were at The Cedar Tree hotel. The camera panned to the mirror and in the reflection, you could see a man, naked from the waist up, watching Jaci.

'What the—?'

Greg hit pause on the recording. 'Are you OK?' He looked at the image frozen on the screen. 'It's the leading actor, the same guy from the previous recording.'

'Carry on,' said Harri fuming. He watched as the man began undoing the buttons of his trousers and forced himself to remain calm until the end. Same terrible script, same country folk costumes. There were even quotes from *Wuthering Heights* in the dialogue that answered the question about the Dictaphone recording. Jaci had been learning her lines for this pile of crap. When it had finished, Harri folded his arms. 'Well, that was interesting at least. I'll hand it to you Mallory, you were right to watch both films.'

'You mean the *Wuthering Heights* quotes? God, I mean the dialogue is terrible. Do you think Beck wrote the scripts as well as filmed it.'

'Probably, but that's not what's interesting.'

Mallory turned to him. 'What's the matter? It's no different to the previous one.'

'One essential difference is the actors,' said Harri standing. 'They're two different people. The man in the second film is Dylan Bethel, Tomos's brother.'

Harri had the satisfaction of seeing Greg's surprise. 'Are you sure? They look like the same man.'

'They look like twins, but they're just regular brothers. Dylan has a small scar above his lip. You can see it in the second film.'

'Show me,' said Mallory, insisting that the film was rewound to a close-up of Dylan's face. 'I can see it. Now put on the first film.' She squinted at the screen. 'Jesus, you're right. Two different men. I'd never have spotted that.'

Greg nodded. 'Well, you learn something every day. I'll have to amend my catalogue. Tomos and Dylan Bethel. Interesting.'

As he stepped out of Greg's house, Harri felt glad to be back in the fresh air. He took a few deep breaths in the driveway. 'Bloody hell, that was an experience. I couldn't watch that stuff all day.'

Mallory opened the car door. 'It was important to watch the films all the way through, not least because we now have three definite suspects. The Bethel brothers are back on the table alongside Beck. And the "B" Jaci talks about could be any of the three.'

Harri got in beside Mallory and started the car. 'In my mind, I'm veering back to one of the Bethel brothers as the killer. Remember what Bridget said about Jaci being happy occasionally with the male actor and unhappy other times. I thought it might be because they had a volatile relationship, but perhaps she was scared of one brother and not the other.'

'Sleeping with two brothers, though. Three, if we assume she was in a relationship with David Bethel. What the hell is that all about?'

Mallory shrugged. 'I'm not sure. Perhaps only one of the brothers is the killer. It's possible the other had no knowledge of what happened to either Jaci or Gwennie.'

Harri thought of Jane Callender's attack outside her home after the church theft. 'I'm not so sure about that. I think they work as a pair. Anyway, we have enough for all three to be questioned under arrest in relation to both investigations. I'm going to speak to Steph to update Cal Bentley on what we've discovered.' He paused, trying to find the right words. 'I'm sorry you had to watch that stuff.'

Mallory turned her face towards the side window. 'We're going to have to stop working together, you know, Harri. What I just saw was by no means the worst of my career. You were behaving like a country vicar in there. It was harmless stuff.'

'What… you don't want to be on my team any longer?'

'Harri!' Mallory turned to him. 'I was embarrassed about how you were treating me.'

'It's not really my thing. I… I just found it hard to sit there watching that rubbish. I'll never understand what motivates people to take part in that sort of thing. Never.' God, he thought, perhaps he should be having a chat with his son and daughter about what was out there. Warn them about the dangers of pornography. Something else to chat to Fran about.

Mallory had turned back to him. 'This isn't just about one film, though, is it? It's about us working together full stop.'

Harri put a hand out and touched Mallory on the arm. 'I don't want to lose you.'

'It's not about losing me, it's about stabilising our relationship. Ever since I came to Wales, I've been living in temporary accommodation and relying on short-term jobs. And look at the position I put you in when I found Gwennie's key in my house. There's too much conflict.' She took a deep breath. 'There's a job going in the Family Courts Division in Swansea which I'm thinking of applying for.'

Harri temporarily lost concentration and his car veered towards the grass verge. 'What?'

'Hear me out, Harri. Even if I don't get that one, there will be other opportunities. I've been shying away from full-time work because of my injury, but we need to stop working together and I need to get my life back on track. Once I get a permanent role, I could buy a house near you in Carmarthen. We'd see more of each other, not less.'

Harri pulled over and stopped the car. He looked at Mallory and saw she was focused, her gaze on the road ahead.

'You don't need a place of your own; you could live with me.'

Mallory shook her head. 'Not now. Not yet. We've three teenagers between us. Your kids are pretty much sorted, but Toby isn't. For a couple of years, I'd be nearby but with my own space. Once your kids have left home and Toby has found his feet, who knows? Besides, there's Fran to think about too.'

'Fran still has her old house in Cardiff. She's been renting it out ever since she moved in with me.' She'd recently had the house redecorated in between tenancies and had hesitated about putting it back on the rental market. Perhaps she too had been thinking of the future.

'That's something again to think about over the next few years. Let's not rush into anything, Harri. I met Joe, six months later I was married and four months after that I was expecting Toby. I'd like to behave like an adult for a change.'

Harri felt a rush of gratitude towards this damaged woman who had made him live in colour once more after Paula had died. She was being the sensible one, not him. He'd have happily let everything continue. He reached out for Mallory's hand.

'I did behave like a country vicar in there, although I have to say I've arrested a couple in my time for—'

Mallory groaned. 'I really don't want to know.'

Harri laughed. 'Right, next stop Beck Cowan's house.'

# 47

Siân and Cal had been waiting at Beck's office in case he returned there, but when Mallory called them for an update, she was informed that there was no sign of the missing man. Mallory's sense of unease was increasing – Tomos and Dylan were to be brought in for questioning and the location of both suspects had been identified. Dylan was working from home and his brother was at a property near Lampeter. It was essential that they had Beck's testimony too so that they could unpick the events of what had happened to both Jones women.

Beck lived in a purpose-built block of flats not unlike the home of Jaci Jones. Perched on the bank of the river near Richmond, it had an affluent feel, suggesting his film work was lucrative. There was no serviced reception, and Harri and Mallory climbed the stairs to the second-floor flat to avoid the maintenance guy working on the lift. Number twenty-three was at the end of the corridor, its view the opposite end to the river. Pinned on the door was a note: '*I'm sorry about this. Please call the emergency services.*'

'Shit,' said Mallory, pulling out her phone. 'We're going to need help getting in.'

'Listen,' said Harri, with his ear to the door.

In the silence, they could hear a muffled sound, the thud of something being knocked over. Mallory banged on the door. 'Beck, it's Mallory. Open the door for us, please. We can talk this over.'

Mallory continued to bang on the door until uniformed officers arrived five minutes later. The door was opened quickly by one of the constables using an enforcer. Mallory was in first, pushing Harri out of the way until she recoiled at the sight of Beck hanging from the beam in his living room. Harri grabbed the fallen chair and climbed up.

'Help me,' he said to the officers, and the three of them removed the noose from around Beck's neck. Mallory reached out to touch Beck and found his body warm, as if he'd just fallen asleep, although his face told a different story. He must have still been alive when they arrived at the door. She wondered how long he'd been standing there, willing himself to make that fatal drop. Her gaze moved from his prone body to the piece of paper lying on the coffee table.

'He's left a note,' she said. Before anyone could take it off her, she bent over it, careful not to disturb its position or touch the surface, and began to read.

*If you're reading this, then I plucked up the courage to do the act. I need to tell you straight away that I don't know which of the Bethels killed Jaci. I think it was Dylan; he was the more interested in her and had his career to protect, but Tomos is the more violent and had begun his ministry as a lay preacher. Perhaps they did it together. I suspect they're also responsible for the killing of Gwennie Jones, but I've no information to help you with that. I can, however, tell you about our films with Jaci, aka Lady Gemma.*

*I met Jaci in a bar when she was out with her work friends. Despite her shyness, she was desperate for some adventure. I never hid what I did for a living. I had my own film company and was dabbling in everything, erotica, artsy films, gritty documentaries. The only thing that made me any money was the erotic stuff. Jaci jokingly said she'd like to appear in one and I thought she was just kidding, but she was up for it. The only thing was she said she wouldn't be able to sleep with someone she didn't know, but she knew someone back in Wales who was the brother of her ex-boyfriend and might be up for it. So we arranged to go to The Cedar Tree – yes, I know you've been there because Bridget tracked me down – and I filmed her having sex with Tomos. It sold well and I booked them both for another stay in the hotel a month later. I didn't even realise it wasn't Tomos until I was editing the film and saw the scar on the actor's face. It was too old to have happened between filming. I rang Jaci and she started to laugh, telling me about Dylan having to stand in for his brother as he had the flu.*

*I think she met the brothers after her ex died. There was some unfinished business there that encouraged her attraction to his brothers. Who was I to judge? Sharing between brothers happens in some countries, and it was all a bit of fun. Until it wasn't. Jaci said it needed to stop because one of the brothers said he'd been recognised and the person had started blackmailing them. I never even knew which brother it was that had been identified, but this person had recognised either Tomos or Dylan.*

*I can't tell you the identity of the witness, but I guess they were very, very sorry.*

*Now I think back, I'm not sure which brother appeared in each of the five films I made, but one of them made Jaci uneasy. She was less her bubbly self, but she acted well enough, and we got the films completed. I paid them five hundred pounds each for their troubles and I thought everyone was happy. However, when I saw Jaci around the time of her disappearance, she said that one of the brothers had accused her of being behind the blackmail and that she wasn't going to get a penny from him.*

*When Jaci went missing, I thought it might be one of them, but I was frightened and buried my head in the sand. Over the years, I've thought a lot about Jaci, and I've made a name for myself, including a BAFTA nomination for my work on a documentary about the Sudan. I encountered frightening situations there, and I felt more confident about tackling difficult subjects, so I thought it time for a documentary on Jaci focusing on the impact of her death on her family. I suppose I hoped that I could tease out the involvement of the Bethels and Jaci would finally get justice.*

*When I spoke to Gwennie, she said she'd got a photograph of Jaci, recognising it from another photo of Jaci she'd found while babysitting. She said she'd show it to me, but she wanted to speak to the man in question first. I said I'd come down and see the man, but she said it was a chance to get some money from him. I don't think she meant babysitting! It wasn't me she was meeting that night but almost certainly one of them.*

*Last week, after I spoke to Mallory, I came home to find my flat trashed. I think one of them was sending me a message, and I had hoped it was just a warning. But my cat has gone missing and I think they're coming for me now. I think it's best I go this way. What I started led to two women dying, and it's just too much. I'm sorry.*

*I hope you find out which one of them killed her, but I know they're both in it together. I do suspect where you might find her body. This is my parting gift. One of the Bethels used to take Jaci to a caravan park by a lake in Monmouthshire. She laughed when she first saw The Cedar Tree and said how different it was to the caravan. I believe a lake is a good place to hide a body. I know because Jaci joked about it once.*

*I'm sorry for everything. Jaci was a nice girl, but she danced with the devil.*

*Yours, Beck*

# 48

Mallory accompanied Siân to the house of Eleri Jones to let them know about the arrest of Tomos and Dylan Bethel. Harri stayed at the station. Given the high-profile nature of both investigations, Harri had needed to be on hand to oversee the interviews and deal with any problems as they arose. But before the press got to the Jones family, they needed to be informed of the investigation's progress. Siân had telephoned ahead to tell them that there was news in respect to both Jaci and Gwennie, but details would have to wait.

Eleri opened the door, looking better than when Mallory had last seen her. She'd had her hair cropped and tinted a light copper colour, giving her a youthful appearance. Mallory had seen this before as part of the grieving process, often before a funeral. Gwennie's body had not yet been released for burial, and it was likely that a defence lawyer might ask for a second post-mortem. However, Eleri had decided to face the world afresh with a new hairstyle and determination.

Marion was sitting on the sofa, crocheting a blanket. 'She's having one of her bad days,' murmured Eleri, closing the door to keep in the heat. 'She'll want to hear what you have to say, but if it's bad, I'll have to intervene and you can update me by myself.'

There was no offer of tea or coffee. Eleri perched on the arm of the sofa while Marion continued to crochet.

'This afternoon, we made two arrests in relation to the murders of Gwennie and Jaci,' said Siân. 'They are currently being questioned, and until that process is complete, we can't give out any more information. I hope you understand.'

'I knew it,' said Eleri through gritted teeth. 'Just tell me, do I know either of them?'

'We can't answer that,' said Siân. 'There's little we can tell you as suspects are entitled to anonymity until they're formally charged.'

'Of course we'll know them,' said Marion, her head still bent over her blanket. 'It's those Bethel boys. Jaci was up to something with the pair of them. I saw what she was like when she attended David's funeral, all over the boys. Old Mrs Bethel was furious with her, but she didn't dare say anything.'

'There's the possibility,' said Mallory, 'that Gwennie might have identified the other man in the photo that you gave us by spotting a similar image while she was babysitting. Did she childmind for anyone other than Dylan Bethel?'

'Nope.' Eleri crossed her arms. 'I'll kill that bastard. Did he murder Gwennie because of the photo?'

Siân glanced at Mallory. 'We're investigating the source of Gwennie's money. We're not convinced it came from the film company.'

Eleri stood. 'I'm going to have it out with Mrs Bethel now. All that family are warped.'

'Sit down,' said Siân. 'It won't help Gwennie. I need to ask you a question which you may find difficult to answer.

Were you aware that Jaci had another income stream? She made films, art type, shot by Beck Cowan.'

Eleri looked over at her mother. 'The bastard. Are you listening to this, Mam?'

Marion shook her head. 'I don't want to know.' She got up and walked out into the kitchen, slamming the door behind her.

'We think,' said Mallory, 'that the Bethels were involved too. Do you think Marion knew about the films as well?' she asked Eleri. 'Is that why she froze out the original investigation team?'

Eleri shook her head. 'I don't know. Maybe. Jaci was always her favourite, the golden girl, but it did her no favours. She was desperate to get away from here, live a more interesting life.' She paused. 'Have you seen the films?'

'I have,' said Mallory. 'Only recently, but I've seen them.'

'Were they terrible?' asked Eleri with a whisper.

Mallory shook her head. 'Not terrible, but they put Jaci in danger because one of the Bethels became paranoid that Jaci was behind a blackmail attempt. Once she was dead, they probably thought that was it until Beck made contact about the documentary and Gwennie made the connection between the torn photo and the one in Dylan's possession.'

'So Gwennie died because of Jaci.'

'No.' Mallory's voice was louder than she intended. 'She died because she came into the path of a killer.'

# 49

It was a beautiful spot, on the edge of the national park. In the distance, Mallory could see the white-topped mountains of Bannau Brycheiniog. Harri would probably be able to name the peaks, but Mallory's gaze kept returning to the surroundings of Hafan Holiday Park, blighted by row upon row of green tin caravans. All right, they might not actually have been made of tin, but they looked flimsy and unloved. The whole place had a 1970s feel to it, and it turned out that the Bethels' grandparents had bought one of the caravans in 1975 to spend part of their retirement in. On their death, the caravan was bequeathed to David, Tomos and Dylan equally. If Beck's note was to be believed, one of the brothers had brought Jaci here too: the first time when they were in a relationship and the second time to kill her.

The caravan was still owned by the Bethels and was now subject to an intensive search. A spray of the interior with luminol had indicated blood spatter in the sole bedroom near the door. A possible scenario was that Jaci had been attacked either walking in or out of the bedroom and wrapped in some kind of sheeting, as the only other discovery of blood was a single spot by the door to the outside. It would take days, even weeks, to get a positive DNA match to Jaci, but the place was being treated as a crime scene.

This is where everything finishes, thought Mallory. It all concludes here. It has to.

Marion and Eleri had been informed that a search was taking place, but its location had not been revealed. Luckily, the caravan park was shut for the season, its licence only valid from March to December, otherwise news of a police presence would have been all over social media. They were also sufficiently far enough away from Ceigwyn to proceed without the presence of family looking on. Mallory would have been unable to send them away, and it would have been up to Harri to put his foot down, an unpleasant task made worse by Marion's fragility. The search, for the moment, remained a secret, but she and Harri would be travelling to the Jones household later that day to update them on developments.

Mallory was standing on an incline watching the search of the lake, conscious of Siân shivering next to her.

'Do you think it's colder or warmer in the water?' asked Siân. 'How do they do it? Me, I can't even get into a lukewarm shower.'

Mallory glanced at her. 'I had you down as one of those who finishes their wash with an icy blast of water.'

Siân shuddered. 'Definitely not me. I like it hot, hot, hot. I'm dreaming of the hot bath that awaits me when I get home.'

Their gazes were on the lake, which was beginning to dissolve in the poor weather. Snow had begun to fall softly, and there was talk of calling off the search at the end of the day and waiting until the weather improved. Mallory had never met a police diver in the course of her work before, and she was struck by how hardy they were. Focused and professional, too. They'd been diving all day alongside two specialist boats with sonar and other imaging equipment.

'There surely won't be any remains left,' said Mallory.

Siân shrugged. 'The search lead says the water is alkali here, which helps, as does the cold. Warmer water speeds up bacterial activity to break down organic matter. Even in summer that lake is deep and cold.'

Harri walked over to them, his face pinched with the cold. He was carrying a tray of mugs filled with instant soup, which they both accepted.

'Sonar has shown a strange mass near the centre. Of course, it's the deepest point, which is why progress is slow. The Bethels didn't have a boat by all accounts, so they must have borrowed one to get into the middle of the lake.'

'It was a risk,' said Mallory, squinting to see the spot where the activity was taking place. 'If Jaci had been found here, suspicion would immediately have fallen on the caravan owners, which would have led us to the Bethels eventually.'

'They had to dispose of the body somehow,' said Harri. 'We know killers like to use familiar but isolated settings – woodland, lakes, gulleys. The Bethels probably thought that by ensuring the body was deep enough to prevent re-emergence, no one would actually be looking here.'

Mallory nodded. 'I wonder if Mrs Bethel knew what her sons were up to. What does she have to say about the place?'

'She never comes here, apparently,' said Siân. 'Hasn't visited since the late Eighties, which isn't to say she didn't know her sons were in some way involved in Jaci's murder. That family are tighter than an oyster. We'll get nothing from her.'

The clouds overhead darkened and it looked like the visit to the Joneses would be for an update only. Suddenly, across the lake came a loud cry. A diver had emerged and was holding his thumbs up.

'They've found something,' said Harri. 'We need to get closer.'

The three of them hurried down the incline, all thoughts of the cold gone. The diver had been helped onto the boat and was showing his colleagues his find while gesticulating at the lake.

'What have you got?' asked Harri, shouting across at the men.

The dinghy moved towards them, its progress frustratingly slow. The diver handed him an evidence bag containing a dirty object about six centimetres in length.

'It's a metacarpal bone,' he said. 'A bone expert will be able to tell you from which finger. It's like looking for a needle in a haystack down there. Visibility is terrible, but my torch found this sticking in the bed. I think we're broadly in the right place because it looks like there's other debris down there, including scraps of fabric. We'll push on tomorrow if the weather's OK, but I also found this.'

He opened his hand to reveal a small glass object.

'It's a perfume bottle,' said Siân. 'It's tiny. Do you think it might belong to Jaci?'

'She carried scent around with her,' said Mallory. 'Her colleagues commented on how nice she smelt. I know what perfume she wore. What does the label say?'

'There's just a scrap of gum where the label once was. I doubt we'll be able to identify the perfume from that.'

Harri took the bottle. 'The perfume is still inside. I'm going to take the stopper off.' With a gloved hand he removed the glass top. He smelt it and recoiled. 'It smells of grannies and grass.'

Siân gave him a look, but Mallory pulled his hand towards her face. 'Let me smell it.'

The aroma was overpowering and transported Mallory back in time to the perfume counter of that Wimbledon department store. It was the scent she'd inhaled all those years ago. 'It's Je Reviens,' she said. '"I'll be back."'

–

'We'll find more of Jaci's remains,' said Harri, as they trudged back to the car. 'It's a matter of combing through the area, even if the snow temporarily slows us down. We've enough to charge both brothers with preventing lawful and decent burial. We can build a decent scenario for what happened that night.'

'Either Tomos or Dylan travelled to Wimbledon, determined to silence Jaci. It must have been preplanned rather than an act of passion, as Jaci had booked the day off work. I suspect he turned up a day earlier than she expected, though, given it looked like she'd settled in for the night. He told her to pack a bag, which she did in haste.'

'Containing her hair straighteners, sponge bag, nightie, perfume and phone. I'm not sure why she left her purse at home.'

'She probably thought she didn't need it.' Mallory gestured around her at the whitening holiday park. 'There's nowhere to spend it here. Her lover told her he'd be returning her to Wimbledon the next day. However, he killed her here, possibly attacking her around the head.'

'Like Gwennie and his previous victim,' said Harri, opening his car door. 'The woman who suggested Tomos might be responsible for the theft from the church roof. It's

Gwennie, however, that will be the key to bringing them to justice. A murder case will be harder to build in relation to Jaci, but we've the CPS agreement to bring a charge in relation to Gwennie's death. This is partly based on the note left by Beck Cowan, and we have Dylan on CCTV walking up the path behind Toby. He'll be charged with her murder, but I can't make a murder charge stick in relation to Jaci.'

Mallory sighed. Gwennie's case was a tragedy, but it wasn't her tragedy. It belonged to Marion and Eleri and anyone else who knew the teenager. But Jaci's death had insinuated itself into Mallory's life for the last seventeen years, and the fact that she'd never get justice was galling.

Mallory said, 'I've heard that the scar on Dylan's face was the result of an argument with Tomos as a child. That's the reason why my guess, for what it's worth, is that it was Tomos not Dylan who killed Jaci to keep her quiet about the films and Dylan helped his brother dispose of her body.'

'Possibly.' Harri turned the heater up in the car. 'Did you know that Tomos put his carpenter skills to use by making cricket bats? We've not found Gwennie's murder weapon, but it's another line of enquiry as we build a case. Neither is going to confess nor implicate the other.'

He pulled out onto the main road and set off towards Ceigwyn, passing through the mountains Mallory had seen from the holiday park. They were both majestic and foreboding. 'It's a beautiful spot. Wales is full of these stunning places.'

'You don't regret coming?' He glanced at her.

She shook her head. 'Never.'

'But it is the end of an era.'

Mallory put her head on his shoulder and let the tiredness wash over her. 'It is the end of an era, but the start of another. I've a lot to be thankful for. I have a life that Jaci never got to live. I'm grateful for that. It's time to look to the future again.'

'With me?'

Mallory smiled. 'Of course.'

# *Acknowledgements*

My agent Kirsty McLachlan at Morgan Green Creatives has been a great supporter of this series and thanks also go to Siân Heap for editing *The First Mistake* and to Louise Cullen and Aidan Kavanagh at Canelo for their input into the book.

Thanks to Tony and Judith Butler, my invaluable first readers. Also, Marion Todd, Sheila Bugler, Rachel Lynch and Jeanette Hewitt, who provide much-needed writing support as do Julie-Ann Corrigan, Michael Wood, and Karen Meek. Thanks also to Dea Parkin for her continued support. My local independent bookseller Gwisgo Bookworm in Aberaeron run by Karen and Niki is always a delight to visit and you can always request a signed copy of any of my titles from them. Thanks too to all the other supportive booksellers. Working as a Bridge Fellow for the Royal Literary Fund has provided me with invaluable time and funds to dedicate myself to my writing.

We have a lovely community talking about books each Saturday on Facebook. Do come over and say hello if you have a chance – https://www.facebook.com/SarahWardCrime

Finally, thanks to all my family for supporting my books especially Andy and Dad.